ShadowCast

V.P. Morris

Black Rose Writing | Texas

ISBN: 978-1-68433-638-8
PUBLISHED BY BLACK ROSE WRITING
www.blackrosewriting.com

Printed in the United States of America
Suggested Retail Price (SRP) $17.95

ShadowCast is printed in Garamond

*As a planet-friendly publisher, Black Rose Writing does its best to eliminate unnecessary waste to reduce paper usage and energy costs, while never compromising the reading experience. As a result, the final word count vs. page count may not meet common expectations.

Acknowledgements

Among many things, this book is about determination. My mother, Dr. Mary Kelly Mohr and grandmother, Mrs. Dorothy Mohr taught me most of what I know on the subject. Both remarkable women have been advocates for my education and my aspirations as a writer. Without them, I wouldn't have the determination and courage to work towards what I want out of life, including the completion of this book.

I also would like to thank the many great teachers I've encountered over the years who helped shape my interest in the written word. Most notably, Ms. Helen Dunne and Ms. Jessica Richter-Furman. Thank you both for being such excellent educators and believing in your students.

To everyone at Black Rose Writing, you have given this book a home and championed it in many ways. Thank you, Reagan Rothe, for seeing what this novel has to offer.

To Gabi Coatsworth for letting me pick your brain on so many writing topics and providing the writers of Fairfield County with a community of support.

To my beta readers, editors, and proofreaders, thank you for helping me shape this story into a finished product.

To the amazing and uplifting creators in the Twitter writing community. I'm proud to have been a part of this special group for almost five years. The positive encouragement and inspiration you all give each other on a daily basis has helped me continue on my writing journey especially when I felt lost on my path.

Last but certainly not least, to my husband, Aaron. Thank you for being there for me to talk endlessly at you about my character ideas and plot problems. Your support means the world to me and I'm so grateful that you continue to believe in me through thick and thin.

ShadowCast

Chapter 1

I always thought women looked more beautiful dead than alive. That was until I met her. My angel.

What a beauty she was, with her long raven hair and alabaster skin. And I loved the way she dressed: Long, flowing old-fashioned dresses with her favorite cameo necklace carved from pure ivory. She was nothing like those stupid girls I see around town on their way to the beach, with their short skirts and sundresses, sipping soda they purchased with daddy's credit card.

It's like they know they're tempting me. It's like they know I can't have them any other way. I tell myself, "No. I promised Ma no more." But I know they want it, those harlots.

The only thing that makes me feel better, when I miss my angel, is heading down into the cave. That's what Ma calls it. I'm such a night owl that I'd keep Ma up if I slept upstairs. So, she let me fix up the basement all those years ago and now it's all mine. I blocked off a portion of it with a fireproof door. I found it at this consignment shop, it actually used to be in a real prison before it was demolished. It's dark and dry down here, perfect for hiding my treasures. The treasures Ma doesn't know I have. But that's the rules. The cave is off limits to her, even for cleaning.

Today, I need to be here.

Ma has dinner on the table. But she'll have to wait. I open the creaking door and plod down the wooden steps to the cave, and I smile. Just looking at them makes me calm down.

I press my hands up against the photos on the wall. The faces of the girls stare back at me from newspaper clippings and Polaroids. Dumb bitches, every last one of them. Except one, of course. She could have been my salvation, but she couldn't stick around.

I admire the photos I have of her, dressed in a bridal veil and not much else. Oh, what could have been! I notice the deck of cards she would entertain herself with on the nights I couldn't spend with her. Ma might want these, I think, and toss them in my pocket.

The last thing I see is the angel wings pinned to my wall. I untack them and hold them against my chest.

It's been twelve years and I still miss her so.

It's been twelve years and, in my heart, I know I have to do it again.

• • •

There isn't enough coffee in the world to make today any less painful, thought Dakota Kilroy as she stared into the bottom of her coffee mug.

She had just drunk two cups of the bitter liquid, but her empty stomach craved something more.

Dressed in shabby plaid pajama bottoms and a black tank top, Dakota made her way over to the fridge. The chilled breeze from the appliance made her shiver as she gazed over the limited selection: An apple (a week passed its prime), a milk carton with only a splash left in it, a bottle of ketchup, and some oily salad dressing. She grabbed the apple and bit into its soft flesh. It tasted dull and lifeless, but now that she was three months unemployed, she couldn't afford to complain.

She couldn't afford a lot of things — like her rent, health insurance, and phone bill. To make matters worse, her landlord just informed her that her building would go co-op in the spring, meaning she'd have to buy her apartment or get out.

She felt tears well in her eyes as she read over the coffee-ring-covered notice that began with "Dear Tenants," someone had shoved under her door a few weeks ago. Normally, when she felt like crying, she had one person to talk to, one person who understood her life and her passions as well as she did: her boyfriend, Seth. But now, he was gone and possibly for good.

"No, you're not crying. You will find a solution to this," she told herself out loud as if she was a coach in a sports movie about to give a pep talk to his team of underdogs. "There has to be a solution. There has to be!"

You know what the answer is, a little nagging voice inside her head said. *You need to call your dad and ask for help.*

Dakota let out a moan, reached under her sink and slammed a half-empty bottle of whiskey on the white countertop. "If I'm going to do this, I'm not doing it sober," she told herself as she mixed room-temperature coffee and whiskey in her mug.

She shot back the drink in two gulps, and the brown liquid burnt her throat. The drink worked fast and within a few minutes, she already felt numb enough to make the call. She picked up her phone and dialed her parents' home phone number into the keypad on her shattered iPhone screen. After two sharp rings, her father, Ken Kilroy, answered the phone with a chipper, "Kilroy residence! How can I assist you on this fine morning?"

"Hi Dad, it's me," she said.

"Hey hon, it's about time you called," he said in his firm but warm voice.

"Sorry, I haven't called in a while, but things aren't too great here," she told him.

"How come?" he asked.

"Well, we're in the middle of the biggest industry-wide layoffs in history and…" She braced herself, "I'm one of the thousands of writers who got cut," she confessed.

"I'm sorry about that, but I'm sure you'll find something soon," he said.

"No, I won't, Dad. I got laid off in late October. I've been to every interview I can get… and nothing. On top of that, my landlord is kicking me out soon. He sold the building to some real estate company. Plus, Seth is…" she paused, feeling the embarrassment creep up inside her gut.

"Yes, Seth, how is he? Can't you move in with him until you get on your feet?" her dad asked.

"Seth is away right now," she said.

"When he returns, I'm sure you can go live with him. It's about time you got serious with someone after all…"

"Dad," Dakota paused, bracing for her father's I-told-you-so tone of voice. "Seth is in rehab. You see, when we were covering our last story on heroin dealing and—" Dakota didn't know how to finish her sentence.

Ken took a heavy sigh. "I told you that would happen. This is exactly why I never liked this so-called career of yours. All that poking your nose into other people's business and pretending to be someone you're not is dangerous."

The screen of her iPhone felt hot against her face. The cracked glass lightly dug into her cheek. She remembered how she dropped it. The alleyway, the knife, and the needle. Seth running, Dakota scooping up the phone and chasing after him. Later she found herself sitting in a musty courtroom, hearing a judge sentence Seth to six months in a rehabilitation facility upstate. He was whisked away by two huge guards. She didn't even get to say "Goodbye."

Ken continued, "Why don't you do something a little less exciting with your writing skills? I hear writing children's books can pay well."

"I'm not calling for career advice, Dad," she said.

His voice stiffened. "Then why are you calling?"

"I need to ask you if you can loan me some money. I need to pay my last month's rent and I have to find a new place. They'll need first month's rent and a deposit. I can't afford that after three months of not working. I barely have any food in the house. The bills are stacking up. Dad, I'm desperate," she pleaded.

"I knew this would happen," he began in that condescending voice Dakota hated as a teenager and still hated as a twenty-eight-year-old. "I told you when you moved there that New York City would be too expensive for you. You simply can't have a comfortable life in that rodent-infested metropolis. And — surprise! I'm right."

"You have no room to talk," Dakota began. "Santa Monica isn't exactly a cheap place to live. If only I had gone into something more stable like Pro-Golf like you, I wouldn't be in this situation."

Irritation boiled in Ken's voice. "Don't talk to your father that way, missy. I worked two jobs just so I could afford golf lessons as a teenager. Don't act like I didn't earn my career. How can you expect me to give you money after disrespecting me?"

"You gave Capri thirty grand for her wedding," Dakota fired back. "You bought Cassidy a new car, and you bought Mom a new face! All within the last two years. And you're telling me you won't help your other daughter out with a few bills?"

Her father took a breath. He had forgotten how Dakota always felt left out. "Okay, I'll help you, but you have to come home."

"Where? California?" Dakota's voice almost squeaked.

"Yes, home."

Dakota grimaced. California hadn't been her home in almost eleven years.

Ken started up again. "If this is an industry-wide problem, staying in New York won't do you any good. I can't afford to pay your rent for God-knows-how-long until you find work again. I've got retirement to think of here. Come live with Mom and me, and we'll get you back on your feet in no time."

4

Dakota leaned over and held her head. In the fall of her eighteenth year, she had packed up her belongings and left for New York, swearing she would live nowhere else. But now, she had no choice.

"Fine. I'll come home," she said between her teeth.

"Great, I'll book your ticket home for Friday. Sound good?"

"Yes, Dad. See you soon."

•   •   •

Dakota walked out of the sliding glass doors at LAX in a thick winter coat, army-green jeans, and black jackboots. The California sun was stronger than she remembered as it beat down on her back. Moments later, her mother's white Mercedes pulled up curbside with the trunk popped open.

The window rolled down and her mother, Debi, shouted across the passenger seat, "Welcome home, sweetie!"

"Thanks, Mom." Dakota loaded her luggage into the trunk.

Now in the passenger seat, Dakota leaned in to give her mother the obligatory hug only to jump at what she saw.

Her mother had another facelift since the last time she saw her, and her skin was spread across her skull like silly putty, making her look like a melted wax model of herself.

"Mom! What did you do? You look just like Joan Rivers," said Dakota.

"Oh, it's not that bad," Debi laughed. "Besides, this will keep me from having to get another one in five years."

Dakota puffed out her cheeks in frustration. For years, she'd had to live with her mother's obsession with looks. Now, she had to endure the twelve-mile car ride that would take 45 minutes in California traffic, hearing about Botox, lip-fillers, and the amount of skin the surgeon had cut from her mother's face.

When traffic had slowed to a complete stop, Debi reached over and poked Dakota in the middle of her brow. "Looks like it's time for you to start with some injections. I can make an appointment for you while you're here. I'm sure it won't hurt as bad as all those tattoos." Her mother gave a disapproving glance towards Dakota's body.

"Mom! I don't need or want—" she stopped herself. Arguing with her mother was pointless: Dakota would fight fire with fire and say something equally insensitive back to her mother. This would hurt Debi's feelings, forcing her to run to Ken crying. Ken would take his wife's side over his daughter's and scold Dakota for being cruel to her mother.

As they pulled up in front of the Kilroys' terracotta mansion, three figures emerged from the front door. The middle figure was her father; his tall, broad build was as easily recognizable as his uniform of a bright polo shirt and khaki pants. On either side of him stood two blond beauties who wore matching blue and white striped maxi dresses. They were identical in every way, except one of them was six months pregnant. They were Capri and Cassidy, Dakota's older sisters who happened to be identical twins.

The sisters rushed forward, and Cassidy gave Dakota a big hug with her pregnant belly poking into Dakota's stomach. "Welcome home, little sis," she said.

"Look at you! You're so big!" Dakota smiled at her sister.

"Um, don't forget about me," said Capri whose voice had somehow developed a more pronounced 'Valley girl' accent than her twin.

"It wouldn't be possible to forget about you, Capri," replied Dakota, in a partly sincere tone.

Her father welcomed her into the house and after putting her bags into her room, her family sat her down at the kitchen table.

"Now, Dakota," started her mother, "the twins and I were talking earlier about how we can't stand that army-girl wardrobe you stomp around in. Have you ever considered changing it? I thought New Yorkers were supposed to wear sexy sling-back heels and tight dresses as they rush off to meet their boyfriends for drinks."

"Mom, real life in New York is not a *Sex and The City* episode," said Dakota.

What she wanted to say was that she dressed like she was going into a war zone because New York *was* a war zone. There were people everywhere willing to elbow you in the gut for the last seat on the subway, and young urban professionals willing to backstab their coworkers just to get a better assignment or a cushier office. You'd have to make your way through the cracked and crumbling concrete, down steep subway steps, or stand in a puddle of brown curb water just to hail a cab. The New York City Dakota knew chewed up and spat out girls who dressed and behaved like Carrie Bradshaw.

Capri opened a bottle of white wine. With her acrylic nails grasping the bottle, she poured everyone, except for pregnant Cassidy, a glass. Dakota took her glass gladly and gulped the dry Sauvignon Blanc until her mouth felt numb. Anything to ease the pain of moving home was welcome.

"Jeez, Dakota, slow down," said Cassidy.

"It's just been a long day." Dakota poured herself a second glass. She knew she would need to be at least a little drunk to handle the non-stop questions that her family would throw at her. They wouldn't rest until they learned every little detail about what had happened in New York, what had happened with Seth, and what she was going to do now.

Her father came over from the kitchen and placed a cheese and cracker plate down in front of the women. "So, what's the plan now, Koty?" he asked.

Dakota recoiled at the sound of her childhood nickname. 'Koty' sounded too much like 'Cody,' which was a name for a boy or a dog. She took another sip of her wine, now careful not to drink too much for fear of Cassidy's reaction.

"I don't know right now. I literally just got here, but I want to get back into journalism any way I can. After saving up enough money, I want to go back to New York," she told them.

They all chattered at once, giving their opinion about her current situation, but her father's voice rang out louder than the rest of them. "New York? Again? Haven't you had enough of the place? Don't you think it's unreasonable to pay almost all your salary to live in a shoe closet? You should stay out West where there's room and fresh air."

"New York is my home and I don't—" Dakota attempted to say.

"Journalism?" Capri chimed in. "Didn't Dad convinced you to write children's books? You know, Peter is golf buddies with an editor at Harper Collins and he said children's lit is extremely popular right now. I should know — Trevor loves story time. But anyway, I'm sure Peter could get you a meeting with him to pitch ideas."

Dakota felt her anger bubbling up in her chest. "Let's get one thing straight, Dad didn't convince me of anything. I still want to be an investigative journalist. It's what I'm good at. For the love of God, I've gotten awards and Mayor Bloomberg personally thanked me for the work I've done. I'm not going to give that up."

"Even after what happened to Seth?" asked Ken, as he took a sip from his glass and glided into the kitchen.

"What happened to Seth?" asked all three Kilroy women at once.

"I really liked him," said Debi.

"Oh please. He was slimy and untrustworthy," said Capri.

Dakota remembered the day she mistakenly let Capri and her husband, Peter, meet Seth.

Peter Cunningham was one of the most successful real estate developers in Southern California. About two years ago, he flew to New York for a business meeting and brought Capri along. Capri assumed it would be great fun to surprise her little sister at her apartment.

Dakota and Seth were in the lust-fueled honeymoon stage of their relationship where they spent little time with their clothes on behind closed doors. She remembers being on top of Seth, seconds away from finishing when there was a knock on the door.

"Those fucking Jehovah's Witnesses," hissed Dakota. Her building's buzzer system broke causing various religious groups to take it upon themselves to go from door to door asking if the residents had been "saved" or "heard the good news."

"Go away! We told you we're not interested," yelled Seth, in his thick Brooklyn accent.

They knocked again, and Dakota heard a familiar voice say, "Dakota? Are you in there? It's me, Capri."

"Fuck," Dakota whispered before she called out, "Just a minute." Dakota got up and searched for the pair of sweatpants Seth had pulled off her moments ago. She found her 'System of a Down' t-shirt and threw it over her head.

"Who the hell is Capri?" asked Seth, as he put on his boxers.

"My sister," she answered, lifting a fallen couch pillow from the floor to find her crumpled sweatpants.

"You have a sister? Why didn't you tell me?" he asked.

"Two actually, but once you've seen one, you've seen them both," she said while gathering Seth's jeans and Rangers' jersey from the floor and tossing them to him.

"What does that mean?" he asked.

"Go hide in the bedroom until I can get rid of her," she commanded.

"She already knows I'm here," Seth pointed out.

"Just do as I say," she said, pushing him into her room and shutting the door.

"Hey Capri," Dakota said with a smile as she opened the door.

Capri leaned in and gave her sister a hug. She looked up to see that Peter was with her as well and leaned in for a hug hello.

"Sorry to barge in on you like this, I thought it would be a nice surprise," she explained.

Peter peeked in her dark apartment. "Who's the guy who told us to go away?"

"That was my boyfriend," Dakota answered.

"Oh my God, sis, I didn't know you had a boyfriend. How long has this been going on? Can we meet him?" she asked.

"About three or four months — and sure, he'll be right out." Dakota stepped back and waved a hand over the entryway, ushering the couple into the apartment.

Hearing all of this, Seth stepped out of the bedroom. The look of shock on these three people's faces as they saw each other for the first time was painful for Dakota to watch. She knew none of them was what the other was expecting.

Seth's eyes widened as he stared at Capri's tall and tan frame, her flat-ironed blond hair, her tight mauve dress and sparkly manicure. He frowned a little out of confusion, looking at Peter who was significantly older than Capri with salt and pepper showing in his hair. Peter was stuck in the 80s and was dressed like he was an extra on Miami Vice with a white suit set and a bright pink shirt.

Dakota motioned towards the couple. "Seth, this is my sister, Capri, and her husband, Peter."

The three of them shook hands.

Capri's judgmental eyes told Dakota she did not approve of the dark-haired, goatee-sporting 'Guido' she was seeing.

Seth scratched at his head before saying, "So, how long you two in town for? Need any pizza recommendations? I know a few spots only the locals go to."

Dakota told Peter and Capri, "Seth is a New Yorker, born and raised."

Peter smiled politely. "Actually, we have reservations at the Plaza with a few business contacts of mine and we're going to Tavern on the Green tomorrow before we fly home, but next time."

Seth nodded and all four of them stood in silence for a moment.

Capri started, "Well, we don't want to keep Peter's colleagues waiting. It was nice to meet you Seth. I'll talk to you later, sis." She hugged her sister and the couple left.

"Thank God that's over," Dakota sighed as she shut the door.

"Wow, that was not what I was expecting. I mean you said you were from California, but I didn't think your sister was a freaking Playboy Bunny," he laughed as he pulled her back to the couch and tried to kiss her.

She stopped him. "How did you know about that?"

"About what?" He wrinkled his forehead.

"She and her twin sister, my other sister, Cassidy, did a spread in Playboy once," Dakota admitted.

"Really? No way! I was just saying she looked like one of Hef's girls, I didn't know it was true. And two of them, Jesus Christ." He ran his hands through his hair and smiled.

"Hey!" Dakota smacked his shoulder.

"What? I still like you better. You're like a real girl. They're a little too plastic for my liking. Plus, those tats are hot," he said looking her up and down.

She threw her arms around him and hugged him, "Glad you think so."

• • •

Now in California, Dakota smiled to herself. Remembering Seth that way warmed her heart, but only for a moment.

"Just because he isn't some businessman or ballplayer doesn't mean he's slimy," Dakota said in his defense.

"Don't bring Blake into this," said Cassidy who mistook Dakota's 'ballplayer' comment for a jab at her husband, Blake Jackman, a linebacker for the Rams.

"No, I wasn't. I just know which types of guys you two, well you three," she said while glancing at her mom, "go for and I'm saying that just because he's not someone you find attractive doesn't mean that he isn't attractive to someone else."

Ken popped his head in from the kitchen. "Is getting addicted to heroin attractive?"

"Heroin?" Debi screeched.

"He's a junkie? Are you kidding me?" asked Capri.

Dakota stood up. "I don't have to take this incessant questioning from all of you. What happens in my personal life and Seth's life has nothing to do with you!" She stomped away and ran to her room feeling like she was a seventeen-year-old again.

• • •

Dakota sat on her bed with her hands on her head. She felt like crying, but the tears wouldn't come. She wanted to scream, but her mouth wouldn't open.

She closed her eyes for a moment, only to hear soft footsteps coming closer and feel someone brush up against her side.

It was Cassidy. She wrapped an arm around Dakota. "Hey, it's okay. They just get over excited about everything. If you aren't ready to tell us what happened with you and Seth, you don't have to."

Dakota nodded and her eyes watered. She never really got along with her family, but at least Cassidy understood her a little better than the others.

Cassidy looked around her little sister's bedroom. Nothing had changed in the eleven years since she left home. Posters and magazine clippings about grunge bands Cassidy had never listened to were still plastered up above the headboard. The bed had the same red flannel sheets, and her wooden desk was still littered with papers and used-up journals. The wall next to it was completely covered with photographs from Dakota's high school days.

Cassidy got off the bed to inspect the photographs. Most of them contained a few other girls from Dakota's class, but there was one common denominator in every single one of them: Maddy. She pulled one photo off the wall — it was of Maddy and Dakota in a side embrace.

"They never found her, did they?" she asked, handing the photo to her sister. Dakota shook her head.

Cassidy touched Dakota's hand. "Do you still miss her?"

"Of course, every day. What do you think all of these are for?" Dakota took off her sweatshirt and stood before her sister in just a black bra and a pair of pants.

"They are all for her?" asked Cassidy, as she stared at Dakota's tattoos.

"Most of them." Dakota pointed to the string of pearls etched across the bottom of her sternum, down her stomach and ended with a cameo of a woman. "This is the face of the woman on her favorite necklace."

She extended her left elbow. "Angel wings, like the costume she was supposed to wear that night."

Dakota put her hands up to show the back sides of her forearms. "The violin and the bow, Maddy's favorite instrument."

"This one was my first tattoo," she said, showing her sister a red cherry etched into her left wrist. "Cherry was her favorite flavor of everything. Cherry soda, cherry pie, cherry lip gloss." Dakota smiled. The scent of Maddy's very-cherry lip balm was so familiar to her she swore she could still smell it now.

"What about the biggest one?" asked Cassidy, motioning towards Dakota's chest.

"That one's my favorite," said Dakota, putting her hand across her sternum tattoo. "It's supposed to mimic this playing card."

Dakota reached for her purse and pulled a single playing card out of her wallet: The Ace of Hearts.

She turned it around and showed the artwork on the back of the card to Cassidy.

The card's slick parchment showcased the mirror image of the same face, one side up and the other side down. It was a woman, clearly a fortune teller. She had a beautiful face, one brown eye and one bright blue eye that gazed down at a glowing crystal ball. She wore a blue and purple headscarf and was decorated in green jewels and dark red flowers that formed a half-moon frame around her face.

Dakota had that same face printed across on her chest, just hovering above her breasts, meeting the web of pearls on her stomach at the center of her rib cage.

"What's this got to do with Maddy?" Cassidy asked, as she compared the drawing on the card to her sister's tattoo.

Dakota's memory turned to the first time she went to Maddy's grandparents' consignment shop.

•　　•　　•

Maddy burst through the door of the little white building beside the church. "Grandpa, we're here!" she called out.

A short man with buzzed gray hair came out from behind the counter and gave her a pat on the head.

"Oh look, you brought a friend," he said. "And a tall one to boot." The old man was about chest height next to Dakota.

"Can we look around?" Maddy asked, her voice was as sweet syrup.

"Of course. Just don't wreck anything," her grandfather told the two girls.

"We won't," Maddy and Dakota said in unison.

The girls dropped their book bags at the door and rushed through all the racks of clothing, pulling out anything that caught their eye.

Dakota remembered the scratchy taffeta from trying on a neon pink prom dress from the 80s. Maddy tried on a pair of bright floral-patterned bell-bottoms from the 70s that were clearly not her style.

Later, Maddy settled into a long white Victorian-era wedding dress that her grandmother had hidden in the back of the store.

"She says it's too beautiful to sell," said Maddy, as she tried to walk in the flowing white gown that was adorned with white pearls and lace.

"You need some high heels for that, you'll trip all over the place without them," said Dakota, who reached for the shoe box that came with the dress.

She handed over a pair of white satin-heeled boots with ivory buttons that ran up the side. As Maddy was trying to steady herself in the heels, something in the box caught Dakota's attention. It was a pack of playing cards.

"Look at these," said Dakota, showing the cards with the bohemian woman on the backside.

"Wow, that's so pretty. Those must be so old." Maddy loved anything with a history.

They both sat down on the rust-colored carpet that smelled of mothballs, and Dakota dealt out a game of Go Fish.

As they played, Dakota said, "I bet Gabriel would love to see you in that wedding dress."

"Stop it," Maddy squealed, pulling her veil over her face.

"What? He'd be stupid not to go out with you," Dakota said.

"I doubt it. Right now, the only guy who likes me is Connor," said Maddy. Both girls let out an "Ew."

"I'm surprised you don't have a boyfriend," said Maddy.

"That's the last thing I want right now," Dakota replied.

"Why?" Maddy asked, as she took the two of diamonds away from Dakota. Dakota fired back, asking if she had any fives — which Maddy did.

"Because," Dakota continued. "I don't want a boyfriend keeping me here. The first thing I'm gonna do as soon as I graduate is move to New York, so I can write."

"Write novels?" Maddy asked.

"No, for a newspaper. I want to get at the truth. The real part of everything." Dakota snatched another card away from Maddy, who was about to lose the game.

"I think that's really cool," said Maddy.

"My parents hate the idea. Everyone else who knows about my plan tells me it's never going to happen or that I should get into a more stable career." Dakota rolled her eyes.

"Don't listen to them," said Maddy. "I think you can do it."

"Thanks," Dakota beamed at her. It was so refreshing to have someone understand her for once.

"What are you girls doing?" asked Maddy's grandfather, who was standing over them.

"Playing cards," said Maddy.

"But look what's on the back of the cards," the pastor said. "Do you know who this is?"

"No," the girls told him.

"The Witch of WoodBurn." The weathered man stood back, waiting for a reaction, but none came.

"Of course, you girls are too young to know about this," he continued. "In our day, we were all told legends of a fortune-telling witch that could give you everything you wanted if you turned away from Jesus Christ and sold your soul to the Devil! Playing a card game with her image on it is a sin. Now, I want those cards back." The pastor reached out his hands, expecting the girls to surrender them.

"No." Dakota was not about to let some superstitious old preacher tell her what she could and could not have.

"No?" His mouth hung open. "That's no way to talk to your elders."

"That's no way to talk to a paying customer." Dakota rose to her feet. "How much do you want for them?"

"One hundred dollars," he said, expecting no teenager to have that sort of cash on them.

"Coming right up." Dakota stomped towards the entrance until she found where she left her bag. Inside her wallet, she kept several hundred-dollar bills. This was nothing unusual in the Kilroy house.

She handed over one of the crisp bills to Maddy's grandfather who snatched it from her fingers.

"All right, you can have your disgraceful cards, but don't let my granddaughter play with them," he said.

"It's just a superstition, witches aren't real," Dakota said.

"You don't know what insidious ways the Devil works!" shouted the pastor. "Either you keep these cards to yourself or I'll make sure you two never see each other again."

She shrugged. "Fine, have it your way."

But of course, the girls would break that rule. At lunches or at hangouts at Dakota's house, they'd play with the cards, learning other games that were more complicated than Go Fish.

And on the day before Maddy disappeared, they had played a game of Poker. Instead of betting pencils and pennies like they used to, they bet the cards themselves. Winner takes all.

The witchy woman on the cards entranced both girls. Maddy was always badgering Dakota to let her borrow them despite her grandfather's threats. Sick of her constant requests, she put the cards on the line. But Maddy had drawn a full house while Dakota had nothing put a pair of Aces. She handed over the cards to her best friend. She had won them fair and square. It wasn't until after Maddy returned home for the night that Dakota discovered they had left one card on the bed: The Ace of Hearts. It wasn't winner take all, after all.

·   ·   ·

Back in her room with Cassidy, Dakota attempted to tell this story, but the words wouldn't come. Instead, the tears finally came, and they poured tiny rivers down her face. Cassidy put her arm around her little sister and pulled her next to her on the bed.

Dakota shamelessly let herself cry on Cassidy's shoulder until she felt the sadness give way.

She sat back up and looking at the tear stains on Cassidy's dress, she said, "I'm sorry about that." She blotted at the wet spot with the edge of her sleeve. "I'm sorry about all of this."

"It's okay, Koty. It's good to have a cry once in a while. You have to let this stuff out." Cassidy smoothed back Dakota's dark brown hair.

"Thanks." Dakota wiped her eyes. "If you don't mind, I think I need to be alone for a minute."

"Of course," said Cassidy as she left her sister alone in her room.

With Cassidy out of the room, Dakota studied the picture of Maddy once again. It was as if she could hear Maddy's high-pitched laugh and smell the cherry blossom shampoo that radiated off her long black hair through the picture. She loved the way being around Maddy had made her feel: competent, protective, and understood. If only she could feel that way again.

Dakota walked over to her desk and picked up the black fuzzy diary she used to write in every day as a teenager. She flipped through the pages, searching for

Maddy's name. She stopped at the entry marked "December 5, 2000," — two days before Maddy's disappearance, and she read the entry:

Selena Diaz is at it again. I couldn't believe what she did this time. The nerve of that bitch! Maddy and I were in the library, studying in our favorite spot when Selena and her idiot best friend, Tiffany Kowalski came up to us.

They were both breaking the dress code with their rolled-up skirts, slutty hoop earrings, and black bras showing through their white button downs. Selena's ponytail made her face even more dog-like than normal and I wish I had told her that.

Anyway, she walks up to us and says, "We want to make a deal with you."

"What would that be?" I asked them.

But Selena snapped back, "I wasn't talking to you."

"What do you want?" Maddy asked, I could tell she was getting nervous.

"I want to make a deal with you." Selena flopped one butt cheek on the table, so she was half sitting on the table and half standing on the floor.

Tiffany moved in closer and crossed her arms.

"How about you do all our assignments and we cheat off of you for every test next semester, and... we'll do something for you?" Selena said.

"I don't think that's—" Maddy began.

"I'll introduce you to Gabriel." Selena began. "And I'll convince him to date you. Half the school knows you've got it bad for him, but he's a hot commodity. He's handsome, he's a soccer star, plays the guitar, the whole package. I'm proud to call him my little brother, but that's the thing, I don't let my little brother just date anyone, and he's always looked up to me. Plus, you might have ended up in the same class as him if you weren't miss smarty-pants and hadn't skipped two grades. Oh well. But now's your chance."

Selena was leaning over Maddy like some kind of wild animal waiting to pounce and said, "What do you say?"

"That's ridiculous. You idiots need to do your own work." I told them. I wanted to rip those ugly earrings out of their heads.

"Here's the problem — you can't say no," said Tiffany. "If you refuse, we'll turn it up a notch. You think this last year has been bad. You haven't seen nothing yet! Your life will be a living hell."

Then, that psycho pulled out a lighter from her leather bag. She picked up a sheet of Maddy's homework and lit it on fire! And she dropped it on the table in front of us.

I took off one shoe and stamped out the flames.

Selena said, "Think about it. This can end one of two ways. You leave school for summer break next year with the boyfriend of your dreams and two bad-ass chicks on your side... or you leave school in a body bag! You choose."

The two girls flashed a fake grin and left.

"Don't listen to them. They're bluffing. You don't have to do anything for them," I told Maddy who was practically shaking with fear.

"I don't think I have a choice," she told me.

I can't believe those psychos can act this way and get away with it.

Dakota closed her diary. *How have I not remembered this?* she thought, sitting back down on her bed.

It was Selena. It had to be Selena.

Chapter 2

I'll have to make this one quick. Ma will wonder what's taking me so long. I said I had to shower after work, but that's just what I tell her.

It's wrong and dirty, but I can't help myself. It's really not my fault. I'm not the one who walks around town in low-cut tops and short shorts, just begging for men to leer at me. I'm just minding my own business, trying to do my job and go about my life. I don't want to be tempted or turned on but there they are, dressed like tramps.

I was leaving the grocery store and I see a few cars down from me, two bimbos loading up their trunk. One of them is a brunette and she is wearing a tight white sundress. A girl like that should not be allowed to wear white. Next to her, her blond friend is bending down, and I can see straight up her jean shorts.

My face got flush, and I didn't know what to do. I couldn't move. All I could do was stare at that perfect ass hanging out of those Daisy Dukes. She stood up and I see she's wearing one of those crop tops.

Worst of all, she noticed me staring at her. She laughed and gave me a little wave. And in that moment, I could have sworn it was Rebecca. But no, it wasn't, it couldn't have been. Rebecca has been long gone for decades now. But why do I still see her face in the crowd from time to time? Either way, I got so flustered and confused that I got in my car with my groceries and sped off. As I drive, I feel nothing but anger and arousal.

I fling the bags on the counter and tell Ma to put the groceries away. Then, I pound the wooden steps down to my room. I open the metal door that leads to my cave and see my wall of photographs. I pick a handful off the wall. Sitting down at my desk, I open my fly and start working on myself with one hand while the other hand flips through the photos.

The first one is Hedda, the Swede. She's in my favorite position. Tied up and bent over. The second one is Sophie whose big dark eyes are looking up at me while she kneels on the floor. That one is helping but I'm not there yet.

I flip to the last one. It's Rebecca in the summer of '69. She was sixteen and perfect. Her and her douchebag boyfriend, Chuck, and her loser hippie friends are gathered around Chuck's wood panel station wagon with a faded orange and yellow surfboard strapped to the top. The girls were all in polka dot or paisley patterned bikinis. Rebecca stands out as the least dressed one in the photo in a multicolored crocheted two-piece that barely covered her nipples and privates.

My eyes wash over her body. I remember how badly I wanted to touch her. How good it felt when I finally did. Her memory is what does it for me. I finish.

Sweaty and lightheaded, I zip up and try to keep my cool for Ma. She thinks I've been able to keep my desire to sin under control this whole time. Back upstairs, we sit at the large dinner table. We eat our mashed potatoes and peas in silence. Then, I stand to help Ma cut her meat. She can't chew too much these days.

I glance around the room and say, "Ya know Ma, this is a lot of wasted space. This big table. It's just us two, no one ever comes over. Why don't we get rid of it? I can sell it for a few bucks and we can turn this into a craft room for you. We can put a smaller table in the kitchen and have meals there."

"Oh, you're talking crazy. I don't need a craft room. I do my knitting in the den," she says, with bits of green pea lodged in the gums of her dentures.

"Well, you say you're having trouble going up and down the stairs to get to your room each night. Why don't we bring the bed down here, so you don't have to anymore? It'll be nicer on your joints." I tell her as I finish cutting her chicken into little squares.

"I'm not getting rid of the table. The kids need it. I don't want any more crazy talk coming out of you, Edward." Ma sits back and puts her hands on her hips.

I furrow my brow. "Edward? Ma, it's Freddy. Your son. Edward was your husband. He left us, years ago. Remember?"

"What?" Her mouth falls open. "Edward left me. How could he? What will the kids think? Where is he? I'll call him and get him to come home."

"Ma, he died," I say.

"What? When? How did—" She buries her head in her hands and cries.

I hug her. "Ma, it's okay. Dad was not a nice man. It was better for us that he left. He got sick a few years after and died. But we were fine. We got through it together."

"Does your sister know?" she asks.

I take a deep breath. "She knows." I grab her by the shoulders and coax her to her feet. "Listen, Ma. Everything is going to be okay. Why don't you sit down on the couch and I'll clear the plates? I think Jeopardy is on in a bit."

"Oh good. I sure like that show," she tells me, as I guide her to the den.

After I've scraped the plates and stuck them in the dishwasher, she calls out:

"Freddy, this damn remote isn't working again. Can you fix it?"

I rush over. She looks different. There's life back in her eyes. She looks mad and mean, like always. As I play around with the remote, she wipes her eyes and asks, "Was I crying?"

"Yes Ma, you cried." I bang the remote against my palm.

"What for?" She's looking right at me, trying to tell if I'm lying, but I won't look back at her.

"You forgot Dad left," I say, matter of fact.

She throws her hands up in the air. "That's crazy. I'd never forget a thing like that."

"Well, you did."

"There are things you don't forget. I'll never forget the day he left or the day the incident occurred."

"Yes, I'm aware. We've talked long and hard about the incident, okay? You don't need to keep rehashing it." I press a few buttons on the remote and the channel changes. I hand it back to Ma.

"Fine, just promise me, you've stopped having incidents for good now?" she asks.

"Yes Ma. For God's sake, it's been twelve years since the last one, I told you I'm finished."

She looks at me dead in the eyes for a moment and smirks like she knows something I don't. She turns back to the TV and I walk away.

• • •

Dakota was pouring herself a cup of lukewarm coffee when her parents came through the door, chattering and laughing. Debi wore a white tennis outfit that showed off her toned and tan figure. Ken had a white polo shirt with a tiny crocodile emblem on the pocket that stretched over his muscular physique.

"That was quite a game there, honey. You're glad I let you win," he said while patting his wife on the butt with a tennis racket.

"You didn't let me win, you silly goose," she said.

"Babe, I'm a professional athlete. I let you win."

"At golf, not tennis. I beat you fair and square." Debi poked him in the chest.

"Oh come here, you." Ken grabbed Debi and kissed her.

They turned to see Dakota staring at them as she sipped from a mug.

"It's great to wake up and see that, first thing in the morning." Dakota took a seat at the kitchen table.

"If you had gotten up earlier, it wouldn't have been first thing in the morning," said Ken.

"Don't give me that guilt trip. I'm jet-lagged," Dakota quipped.

"All right, you two." Debi poured herself another cup of coffee. "Enough of the fighting. I know you and Dad... well, you and everyone, buck heads but try not to get each other too riled up."

"Fine," Ken and Dakota said in unison.

"I'm sorry, I'm not in the best of moods this morning," Dakota said, offering an olive breach to her father.

Ken sat down at the breakfast table next to his daughter.

"Listen Koty, what you've been through in the last few months wasn't easy. I just don't want to see you waste your time," he said.

"Thanks Dad," said Dakota, "but that's not the whole reason I'm in a bad mood. I was thinking about Maddy yesterday. After looking through some old stuff in my room, I found something in my diary, something I didn't tell the police."

Debi rushed over and took a seat. With wide-eyed enthusiasm, she asked, "What did you find?"

"Selena and Tiffany—" Dakota started.

"Man, I hated those girls," Debi chimed in.

"Yes, so did I. But anyway, I wrote down two days before Maddy went missing that they threatened her in the library in front of me. They said if she did their schoolwork for the next semester, Selena would convince her brother to go out with Maddy. Maddy seemed to be all for it since she was crushing on him hard, but they implied that they'd physically hurt her if she didn't agree to the deal."

"What do you mean by implied?" asked Ken.

"They said they'd make the next semester a living hell and that she might even leave the school in a body bag," she answered.

"Dakota! Why didn't you say anything at the time?" asked Debi, almost rising out of her seat.

"I honestly don't remember, but I'm pretty sure I thought they were bluffing. Plus, after Maddy disappeared, I became so focused on finding her, everything that happened the few days before that night didn't seem to matter."

Dakota stared down at her coffee feeling guilt wash over her. Then, she got to her feet. "But I'm going to make this right. I'm going to find that Selena bitch and make her tell me everything."

Ken's face froze. "That's not a good idea. If you think she did something to Maddy, you should talk to Detective Muldowney."

"Oh please, that detective has had twelve years to find Maddy. And he's produced nothing." Dakota's voice raised along with her blood pressure.

"I'm sick of waiting, I want answers *now*." She dashed through the kitchen and down the hall, her weathered flip-flops smacking against the terracotta tiles. She scooped up her purse and her mother's car keys from the entry hall table and rushed into the garage. In seconds, she backed the S-class Mercedes out of the driveway and down the street, leaving her parents standing at the front door with mouths open.

•   •   •

Dakota remembered every twist, turn, and side road in her childhood neighborhood but a few things had changed. The local grocer was now a Whole Foods, and some developer leveled the row of 1920s-style bungalows at the end of the road for luxurious condos. Nevertheless, she found Selena's house.

She pulled the white Mercedes into the circular drive of the Diaz home. It had the same faux-Spanish style exterior as the Kilroys' home, only bigger and with more garage space for Mr. Diaz's classic cars.

At the front door, an elderly Hispanic woman answered the door.

"Mrs. Diaz?" Dakota asked, surprised that Selena's health-nut of a mother had aged so poorly.

"Si," the woman replied.

"I'm trying to find your daughter, Selena. Is she here or do you know where I can find her?" she asked.

"Lo siento, no hablo inglés. Déjame buscar a mi hijo," the woman said, before she called out to someone behind her. Mr. Diaz came to the door. Dakota recognized him right away. He had ruggedly handsome good looks that had barely changed over the years save for some gray on his temples.

"My mother said you needed something," he said to her.

Dakota paused for a moment, realizing she had been speaking to Selena's grandmother instead of her mother.

"Hi, Mr. Diaz. I'm Dakota Kilroy, I went to school with Selena at St. Philomena's. I wanted to say hi to her since I'm back in town," she explained.

Mr. Diaz looked her up and down and smirked at her appearance of yoga pants, a stained NYU sweatshirt, and a messy bun.

"Selena is away right now," he replied.

"Will she be back soon?" Dakota asked.

"Three months or more. But I'll tell her you dropped by." He moved the door closer to the threshold.

Dakota put her hand out to stop it from closing. "Is there a way I can call her or text her?"

"Why do you want to speak to her so bad?" He put his hands on his hips and stuck his head out further.

"I just have a few questions for her," said Dakota.

"About what?" His tone was snide.

"What happened the night Madeline Montgomery went missing?" she admitted.

His eyes turned cold. "Are you a cop or something? Did you even know my daughter?"

"Yes, I did. See?" Dakota pulled out her wallet and held up a coin-sized medal that depicted a young woman crowned in a halo holding an armful of arrows. Mr. Diaz recognized the item. It was the likeness of St. Philomena and every student got this medal upon graduating the school.

Dakota continued, "You see, Maddy was my best friend, and I was just trying to get back in touch with some people from high school to see if they remember anything from that night. Maybe something they forgot about or didn't tell the police."

Mr. Diaz rubbed his forehead. "Listen, my daughter had nothing to do with it. I remember hearing about Maddy's disappearance and I'm sorry about whatever happened to your friend, but Selena won't be answering any questions. You couldn't talk to her if you wanted to."

"What is that supposed to mean?" Dakota didn't like people who gave vague answers.

"She's in rehab, okay?" he yelled. "Court-appointed rehab. And she isn't allowed visitors or any contact with the outside world until she is at least three months clean. Now, can you leave my family in peace? This is embarrassing enough for us."

"I didn't mean to upset you," Dakota began. "I'm sorry for what she's going through, and I didn't mean to intrude."

Mr. Diaz nodded and closed the door.

●　　　●　　　●

Back at the Kilroy residence, Dakota parked the car in the garage. Her parents were there waiting for her with crossed arms and angry faces.

"What the hell was that?" shouted her mother.

"Don't you ever take off like that again!" Ken yelled.

Dakota stepped out of the car. "I'm sorry. I just had to find out. She wasn't even there. She's in rehab."

"Jesus, Koty, you can't do that." Ken's face wrinkled with frustration.

"This is what I'm like. This is how I am on the job. I get a lead and I track it down," she explained.

"You're not on a job right now. In fact, you don't have one," shouted Ken.

Dakota didn't answer and instead stomped back inside the house. She entered the kitchen, only to see Detective Muldowney sitting in her seat.

"Dakota Kilroy. It's been a long time." He stood up and stretched out his hand.

She shook his hand, but Dakota's body tensed as they touched.

"I'm impressed of what you've made of yourself. And at such a young age." He sat down again.

"What do you mean?" asked Ken.

"Have you been following your daughter's career closely?" asked the detective.

"Yes," lied Ken. He hadn't been. Mainly because he found hard journalism too depressing.

"She almost single-handedly exposed a modeling agency as a covert brothel as her senior journalism project in college. I'm surprised you don't know this," he said.

Both of her parents looked at each other with empty expressions on their faces.

"I'm sure you know she is the youngest investigative journalist ever to be hired by *The Village Inquirer*. Not to mention the latest story about the drug wars in New York is up for several journalism awards. Good stuff!"

"Then how come she can't find work?" asked Ken.

"The industry is tough right now," said the detective.

Dakota looked at the old man, grateful that he was sticking up for her, even though everything about him repulsed her: His shaggy gray mustache harbored coffee stains and muffin crumbles around his lips. His eyes haloed by a half circle of deep wrinkles and liver spots. He was at least 20 pounds thinner than he was in 2000, as if years of detective work had gutted his body of health.

"I didn't know you were such a fan," Dakota quipped.

"And I sense that the feeling isn't mutual," the detective said. "I realize you blame me for not finding Maddy. I get how it must feel but believe me, I've tried my best. I've worked every angle, followed every tip I could get. But I haven't given up hope even after retiring. That's why I raced over here when your parents called me and told me your theory about Selena Diaz."

"It isn't really a theory," Dakota said, recounting what she wrote in her diary and what Mr. Diaz told her about Selena's whereabouts.

"That incident of bullying is alarming, but she did have an alibi for the night of the play. She was supposed to be another angel alongside Maddy in the pageant, but Mrs. Diaz had called the music teacher, Mrs. Pruitt to tell her that Selena was home sick with a high fever. But I'd like to speak with her again. I'll track her down in rehab and see if they'll let me talk to her," he said.

"That would be lovely, thank you," said Debi. "Would you like another cup of coffee or a muffin?"

"No, I better be on my way. But keep me in the loop the next time you find something pertaining to the case," he said, giving Dakota a quick glance.

She nodded but didn't move.

Ken ushered the detective out the door, before returning to the kitchen.

"The detective is on the case, so you don't need to worry about investigating Selena or anyone else for that matter," said Ken.

"But—" Dakota started.

"That's enough. You're making things harder on us and things harder on that poor old man," Debi scolded. "Do you have any idea what he has been going through? His son got injured in Iraq and now, that wild child daughter of his is flunking out of Stanford after he paid her tuition for the whole year."

"I don't care about his personal life. I want him to solve the case," she said.

"He will. We're sure he'll follow up with Selena. You just focus on getting back on your feet," said Ken.

"Fine, I'll lay off it," Dakota sighed. "I just want to find her so badly. This is what I do, I investigate."

"And we want you to, just not with this case — you're too close to it. Why don't we try to find you a job around here to get your mind off things and get those journalism fingers a-typing?" her mom said.

"Fine, I'll look at some jobs."

•　　•　　•

"The job entails reporting on local interest items: High school football games, community bake sales, church gatherings." A woman sat across from Dakota in a pale brown blazer with puffy red hair. She was the news editor for the *Santa Monica Bulletin*, the second most trusted news source for the town. There were only two local papers.

When Dakota first arrived at the *Bulletin's* headquarters, she was certain her mother dropped her off at the wrong address. The building was a yellow craftsman-style house that looked like it belonged to the perfect nuclear family instead of a news outlet. If it wasn't for a gust of wind that pushed back the drooping branches of the willow tree out front to reveal a sign that said, "*Santa Monica Bulletin*," Dakota would have ventured down the street looking for a different office.

Now, she was sitting in front of a glass desk in the editor's office, which clearly used to be a children's bedroom when the house had operated as a home. She could even see the faint outline of where the mother painted little pink bunnies at the corners of the room. The idea of working in this tiny office day in and out while reporting on community events made her sick with dread.

"What about local crime?" Dakota asked.

"We have two reporters who work on that already but there isn't much to cover, anyway. Perhaps the occasional car break-in, loud parties on the beach, illegal bonfires, that sort of thing," the editor explained.

"When I was in New York..." Dakota began.

"But you're not in New York anymore, are you?" The editor interrupted. "We don't need the same level of investigation in this peaceful town. The people here want to read about what's happening in their neighborhood. They don't want to read about something that might upset them," she explained.

The two women sat for a moment of uncomfortable silence before Dakota said, "Right, well, I think I'll see myself out then."

She exited the house to see her mother's Mercedes parked down the street. Dakota got in the passenger seat. Her mother turned to her with hope in her eyes.

"So?" Debi asked.

"No, I didn't get it," Dakota told her.

Debi put the car into drive and sped off in a huff.

"Are you kidding me? You have so much experience and worked at a much larger paper. They've got to be insane for not hiring you." Debi stomped on the brake at a red light and turned to her daughter.

"It's fine, Mom," Dakota said. "I walked away from it."

"You what?" shrieked Debi.

"I'm a serious journalist. And if you cared about my career at all, you would know that I'm not going to write about bake sales at some tiny paper," she said.

"I *do* care about your career," said Debi.

"Really? Then how come Detective Muldowney of all people had to tell you about my accomplishments?" Dakota crossed her arms and stared at her mother. Debi kept her eyes on the road, not for safety but out of fear of meeting her daughter's glare.

"And," Dakota continued. "I bet you know every detail of Capri and Cassidy's lives. Back in high school, you went to every single one of their cheer practices, dance competitions, and modeling auditions. But you and Dad would show up late to my photography showcases and would barely look up from your paper when I told you I got straight As on my report card. Nowadays, you know every game that Blake will be in and every real estate deal Peter is working on. But when I work my ass off for almost a year on a story that helped disrupt a major drug trafficking network, you don't even bother to read it."

"Okay, all right." Debi threw her hands up in the air before grasping the soft leather wheel again. "We just don't have that much in common. You know that. It isn't that we aren't proud of you. It's just that we find those dark stories you uncover to be upsetting and we don't like to think of our daughter having to write them."

"The world is upsetting, Mom. Just in case you haven't noticed," Dakota sighed, frustrated at the bubble the people of her hometown inhabited.

"I don't understand," said Debi. "You're from the same family, you grew up in the same household. What happened to you to make you want to deal with all the deep dark stuff in the world?"

"You know what happened," said Dakota. "My best friend disappeared and has never been found. I used to keep myself up at night picturing every sadistic and depraved situation some kidnapper could be keeping her in. Or coming up with all the different places you could dispose of her body without her ever being found. I'd replay that night in my head over and over, combing every detail for some clue about what happened to her. But I can't solve it. I can't save her. But these people, the ones who are victims of crimes happening right now. I can save them by exposing their abusers to the light. That's why I can't give up what I do."

Tears were streaming down both women's faces. Dakota turned away from her mother and wiped away the black eyeliner that had smudged on her lower eyelid.

"I'm sorry, Koty," said Debi with a small sob. "I'm sorry you had to lose her like that. I'm sorry if it seems like Dad and I don't understand. We just love you and want the best for you. I'm sorry if you feel we are pushing you away from your life's calling."

"It's okay, Mom."

"We want to make sure you can provide for yourself. Please promise you'll give another job a try," she said.

"Okay, I'll try," said Dakota.

• • •

Dakota awoke at four in the morning with a pain in her chest. Her lungs struggled to take in air as she sat up in bed. Then, the different pieces of the nightmare she had been having came back to her: Maddy in her favorite white lace dress walking along mounds of dirt. The mounds were made of fresh earth and were about six feet long. They were graves. Maddy stood over a pit and pointed, saying, "Come find me."

Dakota's mouth was dry and her hair clung to the left side of her face with sweat. There was more to the nightmare, but thankfully her subconscious whisked those images away before she could remember anymore. With her heart still racing from her half-remembered dream, she knew there was no getting back to sleep.

Downstairs, she fixed herself up with a nice cup of coffee and her laptop. She spent the next three hours applying for jobs while pushing questions about Maddy's case out of her head. By the time dawn arrived, Dakota was exhausted from typing up cover letters, submitting resumes, and taking required personality questionnaires.

Debi and Ken came down the stairs at a quarter past seven to see Dakota typing up a storm at her computer at the kitchen table.

"Well, you're up early," Ken remarked.

"I couldn't sleep well so I've been applying to jobs for the past three hours. Eighteen total, I think." She beamed at her father knowing he would be proud of her for having such a strong work ethic.

"That's my girl." He kissed her on the forehead. "I knew you had it in you. I'm sure at least one of those places will give you an interview."

"You know what," said Debi, who was pulling items out of the fridge for an omelet. "Mary Beth and I are having a day at the spa she won at some charity auction a few weeks back and she's picking me up in a few hours. Why don't you take the car, so you can drive around and apply for other jobs in person since you're on such a roll today?"

"Sure, Mom. Sounds great." Dakota didn't have the heart to tell her mom that's not how people get jobs nowadays. But after the meltdown they had in the car, she didn't want to rock the boat.

Midmorning came and Dakota felt antsy staying in her parents' large house alone. She picked up the keys to her mother's car, intending to take a drive just to get out of the house. She had a good memory of her childhood town, but it had been eleven years and she found it surprisingly difficult to find her way around Santa Monica.

After about half an hour, she found herself at a four-way stop with no idea which way to go. The driver behind her blasted their horn. Panicked, she took a right turn and hoped for the best. She drove straight for a few more blocks until she recognized where she was: in front of St. Philomena's College Preparatory High school.

She pulled into the parking lot and sat there, looking at her old high school. It hadn't changed at all: Those four long separate buildings with six classrooms each which formed a square. In the center, there was the large auditorium that served as a cafeteria, gym, or theater depending on the day. One of the block buildings had a white-domed steeple on top that bore a bronze cross. That was the chapel where Mass was held for the student body several times a week. The freshmen attended Mass on Mondays. The seniors attended on Wednesdays. And for some reason, the sophomore and junior classes had to share the same small space on Thursdays. This meant at least fifteen or so students had to sit on the scratchy carpet in front of the pews as the local priest blessed the bread and wine.

Laughing to herself, Dakota recalled the time Mr. Lawrence, the somewhat young History teacher, fell asleep in the back of the chapel as Mass was going on. Mr. Kruller, the no-nonsense bulldog-shaped Science teacher, slapped him hard on the knee and he woke up making a funny screaming noise that sounded like a fox being run over by a wheelbarrow.

Dakota's mind flicked back to the conversation with her mother. It was a few years ago, but she still remembers Debi's worried voice over the phone saying, "I can't believe it. Your old History teacher Mr. Lawrence just got arrested for having an affair with one of his students. Please tell me he never tried anything with you."

At the time, Dakota assured her mother that the teacher never did anything inappropriate with her. But now, she wondered if anyone thought to ask if he did anything inappropriate with Maddy?

She reached into her bag and pulled out the moleskin notebook she kept with her at all times. Flipping to a blank page, she made a list of suspects:

• *Mr. Lawrence: Had affair with student. Is in prison. Did anyone question him about Maddy?*
• *Selena Diaz: Is in rehab. Did Muldowney follow up like he promised?*
• *Tiffany Kowalski: Where is she now? Was she ever questioned? Does she have an alibi?*
• *Gabriel Diaz: Did he help his sister with getting rid of Maddy if her bullying went too far?*
• *Connor Freisinger: Strange kid who was obsessed with Maddy.*
• *Mr. and Mrs. Montgomery: Even the parents can't be above suspicion.*
• *Pastor Calvin Shaw: Maddy's grandfather. Strict Baptist preacher. Is ashamed of Maddy for being born out of wedlock.*

Dakota shivered at the thought of seeing Pastor Shaw again. His face was always frozen in a perpetual smirk of disapproval. She hated the way he was so strict and demanding around Maddy. Maybe his anger got the better of him one day.

Dakota shook her head, trying to rattle the image of Maddy's grandfather kidnapping or murdering her free from her mind.

"Think of the other possibilities," she told herself in a low whisper.

The only thing she could come up with was that a stranger snatched her off school grounds. But, according to Mrs. Montgomery, she dropped Maddy off right outside the school and watched her walk into the gates towards the auditorium. The chances of some unknown person wandering onto school property and walking away with Maddy unseen by the dozens of students and staff preparing for the school pageant were unlikely.

Dakota longed to see the police report. A concise summary of all the details of the night she disappeared was her only hope. But Detective Muldowney took the case's files after he retired, and she knew he would not let her look at them, even for a second.

She had to talk to someone else. Someone trustworthy who was there that night she disappeared. Dakota clapped her hands together in the driver's seat of her parked car. "Of course, Principal Bernard and Mrs. Pruitt, the music teacher," she announced, as if she was speaking to someone else in the car. Both staff members had been there that night and knew every detail of what happened. They even worked closely with the police and their search parties in the first few days of Maddy's disappearance.

Dakota jotted down their names on a fresh page in her notebook and sped out of the parking lot.

Chapter 3

I had to get out of the house. It's my day off and I can't stand being cooped up with Ma for too long. She's giving me the silent treatment. She won't talk to me, but I see her giving me that suspicious side-long glance when she thinks I'm not looking. Oh, but I can see — I can see her looking from behind her mane of long gray hairs with her big brown eyes glaring at me. Burning holes in my head. And into my soul.

When I catch her glaring at me, I ask her what's wrong. She'll just shrug her shoulders and turn away. I hate when she toys with me like that. I don't understand how she does it, but she knows when lust for flesh and blood fills my heart. Ever since I was a teenager, I could have sworn she could tell every time I touched myself. She'd give me these glares, the silent treatment, and those random lectures about the Bible for days afterwards.

I'm a grown man now, and she still treats me like an insolent teenager. Well, enough is enough. I had to leave. So I hopped in the Toyota and drove the rusty old thing to my favorite Casino, the Four Peaks. It's outdated with shag carpeting and teal wallpaper, but I love it.

I don't like being out in public much. It's bad enough when I have to go to work every day, go to the store, or take Ma to the doctors. But here, I feel like I can lose myself. The blinking lights, the clinking of slot machines, the sound of the men making bets at the blackjack table help me forget about who I am for a few hours. The best part of all is that you can still smoke inside this casino. That bullshit anti-smoking rhetoric of the 1990s seemed to have taken over everywhere but the Four Peaks.

I sit down at the penny slots and slide a smooth dollar bill into the machine. Placing a cigarette between my teeth and lighting it, I exhale a puff and pull the handle.

Ding! Ding! Ding! I win twenty-five cents.

An hour later, I lost twenty dollars but won back thirty. That's what I call making a profit. And that warrants a drink. Of course, Ma never would approve of me drinking on a random Wednesday, even if it was my day off. "Christmas, weddings, and funerals," she'd say. Those are the only times in life it was morally acceptable to have a drink, and never more than one. But she isn't here, and she'll never know.

I walk up to the bar and order an Old-Fashioned. The bartender hands me the drink and I bring it to my mouth, slowly taking in the bitter liquid. Because of Ma's strict drinking rules, I am what you'd call a lightweight. It only takes this one drink to make me a little lightheaded.

I like it, so I order a second one. I'm a bad boy, I think with a chuckle. But it feels good to be bad sometimes. I take another gulp of the drink, the whiskey no longer burning my mouth, and notice that a woman has been sitting at the bar, two chairs away from me. How long has she been there?

She is about my age and pretty, even though she has wrinkles around her eyes and lips. She has shoulder-length brandy-colored hair with bits of gold highlights. Were they natural or did some hairdresser put them in for her? I couldn't tell.

Maybe it was time to get a girlfriend my own age. Maybe it wasn't too late for me to live a normal life and stop wasting my time on young girls. I got up with my legs shaking and moved to the chair next to her.

"Hi, I'm Freddy. Can I buy you a drink?" I ask her. Every pore in my body leaks sweat and my heart is beating so loudly I almost miss her reply.

"Sure. Glass of white wine, please," she says with a small smile.

I'm stunned. She didn't reject me. I repeat her order to the barkeep, and he delivers the drink to her.

"I'm Marilyn, by the way," she tells me with a hint of a Southern accent in her voice.

"Like Monroe?" I ask, jokingly.

"I wish," she giggles.

"I come here a lot and I haven't seen you around. Are you new in town?" I ask.

"If you couldn't tell by the accent, I'm from Georgia. I'm just in town visiting my daughter and her grandbabies."

"Grandbabies? You don't seem old enough to be a grandma," I tell her. I have to hold back my disgust. It's hard enough forcing myself to be attracted to an older woman, but now I know she's a grandmother, I feel a revulsion towards her.

"Well, I had my first one a little too young at 17. She now has three kids. All boys. They are quite a handful, but my youngest and his wife and expecting a girl in May. I'm quite excited to dress up a little baby girl in pink dresses and bows." She grins, leans in and brushes her hair back.

A grandma with four grandkids, I don't think I can make this work.

She notices that I look upset.

"But don't worry," she continues. "My husband and I have been broken up for years. Say, do you have a room or someplace we can go back to?" Marilyn places her hand on my leg and squeezes.

This wasn't going to happen. The idea of sleeping with a grandma made my gut turn over.

I open my wallet and place cash on the counter. "I forgot I have to be somewhere. Sorry about that. Anyway, I hope you enjoyed your wine."

"Wait, Freddy," she calls after me, but I was already halfway towards the door.

What's wrong with me? Why can't I find her attractive? We're in the same age range. She's sweet and mature... but I can't. I want to go home, but I have a feeling Ma will be there, knowing I drank and tried to have extramarital sex with a strange woman.

I hear a horn honk as I realize I'm behind the wheel of my car, drifting into another lane. I pull the car steady and give an apologetic wave to the guy I almost hit. I focus on the road ahead, but I'm not sure where I am or which direction I should go. Why do I have to be such a lightweight?

I drive for two more blocks and see a sign for the freeway. Maybe I can make it home. I stop at the red light three blocks from the freeway ramp and a cop pulls up behind me.

No, not now. I bet he knows. He has to know I'm driving drunk. And if doesn't know now, he will know the second that light turns green. What if he questions me about where I live? What if I tell him about my senile mother and he comes to investigate, only to find the girls? The light is still red, but I have to figure out something. Up the road, there is a big blue sign saying "Wayfield Mall." The entrance to the mall's parking structure is only a few yards away. Thank God, I'm saved!

The light turns green and I turn into the car park just in time to see the cop pass me in the rearview mirror. Since I'm here, I figure I should stay for a while, walk around the stores and window shop. That way I'll have time to sober up before I have to face Ma again.

Once inside the mall, I'm surprised by the number of teenagers, and families with little kids that are shopping on a weekday. I'm just about to yell "Why aren't you kids in school?" at a little punk who almost ran into me, but then I remember. It's mid-January and many schools have the entire month of January off for "Winter Vacation." We didn't have Winter Vacation in my day. It was called "Christmas Break," and it was only a week long. But now, these little terrors need a whole month off. I roll my eyes at the thought.

After walking the long corridors of this behemoth of a mall, I take a seat on one of the wooden benches that are placed up and down the wide halls for tired shoppers to rest on. Behind me, I hear a girl's voice yell, "But Daddy, that's not fair."

I turn around. A girl with long blond hair, an orange lace top that shows her midriff, and a pair of white short shorts is screaming at her father. The girl continues, "Amy, Jasmine, and Cora are all allowed to shop here. Why can't I?"

"Because I said so," her father, a man who looked like He-Man with a buzz-cut began. "A girl your age shouldn't be wearing stuff like that. Now here's fifty bucks for some school clothes. Clothes, not underwear, understand?" He hands her the money, and she sulks away.

The store the teen wanted to go into was Victoria's Secret.

My face flushed at the sight of the huge advertisement in the store window of a brunette model in a leopard print bra and pantie set. I laugh to myself a little. Her father would give her fifty dollars to keep her out of that skimpy underwear and I'd pay thousands just to see her in it.

At that very second, she sits down on the same bench as me. She has her white iPhone out and is feverishly tapping away at it. My heart pounds in my chest, but I force myself to ask her, "Hey, do you wanna buy some stuff from in there?" I point to the lingerie store.

She flips her long hair behind her ear and turns her sweet little face with a button nose and round blue eyes towards me.

"Yes, I do. Like, really bad. They have me wearing little girl underwear. Like I'm fourteen, I totally think I can wear, you know, grown up underwear," she explains to me.

"Totally," I agree. "Why don't I give you another fifty dollars so your dad doesn't think you spent his money on it? And then you sneak home with the stuff you bought in your purse and he'll never find out."

The girl half-smiles at me. I can tell she's talking herself into it.

"I only ask one thing in return," I reach into my inner jacket pocket and pull out my digital camera. "You take pictures of what you try on in the dressing room for me."

She giggled a little. "I don't know."

"It's a good deal. Free panties for a few photos," I say.

"You won't share them with anyone, will you?" she asks.

"No, of course not, honey. They're just for me."

"Okay," she says.

She is about to take the camera from me when a booming voice calls out, "Shannon!" Her giant father is less than three yards away from us.

"Hey, what are you doing?" he calls after me.

I get up and run.

I spend the next 45 minutes hiding in the handicapped bathroom stall. Once I can assure myself that the coast is clear, I creep out of the mall and back to my car.

• • •

"Dakota, dear, it's so lovely to see you." Principal Bernard leaned in and gave Dakota a quick hug.

"Nice to see you too." Principal Bernard's short and frail appearance shocked Dakota as much as the improvement in her demeanor.

The woman was a force to be reckoned with over eleven years ago. She would watch students report to school every day from the middle of the courtyard and scan them for any signs of misbehavior. She didn't smile, she didn't hug, and she didn't tell her students it was nice to see them.

Dakota walked through the hallway to the sitting room. The place smelled like baby powder and Chanel perfume. Sitting behind the coffee table with a gilded teacup in hand, Mrs. Pruitt lit up as Dakota came into the room.

"Oh my goodness, you're all grown up." Mrs. Pruitt stood and gave Dakota a hug.

In true Mrs. Pruitt fashion, her long blond-turning-white hair was pulled back with a big black butterfly clip and she wore a long flowing lavender skirt with a beige top that was reminiscent of the late 60s.

"Thank you both for taking the time to meet with me," Dakota said, pulling at her sleeves. It was over seventy degrees today, but Dakota wore a black turtleneck to cover her tattoos. The last thing she needed was a lecture from two older women about her body art.

"Nonsense, we're happy to have you." Mrs. Pruitt poured Dakota a cup of tea with two biscuits on the saucer and handed it to her.

Dakota nodded in thanks. "Like I said on the phone, I want to go over what happened the night Maddy disappeared. I'm sorry for bringing this stuff up again. It's been twelve years and we're trying to move on, but I can't—"

Principal Bernard spoke up. "I understand. The things from the past can haunt you and it doesn't matter how much time has passed or how many people tell you to move on. Sometimes, you have to keep digging."

Relief washed over Dakota. Finally, someone understood what it was like.

She reached into her bag and pulled out her iPhone. "Do you mind if I record this on my phone? I want to make sure I have a record of everything that has been said, so I don't mix up my facts later on."

"Oh my, that thing acts as a tape recorder too? What will they think of next?" quipped Mrs. Pruitt.

"It's fine with us," Principal Bernard answered.

Dakota placed the phone in the center of the coffee table and hit record.

"This is Dakota Kilroy recording on January 20, 2012. I'm sitting with Mrs. Jane Pruitt and Principal Alice Bernard, both formerly employed at St. Philomena's College Prep. Both women have agreed to speak with me about the disappearance of Maddy Montgomery on December 7, 2000. All right ladies, why don't I start with something easy first? What was Maddy like?" Dakota asked.

Both women let out a small laugh.

"She was a very sweet girl. Always a pleasure to see around campus, but I never did understand her fashion sense," began Principal Bernard.

"What do you mean?" Dakota leaned forward.

"I'm sure you remember," Principal Bernard began. "Every other Friday was 'Free Dress Friday' where the students were allowed to wear regular clothes instead of their uniform to school. I was, of course, completely against the idea but I was outvoted by the PTA. Most students wore jeans and a tee shirt or some of the girls would try to sneak in with a crop top and a mini skirt, but not Maddy. She dressed up like it was 1902! Long white lace dresses, long sleeve sheer shirts with whale-bone corsets over them, black chokers, and cameo necklaces. I think she even wore her hair in the typical Gibson girl style with her long black hair tucked back on top of her head." The old woman smiled as she remembered the student.

Mrs. Pruitt let out a small giggle. "Yes, I do remember her strange outfits and I admired her for them. It takes a lot of courage to be creative and expressive like that. I loved how she was unapologetically herself and how dedicated she was to her study of music. She wasn't much of a talker but when I had her in choir and in band practice, I could sense her passion and dedication to music. Not only was she fantastic on the violin, she had a voice like an angel. I know that sounds a bit cliché, but it was the truth. I'm sure you remember."

Dakota nodded and thought of listening to Maddy play a complex piece of classical music by a long-dead composer in her room. But Maddy, cursed with extreme shyness, would only sing for Dakota with a door separating the two of them. She said people looking at her while she sang would make her nervous and forget all the words.

"Her remarkable talent and intellect made her a welcome addition to St. Philomena's, but sometimes I felt sorry for her," said Principal Bernard.

"Why so?" asked Dakota.

"Well, outside of your friendship with her, she had no one. Skipping a grade, two in Maddy's case, can be hard on students. They often feel like an outsider or are intimidated by the physically more mature students in their class. Her parents sure didn't seem to appreciate her. Not to say they didn't love Maddy or take care of her. I could just tell she didn't have much in common with her mother or stepfather," Principal Bernard explained.

"Yes, I also got the impression that no one in her home life understood her personality." Mrs. Pruitt took a sip of her tea and continued. "The fact that she was so small — I mean, I don't think she was over five feet tall, and that she was technically the age of a freshman in the junior class led to a sense of isolation for her. My heart often drops at the thought of her in her angel costume disappearing into the night."

"That brings us to the night of the disappearance," said Dakota. "Can you both tell me the events of that day as best as you remember them?"

"Go first, Jane," motioned the Principal. "Since you were in charge of the play."

Mrs. Pruitt nodded and adjusted her expansive hair beneath her butterfly clip before speaking. "I was the music teacher, as you know, so I was in charge of getting the Christmas pageant together. This was a long-standing tradition at the school, and I had been putting it on for almost fifteen years. We'd act out various scenes from famous Christmas plays and stories: A scene from the *Nutcracker*, a scene from *A Christmas Carol*, and a scene from *The Grinch Who Stole Christmas*. In between, the choir would be dressed as angels and sing different Christmas songs: *Jingle Bells, Deck The Halls, The Little Drummer Boy* — you know, the classics. At the end, there would be a nativity scene. One of the choir members would sing the first two verses of *O Holy Night* as a solo and then have the choir and the audience finish the rest. That was Maddy's job. She was the best singer in the choir. We worked on the song for a full month before the pageant."

"When did you notice she was missing?" asked Dakota.

"I asked everyone to be at the school an hour and a half before the play would start, which was at 7 pm. So I wanted everyone in the backstage area of the auditorium by 5:30 pm. School would finish at 3 pm, but there were no after-school activities or staff on duty, so they all had to go home for the two-and-a-half hours before the show and then come back. The backstage was so chaotic with kids showing up late, their costumes missing or dirty. I remember one student got a bloody nose and another needed his inhaler. It was very stressful for me. I didn't notice that Maddy was missing until fifteen minutes before showtime.

"I was angry at her. I'm ashamed about it now, but I assumed she got stage fright and bailed on me. So, I just instructed the choir to sing the first two verses that were saved for the soloist and then they'd motion for the audience to join in. After the show was over, Mr. and Mrs. Montgomery and the grandfather, Pastor Shaw, came up to me with panic on their faces. Well, Pastor Shaw looked more annoyed than panicked. They asked me where Maddy was and why I didn't let her sing. I told them I hadn't seen her since school finished earlier that day. That's when they really started to worry," explained Mrs. Pruitt.

"I wasn't aware Maddy was missing until after the play," began Principal Bernard. "Early that day, I remember talking to a few parents as they came to pick up their children around three in the afternoon. I issued a junior-aged boy, I forget his name, a citation for loitering in the student parking lot after hours around four in the afternoon. Then I returned to my office to finish some paperwork before I went over to the auditorium around 6:30 in the evening to meet and greet with a few of the parents and family members who were coming in early to get a good seat for the pageant. I believe the show was over about fifteen minutes after eight in the evening. That's when you, Jane, and Maddy's family came up to me to tell me you needed to call the police because Maddy was missing. I led the parents into my office, and they placed the call from my phone. Pastor Shaw took his car back to the Montgomery residency to see if Maddy had walked the five blocks from the school to her family's home. When he returned to the school, I remember him telling one of the officers that she wasn't there. I can't recall if they sent a car out to check the house right away or if that happened later. But I remember the detective, Muloney—"

"Muldowney," corrected Dakota.

"Yes, Muldowney," Principal Bernard continued. "I remember he came up to me with his Tom Selleck mustache and told us everything was going to be all right. I didn't believe him. He seemed cocky and arrogant. I wanted hard facts, not reassurance. Mrs. Montgomery said she dropped Maddy off outside of the school before the play and watched her walk in towards the auditorium. That meant whatever had happened to her, happened on school grounds, making it my responsibility.

"Soon, the police shut everything down. They questioned everyone who was left on campus and searched each classroom and the fields outside with flashlights, but no Maddy. The following day I announced that classes were canceled and that the grounds were off limits to anyone who wasn't associated with law enforcement. They brought in the dogs who were given a clothing item from Maddy's laundry basket to sniff. They circled the grounds and found no sign of her. I remember her mother telling me they tracked her scent down the block from their house but then it disappeared. She was known to walk home on occasion so they assumed her scent was left over from earlier in the week," said the principal.

"I have to ask, you said earlier you issued a citation to a junior grade boy in the parking lot that day. You said you can't recall his name, but can you describe him to me?" Dakota asked.

"Well, I know he was not one of my favorite students," chuckled Principal Bernard. "He wasn't a troublemaker, but he wasn't an all-star student like you or Maddy. He was about average height, had dark brown hair and green eyes. Oh yes, I remember, he had one small portion of his hair that was white. I kept asking him if he had dyed his hair that way, but he insisted it was a birthmark. I believe his name started with a C."

"Connor Freisinger." Dakota knew the kid well. Connor had been in every one of Dakota's classes since they started at private school together in the third grade. He had a reputation among his classmates for being repulsive in his physical appearance and in his social interactions. In his younger years, he'd take long strings of boogers from his nose and wipe them across the bottoms of chairs or desks to mark them as his property. In junior high, he got into the habit of whispering sexually suggestive remarks to the girls in his class. This usually involved misquoting lyrics from popular rap songs which led to him saying something awkward about "milkshakes" or "candy shops." In his high school years, he turned his attention to Maddy.

"He had a thing for Maddy which seemed unhealthy," Dakota said.

"How so?" asked Mrs. Pruitt.

"As you might remember, Maddy and I were inseparable, only hanging out with each other most of the time. Whenever we were together during lunch or a study hall session, Connor would lurk nearby. If we sat around a corner outside at lunch, Connor would lean up against the wall, trying to overhear our conversation and get a glimpse of Maddy. In classes that had unassigned seats, he'd always sit right behind her. If he heard us talking about a certain topic, he'd awkwardly bring it up the next day. One time, Maddy was speaking about her favorite book being *Pride and Prejudice*. The next day, Connor cornered her during passing period to tell her all the Jane Austen facts he knew. Sometimes, we found love notes that were just an assorted mixture of song lyrics. I remember one which borrowed from Meatloaf's *I Will Do Anything for Love* and Twisted Sister's *Talk Dirty to Me*." Dakota laughed but her tone hardened. "We asked him time and time again to leave us alone, but he didn't stop until she disappeared."

"I never knew he behaved in such a way," admitted Principal Bernard.

"I'm just thankful he didn't attend music class," said Mrs. Pruitt. "Do you think he...?"

"I don't know." Dakota swallowed hard, almost choking on her words. It was one thing to have suspicions about Connor on her mind, but another to hear two other people wonder whether he could be a suspect as well. Her throat was dry and tight, but a few sips from her teacup helped her a bit. "I want to talk to him — to get his side of the story. Did the police questioned him?"

"I can't remember," said Mrs. Pruitt. "He wasn't at the pageant, and as far as I know, the only students that were questioned were the ones that were there that night. They questioned you as well, right?"

Dakota's mind flashed back to the day she and her parents went down to the police station to submit an official statement. She sat in a dark room with her mom and dad on either side of her. She had her camera in her lap that she slid across the table to Detective Muldowney and another officer who were seated across from her at the metal table.

"This is everything I have from that night. I didn't turn in any film to Mr. Miller," said young Dakota. She was working as a photographer for the school newspaper and was on duty the night of the pageant.

Now, in Principal Bernard's living room, Dakota forced herself to wipe those memories away. She had to stay focused on gathering facts.

"Yes they did, but I didn't know anything more than anyone else. The photos I had taken from the event didn't show any sign of her." Dakota looked right at Principal Bernard. "I do have another question to ask you. It's about Mr. Lawrence. He went to prison for sleeping with a student at St. Philomena's. What do you think about him? What was it like at school when he was arrested?"

"Actually, I was no longer working at St. Philomena's when the whole incident with Ryan Lawrence occurred. He was arrested in 2006 and I retired in 2003," the Principal said.

"Really? I was under the impression you only recently retired."

Principal Bernard straightened her posture as if she was about to brace for a strong headwind. "No dear, you see — I guess I should tell you. You'll find out from someone in this town sooner or later. My son, Will, was an investment banker and he lost quite a bit of money in the stock market slump that followed 9/11. In March 2002, he jumped off a building in downtown L.A. The event completely changed me. I managed to get through one final year at St. Philomena's, but afterwards, I quit. It was too much for me. I partly blamed myself even though everyone tells me not to. But maybe if I hadn't been so hard on him, he would have picked a less stressful career. Or maybe he would have felt like he could have talked to me about his troubles, instead of feeling like there was no way out. His death softened me. It made me realize that the no-nonsense attitude I was inflicting on the students at school was not doing them any good so I stepped down."

"I'm so sorry for your loss. I had no idea that happened," Dakota said.

"But for the record, I was completely unaware of Mr. Lawrence's dirty deeds," the old woman said. "He raised no suspicion while I was in charge. I don't think he was doing anything wrong during the time I was at the school, but you can't be too sure."

"Did the police ask him about Maddy when he was arrested?" Dakota asked.

"I don't think so," answered Mrs. Pruitt. "From what I was told, the girl was 16 years old, and they claimed to be in love with each other. I don't know if anyone from the police realized he was working at the same school that Maddy disappeared from."

"That's exactly what I intend to find out. Thank you, ladies, for your time." Dakota reached over and turned the recording off.

"I hope you find her." Mrs. Pruitt patted Dakota on the back, the way you'd pat a child who scored a goal at a soccer match.

Dakota smiled. "You've been a big help and have given me a lot to think about. Right now, I'm going to try to track down Connor, and then see Mr. Lawrence in prison."

"Oh my! Well, you be careful, dear," said her former teacher.

"Dakota, what will you be doing with the recording?" asked Principal Bernard.

"Just keeping it for my records," she replied.

"I think you should broadcast it, like on the radio. Maybe someone out there knows something about Maddy and can help you find her," suggested Mrs. Pruitt.

"I hope so," said Dakota. "I'll see what I can do."

• • •

Dakota returned home to find Debi and Cassidy sitting among a mountain of cardboard boxes in the living room.

"We're cleaning out the storage area," Debi called out to her. "Go through your boxes when you have a chance, please." She pointed at a few boxes pushed to the corner of the living room with her nickname, "Koty" written on the sides.

"I'm trying to get things ready for Isabelle, and I thought it might be nice to give her something I had as a baby," Cassidy explained, as she sat in the middle of a nest made from half-opened boxes. She reached into one and pulled out a soft pink blanket. Both Cassidy and Debi cooed at it.

"I remember taking you both home from the hospital in those little blankets, scared out of my mind at the thought of caring for two babies at once," said Debi.

"Thanks, Mom," laughed Cassidy.

"Oh, you get used to it. It's not so bad, especially since you're having only one," she added.

Cassidy reached over and opened another box. Reaching in, she pulled out a teal wool sweater with massive orange, yellow and green shapes of all different sizes stitched into the wool.

"Jesus, Mom, how could you ever think this was fashionable to wear?" she asked.

"Hey, don't judge. I'll have you know I was hot stuff back in the 80s with my perm, scrunchies, and stirrup leggings. Even as a mom of three young kids, I stayed with it," Debi bragged.

Dakota took the lids off a few of her boxes and combed through old clothes, grade school art projects, and middle school report cards. Nothing worth keeping.

She grunted as she dragged an unreasonably heavy box to her lap. Opening the lid, she looked down at a mess of black wires. Her hands fumbled over several types of microphones and a large panel with knobs and switches.

"Hey, guys, what's this?" Dakota asked her mother and sister.

"Oh," laughed Cassidy. "You weren't here for this, thank God, but Capri tried her hand at becoming a famous singer. And, well, let's say she's no Mariah Carey."

"More like Mariah Scary," said Debi as she put both hands over her ears and pretended to block out a horrible noise.

All three women laughed.

"Can I use these for something?" asked Dakota, remembering Mrs. Pruitt's radio idea.

"Sure, I'm glad someone else is going to put those things to use. It cost your dad a lot of money and he was not happy when she gave up music after two months," said Debi.

"What are you gonna use them for?" asked Cassidy. "Please don't tell me you want a solo career too."

"Very funny, but God no! I'm considering recording an episode of a radio show idea I have and submitting it to a few radio stations around here to see if it gets picked up," Dakota said.

"Oh no, Koty, that's not how to do it. Radio is dying. It's all about podcasting now." Cassidy came close to Dakota and started taking audio equipment out of the box.

"I have no idea what you're talking about," said Dakota with her hands on her hips. She still loved listening to her favorite classic rock station when she was doing chores around her apartment.

Cassidy continued, "You don't need a radio station to pick you up. I mean, what's the chances of that happening? Pretty much none. It's all morning banter and Justin Bieber songs, nowadays. Podcasters get to talk about whatever topic they want without a radio station telling them what to do," she said.

"How do you know about this?" asked Dakota.

"Blake is constantly asked to be on all these sports podcasts that are popping up all over the place," Cassidy explained as she untangled a knot in a microphone wire.

Dakota imagined Cassidy's behemoth-sized linebacker husband with headphones on, talking with some guys in a studio about running plays or his training regimen. "I'm not sure if that's for me," she shrugged.

"You don't have to have guests on or anything like that. Some people just talk for the full hour." Cassidy pulled out a small mic and said, "This one you can attach to your phone when you're on the go."

"Girls, this sounds real interesting," said Debi whose attention span had never been long enough to listen to one person speak for five minutes let alone a whole hour. "Give it a try, Koty," she said, picking up three empty cardboard boxes and taking them to the garage.

"I agree," said Cassidy. "I'm sure people would be intrigued about a cold case of a missing girl especially one that was as cute as Maddy."

"Is." Dakota snapped, then flushed with embarrassment as the word came out of her mouth. The likelihood of Maddy still being alive was slim, but Dakota saw Maddy only in the present tense and never in the past.

"Sorry, I didn't mean—" Cassidy started. "You're right. Is. She still could be out there. We don't know."

"I didn't mean to snap at you. But to me, she still feels very much real, very much still alive. Even if it turns out she is only alive in my memories." Dakota felt tears gather under her eyelids.

"I think you have to do this," said Cassidy. "You have to tell her story."

•   •   •

The next morning, Dakota sat at the desk of her childhood room with a microphone inches away from her lips. The record button was on, but she couldn't find any words to say. She was nervous like she was about to sing the National Anthem at the Super Bowl.

She had stayed up past midnight getting her recording equipment set up and figuring out how to edit audio from the interview with Principal Bernard and Mrs. Pruitt. But the hardest part of all was figuring out what to call her podcast.

She lay in bed that night with titles like, "Where is Maddy?" or "The Hunt for Maddy Montgomery" coming to mind. Then, she recalled the street Maddy used to live on: Shadow Lane.

"ShadowCast," she whispered to herself. That was it. The name related to Maddy's case, but it came with an undercurrent of darkness and a sense that something would come out of the shadows to see the light.

At her desk, she took a deep breath and forced herself to speak into the mic. "Hello everyone, I'm Dakota Kilroy and you're listening to *ShadowCast*. Since this is the first episode, let me tell you a bit about myself and the case I'm working on."

Dakota paused and took a breath. Her heart was pounding so hard she felt it shake her whole body. This was not a role she was comfortable with. She preferred keeping herself hidden behind the black and white print of a newspaper. It seemed too intimate to have strangers hear the sound of your voice.

But nevertheless, she pressed on.

"I'm an investigative journalist with over eight years of experience, starting with breaking a story on prostitution in the modeling world while I was studying journalism at NYU. Later, I became a lead journalist at *The Village Inquirer* in New York City. I'm now back in my hometown of Santa Monica, California, investigating the cold case of the disappearance of fifteen-year-old Madeline "Maddy" Montgomery."

Dakota muted the microphone to allow her to clear her throat, though really she needed the time to clear her mind. She felt awkward talking about her employment history and how she had to skirt the issue of why she is no longer with the *Inquirer* — or any publication for that matter.

It's not about me, she thought, *it's about Maddy.*

She pressed the record button again and continued, "Maddy was born Madeline Shaw on October 16, 1985, to Jacqueline Shaw and an unnamed father. Jacqueline and the father of her child were only 17 years old at the time of her conception. From what little information can be gathered, Maddy's father had almost no involvement in his daughter's life and soon disappeared from it altogether. Years later, when Maddy was eight years old, Jacqueline married electrician Robert Montgomery whom she met through her father's church. Maddy's last name was changed to Montgomery when Robert legally adopted her soon after the wedding. As the years passed, Maddy became a big sister to two half-brothers, Anthony and Michael. Maddy's home life was simple and peaceful. Her parents lived in the house next door to Jacqueline's parents, Pastor and Mrs. Shaw. The small Baptist church that the pastor ran was on this property as well. Within the affluent town, the Montgomery and Shaw residences were in the section of town that was lower middle-class.

"Despite this modest life, Maddy was far from typical. She was an intelligent girl, gifted in many areas. This caused her to skip two grades when she was ten years old. Additionally, Maddy was a talented singer and violinist who had perfect pitch and could sight-read music from an early age. This won her a scholarship to go to the prestigious St. Philomena's College Preparatory, only five blocks from her house. Maddy was not just extraordinary in intelligence but also in personality, style, and looks. By all accounts, Maddy was a beautiful girl. She had dark brown, almost black hair that fell down her back and framed her face with feathered bangs. Her dark eyes stood out against her fair skin that had a smattering of golden-brown freckles across her nose and cheeks. She was small-boned, petite, barely five feet tall at fifteen years old. When she wasn't in the standard-issued uniform for school, she dressed in vintage clothes. She was known for her long white lace dresses and skirts, and her corset-like tops which she wore with a tee shirt underneath for modesty's sake. She loved vintage jewelry, most notably a black velvet choker with a cameo of a woman's face in white ivory.

"But who she was as a daughter, a friend, and a sister was what made her truly remarkable. While quiet and introverted, she would do anything for the people she was closest to. Often staying up late to help her mother care for her younger brothers if Mr. Montgomery was working a long shift. She had a passion for music and dreamed of one day getting into Julliard. When met with unpleasant people, she never became angry, she remained calm and never met them at their level.

"You may be wondering how I know all this about Maddy. That is because I'm not just an investigative journalist; I was Maddy's best friend in high school. Her disappearance still haunts me to this day. Like all the people who knew Maddy at the time she went missing, I'm constantly bothered by questions about where she is, what happened to her, and if she is still alive. People have told me to make my peace with it and move on. But I can't. That's not what a best friend would do. Twelve years later, I'm finally putting my skills to good use to find out what really happened.

"The recording that you will hear in the next few minutes is an interview I conducted with Alice Bernard and Jane Pruitt. Before I let the interview play, I must first tell you about who they are and what allegedly happened on Thursday, December 7, 2000.

"It was a standard day at St. Philomena's. School started at 7:45am and dismissed at 3pm. A lunch break took place between 11:45 and 12:30, but Maddy did not leave the campus during this time. Everything was normal except that Christmas Break was a week and a half away and the Christmas pageant was happening that night. Maddy had been excused from the last class of the day so she could attend the final rehearsal. Maddy was then picked up by her mother soon after school ended. Her mother has told the police that at home, Maddy did some homework in her room, ate dinner with her brothers, and changed into her costume for the pageant. Then, Mrs. Montgomery dropped Maddy off at the school around 5:30pm as the cast was asked to be at the school an hour and a half before the show's start time at 7pm. Jacqueline says that she watched her daughter, dressed in an angel costume, walk into the gates of the school and towards the auditorium where the pageant was set to take place. That is the last time anyone ever saw her.

"Alice Bernard was the Principal at the time of Maddy's disappearance, and Jane Pruitt was the music teacher at St. Philomena's — she was in charge of putting on the pageant. The two educators graciously allowed me to interview, record and broadcast what they've said to me. Their stories not only shed more light on the details regarding Maddy's disappearance but also raised a few questions about possible suspects who might have been overlooked by the police. Here is the recording."

Dakota added in the pre-edited audio file of the interview.

At the end of the episode, Dakota said, "This interview was very helpful to me, but it raised more questions than it answered. For one, did Mr. Lawrence attempt to strike up an underage romance before 2006 and if so, was it with Maddy? Where was Connor Freisinger on the evening of December 7, 2000? And where is he today? I'll attempt to answer these questions and more on the next episode of *ShadowCast*."

Dakota saved the audio file for the entire episode and uploaded it to several podcast platforms. She leaned back in her chair and smiled at what she had just done, unaware of the fact that in two weeks' time one of the listeners of *ShadowCast* would help her investigation, while another would try to destroy it.

Chapter 4

Dakota found herself sitting in an army-green plastic chair that was bolted to the floor with metal legs. A white table, fastened down in a similar fashion, was in front of her with the number twelve printed on it. She had already been through the metal detector and the pat down. Now, she sat waiting with a visitor tag clipped to her shirt and a cup of vending machine coffee in her hands. A metal door to her left swung open. A guard escorted a tall, lanky man in prison blues to Dakota's table.

"Twenty minutes," said the guard, as the man sat down across from Dakota.

"Who are you?" asked the man. He had a flat face and head of jet-black hair, cut close to the skull.

Dakota looked straight into his eyes. "I'm surprised you don't remember me, Mr. Lawrence. I thought you'd remember the names and faces of every girl you had as a student."

He looked down the frame of his glasses and said, "This again. Okay, are you a family member or friend of Briana's?"

She shook her head. "No, I have no connection to your victim. My name is Dakota Kilroy and I'm an investigative journalist and—"

"Oh great," he cut her off.

"*And* I was one of your students from 1998 to 2002." Dakota started again but she was interrupted once more.

"So, you've come here, six years after my trial and ten years after you graduated to harass me," Mr. Lawrence leaned forward, his small eyes amplified by his lenses stared down at Dakota. A guard across the room took a step closer which caused Mr. Lawrence to draw back into his seat.

"No, if you'd let me get a word in, I'd tell you why I'm here." Anger rose in Dakota's chest. She wanted to punch the bastard in the face, not because of what he did to his student or how difficult he was being but because of the possibility he had hurt Maddy.

"Fine," he said, with his hand outstretched like he was the conductor of an orchestra beckoning the music to start with his command.

"I'm not looking into what you did with this Briana. It seems like that case has been put to bed." Dakota glanced at his prison uniform. "But there is another case I'm working on, and I think you might have a unique perspective on it."

"Listen. I'm not going to help you with some other 'Hot for Teacher' case, if that's what you're thinking," he said.

"It's Maddy Montgomery," Dakota blurted out.

He went deathly quiet.

Dakota leaned closer and made direct eye contact. "From what I've found, the police never questioned you about Maddy. Not at the time of her disappearance in 2000. Not when you got arrested six years later. Detective Muldowney didn't put two and two together. But I have. So, I'm offering you a chance to clear your name before I help *him* put two and two together and they drop a kidnapping or murder charge on top of your original sentence."

"That would never happen." Mr. Lawrence waved her off.

"Really? The man who had a relationship with his sixteen-year-old student was also the teacher of another teen girl who happened to go missing a few years prior? I mean, who else could have done it? The family, that's unlikely. You might be thinking, it's always the boyfriend. Wrong, she didn't have one. Most other teachers at St. Philomena's were questioned and ruled out. But you weren't. You flew under the radar, somehow. From what I found in the papers, your student looked a lot like Maddy. Dark hair, light skin, small frame. The perfect victim. When this suggestion lands in Detective Muldowney's lap, whose phone number I have on hand, he'll be on you so fast. Sure, a jury may have reasonable doubt, but it's common knowledge that child predators, especially ones serving time already for sex crimes, receive little mercy in the court of law. You think you're out of here in three years? You could be looking at life. But..."

Dakota paused. She took a sip of coffee while she stared at Mr. Lawrence. His cocky and relaxed posture changed. He looked five inches shorter and his face hung in a deep frown as he waited with anticipation for Dakota to finish her sentence.

"But, if you clear your name publicly by allowing me to record and broadcast what happened that night, then this could prove you innocent." Dakota pulled her phone out of her pocket with the recording feature already opened and the portable microphone attached. "What do you say?"

He took a heavy sigh. "All right," he said with a grimace.

Dakota pressed record.

"This is Dakota Kilroy recording on Monday, January 23rd, 2012. I'm here in a correctional facility in Southern California with Mr. Ryan Lawrence. Mr. Lawrence is serving a nine-year sentence for the statuary rape of a student in 2006. But he also was the History teacher at the time of Maddy Montgomery's disappearance and was never questioned about her. Mr. Lawrence, would you please tell me where you were on December 7, 2000?"

"Um, well, it's been about twelve years, so it's hard for me to remember everything; but I remember that day for one big reason," he smiled with an expression that said, *gotcha*.

"We'll get to that — just talk me through the day and tell me why you remember it when we get there," Dakota instructed.

"I normally got to school half an hour before class starts, so that would be around 7:15 am. Then, I'd teach from 7:45 to 11:45, then have lunch in the break-room if I wasn't on lunch duty that day."

"And were you?" asked Dakota.

"No. No, I was not," he laughed. "I believe I was scheduled only on Mondays for lunch duty, but anyway, I had ordered Chinese food two nights before and brought the leftovers in for lunch. Well, two hours later, my Kung Pao chicken was kicking the shit out of my intestines, literally. I had to go home with an hour left in the school day. By the time my wife got home, around five that evening, I was extremely sick. So sick in fact, she took me to the emergency room, where I was on IV fluids until early the next morning."

Dakota didn't like what she was hearing. "Do you have anything that would back this up?"

"My ex-wife hates me, divorced me four years before Briana, but I'm sure she remembers it. It was one out of two times I'd ever had to go to the hospital in my life and the only time during our marriage. Plus, there must be records with her or the hospital or the insurance company that shows I was a very sick boy that night," he chuckled.

"Good. I'll check on this. Is there anything else you'd like to say?" she asked, wanting to end this interview after being caught off guard by his chicken story.

"Yes. I didn't do it," Mr. Lawrence started. "Yeah, I like young girls — most men do but don't have the stones to say anything about it or act on it. But I wouldn't abduct or kill anyone. Especially Maddy. She was such a good student and so pleasant to be around. You don't get a lot of kids like that, nowadays. But I swear, I have no idea what happened to her."

Dakota turned off the recording device.

"Sorry I disappointed you. But I didn't lay a finger on her," he insisted.

"I'm not disappointed. I'm trying to find out what happened. And the only way to do that is to rule people out. I just hope everyone else isn't as snide as you," said Dakota as she stood up.

"I really do hope you find her remains and whoever killed her. I really mean that. I want the family to have closure," he said.

"Her body? You think she's dead?" Dakota asked, thinking the perverted teacher was just caught giving away more information than he should have if he was innocent.

"Yeah," he shrugged. "After living with these animals in here for the last six years, I know what some men are capable of. If someone like them got to her, there's no chance she's still alive."

Dakota's heart sank. She pulled off her visitor's pass and left without looking back at Mr. Lawrence.

● ● ●

Dakota was back at home in her room. She plugged in her silver microphone to her computer and placed thick black headphones over her ears.

"Welcome back to *ShadowCast*," she said, as she watched the wavy lines on the audio recording software move with each syllable that came from her mouth. "I'm Dakota Kilroy and I'm investigating the December 7th, 2000 disappearance of fifteen-year-old Maddy Montgomery from the Santa Monica area. In our last episode, I filled you in on the circumstances of Maddy's disappearance and interviewed two school employees that were there the night that Maddy went missing from St. Philomena's private high school. As you recall, there was a teacher at the school, Ryan Lawrence who was arrested for having illicit relations with a sixteen-year-old student in 2006. Since the police never questioned this man at any point about his possible connection to Maddy, I decided to see him myself. Here's what happened."

Dakota inserted the digital file from the interview at the prison into the audio software.

"I followed up on Mr. Lawrence's request. Due to HIPPA, I can't get medical documentation from a hospital or an insurance company without a warrant, but I did track down his ex-wife via email. She agreed to let me read what she wrote on the air as long as I don't reveal her first name or her new surname. Mr. Lawrence's ex-wife says:

"Dear Ms. Kilroy,

I can't recall the exact date but yes, my ex-husband Ryan Lawrence did go to the hospital for food poisoning once around Christmas time in 2000. I remember this because it was the only time in our marriage that he needed to be hospitalized. I believe we were supposed to go to a Christmas play at the school, but we ended going to the hospital instead. While I'm completely surprised by the actions that lead him to where he is now, I don't believe my ex-husband had anything to do with the girl's disappearance."

Dakota closed the email from his ex-wife and continued, "Now I'm interested in what you think. Is Mr. Lawrence telling the truth? Or is it too much of a coincidence? Is his ex-wife's statement enough to give him credibility or do you need more proof to believe him? Let me know what you think by commenting on this episode or sending me an email to the address listed below. Thank you for listening."

Dakota stopped recording. She tinkered with the audio to remove her awkward "ums" and "uhs" and the occasional long pauses so her words sounded smooth.

After she uploaded the file, Dakota went back to work on tracking down more people to interview. Connor Freisinger was on the top of her mind. She hated that creep, but she wasn't sure he could do anything to hurt Maddy. She also wanted to talk to Selena in person. Plus, there also was Tiffany — Tiffany had always been willing to do anything to please her best friend. Dakota remembered how teachers would often ask the students, "If your friends jumped off a bridge, would you jump too?" When it came to Selena and Tiffany, Tiffany would not only jump off a bridge if Selena told her to, she'd build a bridge if there wasn't one in the first place.

But in the back of her mind, Connor's face kept reappearing. Dakota logged into Facebook and typed his name into the search bar. She was scrolling down the seven Connor Freisingers that existed in the world when her father came in.

"What are you doing?" Ken's face looked hard like his irritated expression was permanently carved onto his features.

"I was just—" Dakota explained.

"Goofing around on social media, that's what," Ken said with his beefy arms crossing his chest.

"No, I've been working on something," said Dakota.

"Is that something resumes and job applications?" he asked her.

"No," she confessed, feeling like she was twelve years old again and was getting grounded for some silly little mistake.

Ken now looked confused. "But Mom said you were interviewing all day yesterday and on Friday, yet you haven't been looking for a job. What were you doing?"

"I was interviewing people who knew Maddy to see if they have information they didn't share with the police," she said.

Ken let out a sigh of sadness. He took a seat on the edge of her bed, next to her desk. "When this whole thing happened with Maddy, your mom and I were so scared that this would traumatize you for life. But you seemed to pick up the pieces and move on. You went to college and started a career in a city far from home. We hoped you were over it. But I'm afraid it's catching up with you. Now it seems like you're never going to be able to let it go."

"Dad," Dakota swiveled on her chair to face her father. "I'm not obsessed. Well, not in a bad way. If I don't do this, who will? Detective Muldowney has proven himself to be useless. The other police officers on duty at the time don't care anymore; they have other cases to solve. Her family doesn't have the money to hire their own investigator. I'm the perfect person to solve this case. I have the skills and knowledge — plus, I was there when it happened. I know the people she knew. I know the city she lived in and I know what Maddy was like. I can't let this go because maybe that's why I'm here. Maybe life made me lose my job in New York so I could come back home and figure this thing out once and for all."

Ken put his hand on his daughter's cheek. "I get what you're doing and it's really important, but I don't want you to ruin your career by being unemployed for a really long time. You need to get a job and stand on your own two feet again."

Dakota felt a pang of embarrassment. She was a twenty-eight-year-old woman living in her parent's house, spending her days interviewing child predators. She remembered hearing about how more and more young people were living at home and she thought she'd never be one of those losers. Yet it seemed she had now become one of them.

"Just promise me, you'll spend the rest of the week looking for a job, then you can continue playing PI on the weekend, okay?" said Ken.

"Sounds like a plan," she said, although every bone in her body told her to work on the case more. She was getting somewhere, she knew it.

•　　•　　•

The sun filled the small coffee shop Dakota had holed herself up in. She submitted resume after resume for every job she was remotely qualified for in a thirty-mile radius. This coffee place was the only store open at six in the morning, and thus her only recourse as her father had purposefully woken her from a deep sleep at that time to tell her to get a jump on the day.

Annoyed at his pushiness, she fled for the nearest establishment that had an outlet and an endless supply of caffeinated beverages. "Hit The Spot Coffee Shop" wasn't a Starbucks, but it smelled like one and looked like one with its mixture of dark wood tones and green accents.

After returning to her seat with her second latte of the day, Dakota decided to log in to the email account she created for *ShadowCast*. To her surprise, the little envelope icon that read "Inbox" had the number 121 next to it.

Dakota shook her head. *That can't be right,* she thought. She clicked on the first email and it was from some guy with the screen name, *No-The-Truth*.

His message read: "Hey, I saw the Reddit post about your show and I'm pretty sure I know what happened to Maddy. You see, the government has been hiding their dirty doings for years. They take young girls from their home to do experiments on, so they have more powerful spy technology than the Russians. You really should look into that."

Dakota rolled her eyes. There was nothing she hated more than conspiracy theory enthusiasts. *Wait, what Reddit post?* she thought. She clicked on the link in No-The-Truth's email. It took her to a post by a man whose screen name was *TruCrimeJunkEE*. His post read: "Hey guys, I found this interesting new podcast. It just started, but it's about finding a missing girl. This girl, Maddy Montgomery went missing from St. Philomena's Catholic school in Santa Monica, CA. She was supposed to be part of the Christmas play, but after her mom dropped her off at the school she was never seen again. I already have a bunch of theories as to what happened to the girl, but I really want to hear what you think. Here are the first two episodes."

Dakota was shocked. There were already two hundred comments on the thread. Some of them read:

"That teacher is guilty as sin."

Someone replied with, "No he's not. He's telling the truth. Just because he did one crime doesn't mean he's guilty of another."

A different user asked, "Where are the parents? Ask the parents! They need to be questioned again."

Another user wrote: "I bet you money it's the stepfather. Why? Because stepparent violence is much higher than biological parent violence. Just look at the statistics. This woman needs to talk to him ASAP."

She scrolled down the page and another comment grabbed her attention. "Dakota, please find Connor. Creepy kids like that can't be trusted."

Dakota sat back in her chair, stunned. She felt hot and shaky. She wasn't used to this much attention nor was she expecting this type of reaction. She got herself together and checked her unread emails. Her inbox was filled with people giving their two cents on what they think happened to Maddy — and more specifically, whether they thought Mr. Lawrence is guilty.

Dakota knew she needed to get working on another episode, but Mr. Lawrence was a dead lead. Her gut told her he had nothing to do with Maddy. And if her gut was wrong, he wasn't going anywhere for the next three years, anyway. She needed another lead. The last comment about Connor came to mind. She had to get to him before too much news about her investigation spread.

Back on Facebook, she found a Connor Freisinger who lived in Palm Springs, California. The man seemed to be the right age to be the Connor she was looking for, but his appearance was drastically different from her last memories of that strange Connor from school. In his profile picture, he stood in camo-patterned cargo pants and a tight black t-shirt that clung to his muscular chest and arms. He had shaved his head bald, but Dakota recognized his facial features.

In his photo, Connor held what looked like black assault rifles in each hand. At first, this worried Dakota. Did he grow up to be some overly zealous hunting enthusiast? One of those guys who seems a little too eager to pull the trigger? But after zooming in, Dakota realized that those weren't real guns but instead, paintball guns. In fact, his profile read "Owner of PaintBall Madness" as his occupation.

She breathed a sigh of relief. A quick Google search of the paintball company revealed that it was located in Palm Springs. She punched in the number from the company website.

After three rings, a cheery male voice answered, "Hello, This is Paintball Madness where we are crazy about Paintball. How can I help you?"

"Hi, I'm looking to speak with Connor Freisinger."

"This is he," the voice said in an upbeat tone. "How can I help you, miss?"

"This may seem like it's coming out of left field, but my name is Dakota Kilroy. I went to school with you at St. Philomena's. And I was wondering if I could come down to ask you some questions?"

Chapter 5

Today is like any other day. Boring. Empty.

Ma made her meatloaf for dinner again. It's hard to believe I've been eating that same recipe for over fifty years. It's gotten real old, but I don't tell Ma that. She'd pitch a fit like I'd never seen if I really did tell her what I thought about her cooking.

No, the best way to deal with her is just to smile and nod along.

But sometimes that gets me into trouble. So much trouble. It got me into trouble forty-three years ago and it got me into trouble today.

After dinner, there was a light knock on our door. Ma jumped up to answer it. She's still quick on her feet after all these years. From the kitchen, I see it's our neighbor Margaret at the door. She's about the same age as Ma and moved into our neighborhood a few years after Dad left. She always keeps her silver hair short and curled like most old ladies do. She hides her plump frame under over-sized sweaters that usually have something like roses or kittens or kittens playing with roses on them.

"Hi Marge," says Ma in an overly friendly tone. "What can I do ya for?"

"I just got some of your mail again, that darn postman," she laughs, handing a few envelopes over.

"They always get things wrong," says Ma."

"You know what. I don't think you showed me the Christmas letter you got from Rebecca, this year. She lives such an exciting life, I always loved hearing from her," coos Margaret.

Ma looks back at me, her eyes as hot as hellfire. "We didn't get a letter this year."

"You didn't? Is she all right?" asks Margaret.

"She's fine," I call out from across the room. "She must have forgot to send one this year."

"Yes, but I think she'll write one soon. Isn't that right, Freddy?" Ma asks me, not letting up her accusatory gaze.

"Oh, yeah, we should probably be getting one any day now," I say to the two old ladies.

"Ring me when you get it. Can't wait to hear how she's doing," Margaret smiles. "Well, I got to get back to Frank. I'll see you both later."

"Bye, bye, dear." Ma closes the door.

"Tell me again why you thought not sending the letter this year would be a good idea?" Ma hisses at me.

"It's been so long. I didn't think anyone else would remember that she even existed," I explain.

"Well, clearly people do."

"I'm sorry, Ma," I tell her.

"You better be sorry. After the hell you put me through, you're lucky I've helped you and continue to help you clean up your mess. Now, you need to stick with the plan. Rebecca sends letters from Las Vegas every year at Christmas time and we're going to keep sending those letters until one of us is dead. So, you're going to write the letter, call in sick tomorrow, pack up your car, and send the letter to us."

"But Ma, the drive is long, and I don't want to use one of my sick days for this," I say.

"You will do as I say. No more mistakes." She turns around and heads upstairs.

"Whatever you say, Ma."

• • •

The cool air from the Mercedes' climate control system made the two-hour drive to Palm Springs in 80-degree weather bearable. To her surprise, Connor was more than happy to talk with Dakota about Maddy on the record. She didn't want to give him too much time to think things over and change his mind.

She pulled up on the empty asphalt of the parking lot next to a beige warehouse with a plastic sign for "PaintBall Madness" hung up above the entrance. She opened the metal doors with a screech to find the warehouse that had been turned into a faux battleground with hollowed out Hummers and stacks of tires placed at various ends of the wide space.

To her left, there was a check-in counter with a plethora of paintball guns displayed on the wall behind glass cases. But no one was at the counter and everything was dark except for a few dimly glowing fluorescents that hung above the mock war zone.

Maybe Connor was guilty. Maybe he did kill Maddy, she thought with a shudder. Now he found out about *ShadowCast* and how she was looking into her disappearance. He didn't even have to trap her or trick her. She had come to this empty warehouse alone with no one knowing where she was going.

It was too perfect. She should have seen this coming.

A heavy metal clunk sounded at the far end of the warehouse. Dakota jumped. Her gut was telling her something was wrong. She turned around and headed towards the parking lot.

"Hey, where you going?" a friendly voice asked.

It was Connor, and he was coming towards her with two paintball guns in his hands.

"Dakota, right?" he asked, as he got closer.

She nodded.

"Long time, no see. Come here." He beamed at her and tossed the two guns onto the front counter.

She was about to bolt for the door when he stretched out his arms and gave her a hug.

"Oh, hi." Dakota felt awkward being in this man's embrace. He relaxed his grip and the two parted.

"It's not every day you come across another St. Philomena's survivor. Come in, sit, let me get you a water." Connor pressed his hand to the small of her back and gently guided her to his office round the back of the front counter.

The office was nothing special other than it was painted the same shade of army-green that covered the rest of the facility. On the wall to her side, there was a big white board with numbers, names, and dates written in faded marker. She sat in the chair across from his glass-top desk as he reached into his mini-fridge and handed her a chilled bottle of water.

"Thanks," she smiled slightly.

The wall on Connor's right side was littered with notes held up by metallic thumbtacks including a small calendar with a nearly nude swimsuit model stretched across a tropical beach. Connor noticed that Dakota had seen the calendar and took it off the wall and flung it behind him into a pile of unorganized papers.

"Sorry about that. I don't get a lot of women coming in here." His body tightened in embarrassment.

Dakota ignored his discomfort. "So you own this place?"

Connor patted his knees. "Yep, it's my pride and joy."

Dakota asked, "Where are your employees? It seems like too big of a place to manage alone."

"It's a weekday morning, no one comes in around this time. I have staff for the after-school hours and the weekend." He paused for a moment and then said, "You wanted to talk about Maddy, right?"

"Yes, and you said you didn't mind if I recorded this for my podcast?" asked Dakota.

He pulled his office chair in close to the desk. "No, I don't mind. But to be honest, I didn't want to sound dumb over the phone asking you this but, what's a podcast?"

"Oh," Dakota laughed. "It's like a radio show on the Internet."

"Cool, yeah, I don't mind," he said, resuming his nervous knee-patting from before.

Dakota placed her phone on the desk at an equal distance between them.

"Connor, I'm going to need you to stop that," she said.

"What?" he smirked.

"You keep tapping your knees and the mic will pick it up," Dakota explained.

"Oh, sorry," he said, now turning his nervous energy to picking dry skin on his thumb.

Dakota pressed record on her phone and began.

"This is Dakota Kilroy sitting with Connor Freisinger on Wednesday, January 25, 2012, in his office in Palm Springs, California. Connor was in the same grade as Maddy and me at the time of her disappearance."

She looked up at him. "Connor, it was a bit of an open secret amongst the kids in our grade at St. Philomena's that you had a pretty big crush on Maddy. How would you describe your feelings for her at the time?"

Connor's eyes widened as if he was not expecting such a personal question off the bat. He blinked hard and proceeded.

"Yes, it's true, I had feelings for her. And to be honest, it was way more than a crush. Now that I think about it, she was probably the first girl I ever had serious feelings for. At certain points, it was an all-consuming passion. She was all I could think about for days on end. I'd imagine little scenarios where I'd win her affection and ask her out. I also thought a lot about what it would be like to grow up and marry her." Connor looked away from Dakota.

"This comes as a bit of a shock for me," Dakota said. "I always got the impression that your feelings for Maddy were lustful and predatory in nature.

For example," Dakota reached into her bag and pulled out a crumpled piece of lined paper that had messy cursive writing on it. "I'd do anything for you. Anything to be able to be with you. I'd cut myself. I'd hurt myself or my family. I'd even kill for you. I know that eventually, you'll say yes and you'll be mine. It's only a matter of time. Just you wait."

"You held on to that all these years?" he asked. Connor's brow was sweating, and panic spread across his face.

"Yes, Maddy gave it to me because it freaked her out. I recently discovered it among my possessions in my childhood home. Can you confirm that you wrote it and others like it while you and Maddy attended high school?" Dakota asked, finding eye contact with the embarrassed Connor.

"Yes, I believe I did write that," he started. "You see, at the time, I didn't have the best view of women. I thought they were something to get, like an award or achievement. I thought her ignoring me was her denying me my right to have her as a prize. It was a stupid way of thinking and I'm embarrassed by that. I promise you, I'm not like that anymore."

Dakota uncrossed her legs and moved in more. "Why? Did Maddy's disappearance cause this change?"

Connor answered, "Even though you might say I was a bit obsessed with her and I didn't respect her boundaries, I still cared about her a lot and I had this whole stupid future with us together planned out in my head. I thought one day she'd see that I'm worthy of her and we'd get married, like I said. So when she disappeared and time passed and no one found her, it devastated me. But I couldn't tell anyone. My father left my mom when I was ten, so he wasn't around to talk to. There was no way I was going to talk about my feelings for girls with my mom. I didn't really have any close friends I could trust, so I just kept it inside. I started drinking. It started with a few of the guys I'd skateboard with sneaking a few beers away from our parents, but then I was drinking every day. My mom wasn't around much because of work so I'd steal money from her purse and pay some guy who hung out by the gas station to buy me alcohol. It went from beers to straight Jack every day. About six months later, it was summer, I remember because there was no school to stop me from drinking, so I went hard. My mom came home to find me passed out in a puddle of my own vomit and I wouldn't wake up. After the doctors brought me back to life at the hospital, she sent me to a reform school. There I found fitness. It totally changed my life. It gave me a purpose and a positive attitude. Looking back on my teenage self, I realized I only said those creepy things to Maddy because I lacked the self-esteem to talk to her like a person."

"Well, I'm glad you turned your life around. I still have to ask," Dakota paused. "Where were you on the night of Thursday, December 7, 2000?"

The lines on Connor's brow intensified as his eyes glowed with anger at Dakota. "You think I had something to do with it?"

"I don't think anything," Dakota said in a calm voice. "I'm asking everyone who is willing to speak with me about Maddy's disappearance this question. This way I can put everyone at a certain time and place on that day to further rule people out."

Connor pushed himself farther away from the desk. His arms were crossed in front of his chest with veins bulging. "Well, why don't *you* answer? Where were *you*? Are you sure you didn't kill your best friend because she was prettier and smarter than you?"

Dakota jolted back.

Connor's posture relaxed. "I'm sorry," he began. "I just don't like being accused of something I didn't do."

"I'm not accusing you," Dakota forced herself to remain respectful. She didn't like that he was so two-faced. She didn't want to retell the story of what happened that night again. Investigating this alone was hard enough. But she knew if she was going to gain his trust, she would have to answer his question.

"But if you want me to answer first, I'll tell you my side of the story," she conceded. "It was the night of the famed St. Philomena's Christmas Pageant. I'm sure you remember those silly plays put on for our parents each year. Anyway, I was on the school newspaper and had been given the assignment to take pictures of the show. I got there early and found a seat in the front row. I snapped picture after picture of the scenes from *A Christmas Carol* and all the other skits. I was waiting for Maddy to come out to sing her solo. I wanted to make sure I got a fantastic photo of her, so she would be the main photo used for the article on the play and maybe they'd save the photo for the yearbook. But she never came on. I looked over every single face of the girls in the choir, but she wasn't there.

"I had to sit through all of those Christmas songs, sick to my stomach with worry and confusion. I knew something was wrong. At the very least, this meant she was too anxious to perform and was probably having a panic attack somewhere. After the show finished, I rushed backstage to find her. But she wasn't there. She wasn't anywhere. I wanted to go talk to her parents, but they were already having what looked like a serious conversation with the Principal and Mrs. Pruitt. I assumed her parents were telling them that Maddy had stayed home, too nervous to even make it to the play. I was about to grab the jacket and book bag I left on my seat and leave when I noticed the police were there. They shut the gates to the school and told everyone who was still on the campus not to leave until they were questioned. An hour or so later, I gave a statement saying I hadn't seen her since we left school around three that afternoon. A few days later, they requested that my camera with film from the Christmas pageant was handed over for evidence. I cried and cried for weeks thinking about her being kidnapped and held somewhere or being dead in some unmarked grave. She was my best friend and I wasn't jealous of her. I loved her like she was family, even more so."

Dakota blinked back her tears and cleared her throat. "Your turn. Why don't you tell me where you were that day?" she asked.

Connor was looking at the floor, either too uncomfortable or upset to look at Dakota.

"I wasn't there that day because that was the night I was arrested for the first time," he stated.

"And you're sure of this?" she asked.

"Listen," he said with a laugh. "You never forget your first time. Especially your first time in jail. I remember it like it was yesterday. After the principal busted me for "loitering" in the parking lot, I took off and found a few of my skater buddies. A little while later, we got popped for trespassing and vandalizing the alleyway behind the supermarket with a bunch of graffiti. And not the artsy type of graffiti. The shitty kind that was just giant dicks or the word "fags" spray-painted in cheap black paint. Well, my mom was on a business trip and couldn't come home to bail me out, so I had to spend Thursday night and Friday night in jail. You can look it up, there're records of it."

Dakota looked him in the eye, and she knew he was telling the truth. He may have been a creepy kid in high school, but he was innocent.

"So this means you were in police custody the night Maddy disappeared?" she asked, again to confirm.

"Yes, it does. I got arrested one more time for "disturbing the peace" before my mom sent me away to Miller academy. There's a record of that too," he smirked.

"I will verify everything you're telling me now about your criminal history. Is there anything else you'd like to say?" asked Dakota.

"Not really." He paused to scratch his neck. "I just hope that you find her or find out what happened to her. It's a good thing you're doing and I apologize for being defensive. I just don't want you or anyone else to think just because I liked her and didn't understand how to express it that it means I would hurt her. I do sincerely hope she is okay wherever she is and if someone did hurt her, that they get what they deserve."

"Thank you, Connor, for your cooperation." Dakota ended the recording.

Dakota placed her phone back in her bag and stood up, ready to leave. "Thanks again, you've been a big help," she told Connor.

His eyes flicked over Dakota's tall and slender frame as she stood. For the first time, he noticed she was heavily tattooed.

"Boy, you've grown up a lot. And those tats, I never thought you'd turn out to look like this," he smiled while his face flushed.

"People change," she quipped.

"It must be a drag to have driven all the way down here just to ask a few questions," he continued.

She shrugged. "I've done a lot more for a lot less in other investigations."

"If you don't have to go home right away," he walked towards her. "We could get lunch somewhere. There's a good Mexican place down the block."

Dakota froze. "I don't think that's the best idea."

"Why not? We could catch up on old times. See where things go?" He looked at her with a sweet expression on his face that made him look like a naïve teenager instead of a living G.I. Joe.

"Going out with someone who I'm investigating could compromise the case and my credibility," she explained.

"Oh, come on," he moaned in a half-annoyed, half-joking tone.

Images of Seth flooded her mind. "The last guy who got tangled up with my work almost died," she blurted out.

"Oh," he took a step back. "Okay then, have a safe drive back."

"I will. Thanks again for talking with me." She didn't wait for him to show her out of the building. She left his office, headed straight for the front doors of the warehouse and dashed to her car. As passionate as she was about this investigation, she had had enough of people from her past for one day.

• • •

The following afternoon, Dakota edited and posted another episode to *ShadowCast* that included Connor's interview. Within a few hours, *ShadowCast's* newfound fanbase were leaving their opinions on Connor's interview all over the Internet, including in her Inbox.

Not sure where to start, she opened an email at random:

> Dear Dakota,
>
> I'm loving *ShadowCast* so far. Listening to your interviews with these potential suspects is keeping me on the edge of my seat. But I have to tell you, based on the last two episodes, I have a theory. Mr. Lawrence and Connor were in on it together. Connor was clearly in love with her but couldn't have her. Mr. Lawrence probably lusted after her since he's into young girls. But she didn't have an interest in either of them so they both killed her because they didn't want anyone else to be with her. Please look into my theory.
>
> Best,
>
> Barbara

As flattered as Dakota was by Barbara's compliments, she knew her theory didn't hold any water. Neither did the dozens of emails and comments she got on a daily basis since debuting her first episode. She gave out a disappointed sigh and continued rummaging through her emails.

Moments later, she heard the side door open and two familiar voices call out, "Hello! We're here!"

Dakota jogged downstairs to see Capri and Cassidy standing in the living room. Capri was holding the hand of her three-year-old son, Trevor.

"Oh my goodness, Trevor!" Dakota squealed, as she rushed to give the boy a hug. "You've gotten so big!"

Trevor hugged her back but only for a second before he looked up at his mother and asked, "Mom, who is that?"

"She's your aunt, sweetie." Capri brushed his chestnut hair with her cat-like nails as he buried his face in his mother's leg.

"No, that's my aunt," he pointed at Cassidy.

"Yes, that's Aunt Cassidy, this is your Aunt Dakota," his mother explained.

"It's okay. It makes sense he doesn't remember me. It's been over a year since I last saw him," said Dakota, trying to hide her disappointment.

"Well, we both thought we'd stop by to talk about our newly famous detective sister," said Cassidy. "We're so proud of you!" She gave Dakota a kiss on the cheek before she continued. "Blake listens to podcasts and radio shows when he works out. He clicked on something that said, 'Recommended for you' and — lo-and-behold — it was his sister-in-law's show! He came and got me and we both looked at all the comments and reviews people are leaving. They are all dying to know if you can solve the case."

"Peter and I binged all three episodes yesterday and we couldn't be prouder," said Capri, giving her little sister a rare compliment.

"You're going to get to the bottom of this, I can feel it!" said Cassidy.

"And since you're kicking ass right now, we thought we could interrupt you and take you to brunch to celebrate," offered Capri.

"Really?" This was not typical of the twins. Whenever Dakota came into town, they'd exchange pleasantries and inquire about each other's life until one of them, mainly Capri with the tacit encouragement of their parents, would begin to criticize Dakota for something or other. They didn't hang out with her and they never congratulated her on anything other than graduating college eight years ago.

"Of course, silly," said Cassidy, "Now get your purse and go."

Dakota dashed up the stairs and looked around the mounds of suitcases and unpacked boxes for where she had put her bag. Before she could grab it, there was a pounding on the front door followed by the sounds of her sister's voices speaking to several people.

Dakota came downstairs to see Jacqueline Montgomery flanked by her husband, Robert and Principal Bernard. Jacqueline wore an overall denim dress with a long-sleeved light blue shirt underneath. Her dark wavy hair was halfway pulled back and ran down to her knees. Thick-framed glasses that had been out of style since the 70s sat on her nose as she glared at Dakota.

"How could you do this to us?" she screamed. "Did you not think for one second to talk to us, the family, before you going around broadcasting every detail of the case to the whole wide world?"

"I didn't," Dakota began. She didn't have an answer or at least one she was comfortable sharing. She had considered talking to the Montgomery family and asking if they were on board with her plan to investigate the case. But she knew they would only get in her way.

"You didn't what? You didn't think how this would impact us? We've tried our hardest to move on and live with the fact she isn't going to come back to us.

We don't need someone bringing all of this back up again. We've got two other sons to worry about. We don't want them getting caught up in this. We don't want what happened last time with the media showing up at our door, asking personal questions and drawing conclusions out of nothing," the homely-looking woman explained.

"I'm sorry that what I've done has hurt you," said Dakota. "But I need to find her."

"But we need peace," said Robert Montgomery. He was normally a warm and welcoming, if not boisterous man. But there was no warmth in his dark eyes today.

"Listen, I didn't mean to cause your family any trouble. I will do everything I can to keep the press and the public away from you, but this has to be solved once and for all. And I'm getting close, I can tell." Dakota would not back down. Maddy was just as much hers as she was theirs.

"Asking some people from the school some questions isn't going to help. The police didn't help, how could you?" asked Robert.

"Because I knew her. I know how she would have reacted to certain people or situations. I know what was important to her and who she did and didn't trust. Plus, she isn't just a case to me. I don't have to worry about the rules or the budgets or the thousands of other missing persons cases that come across policemen's desks in Southern California. I can focus on Maddy — and Maddy alone," Dakota insisted.

Tears began to stream down Jacqueline's face. "We just want for all of this to stop. We just want our lives back to the way they were before."

"Before I started investigating?" asked Dakota.

"No, before she went missing," Jacqueline cried.

The dignified Principal Bernard spoke up. "That isn't going to happen."

Everyone looked at her in shock.

"It's painful to hear, but it's the truth. Once you lose a child in whatever circumstances, your life isn't the same. I pray every night that when I'd wake up in the morning, my son would be alive but that's not the case. It can't ever happen. And as hard as it has been for me and my family to deal with Will's suicide, at least we have all the answers. I'm an old woman now. Even if I'm not at death's door, I spend time now in my older years thinking about what I'll regret when I go. And If I were in your situation, I wouldn't want to leave this life before knowing what happened to my child. If there was a possibility someone could find all the answers, I wouldn't stand in their way," the former principal said.

The couple was quiet for a moment.

"Fine," said Jacqueline in a softer tone. "I hear you've become quite good at this sort of thing, so there may be a chance you can do something. But once you've exhausted all your options, please do us the service of letting us be."

Dakota nodded. "Can I interview you? You can tell me what happened that day and how the investigation was handled from your point of view?"

"No," said Robert. "Please leave us out of this."

"All right," said Dakota, knowing the investigation would be hampered by not having the parents of the missing person give an interview.

"Just do what you have to do and let's put this to rest," said Maddy's mother.

Chapter 6

I didn't do what Ma said. I didn't call in sick. It was Friday, and I bet they'd all think I was playing hooky. Plus, I wasn't going to let Ma tell me to use one of my precious sick days for this task. I'd just do it on a Saturday. One more day wouldn't hurt.

I arrive at the shop around nine in the morning like always. I put my lunch that Ma packed me in the employee fridge. But before I can get my gear on to work on a Mustang with a dented hood, Dave, one of the few guys at the shop who pays me any attention, walks up and slaps me on the shoulder.

"Hey, Freddy. Thank God it's Friday, am I right?" he asks with a grin stretching across his lightly stubbled face.

"Yep, TGIF," I say.

"I'm looking forward to the weekend. One of my buddies is getting married — for the third time — but whatever. Me and some of his other friends are throwing him a bangin' bachelor party tomorrow night at that strip joint off Ocean Park. Wanna come? The rest of the guys from work will be there," says Dave with a devilish smile.

My face is burning with embarrassment. I've fantasized about going into a place like this before but I never had the courage. The idea of getting aroused by naked women dancing on my lap while sitting next to my coworkers makes me nauseous.

"I can't," I blurt out. "I have a funeral on Saturday."

"Yeah but you ain't dead," he pokes me in the ribs and laughs. "Funerals are usually in the morning; you're telling me you aren't free on a Saturday night?"

"It's in Vegas. I have to drive all the way there so I wouldn't be back in time," I tell him.

"Oh, I see." he gives me a slight nod. "Well hey, have fun in Vegas for me," he says.

"I'll try but it won't be much fun, not like the fun you'll be having here," I say trying to sound like one of the guys. "It'll just be me and the open road for four hours there, a funeral and then four boring hours home. The driving really gets me. There's nothing to look at or listen to for hours, the radio doesn't even come in for most of the drive."

"You should listen to these new show things," says another voice. It was Larry another mechanic. "They are like radio shows but you put them on your phone, so you don't need a signal to listen once they're uploaded or downloaded or whatever."

"Shows like what?" I ask.

Larry shrugs and takes a drink from his morning coffee. "Like talk shows, they talk about anything. Sports, politics, movies, murder."

"Murder?" The hairs on the back of my neck stand on end.

"Yeah," Dave chimes in. "There's a bunch of these weirdos out there who like to solve old crimes. I don't really see the appeal. A little too morbid for me but hey, you might like it."

"Sure, I'll check them out," I say with lukewarm enthusiasm. Meanwhile, my brain feels like it will bust out of my skull. There are people who look into old crimes for sport? Not even because it's their job but because they want to? What if they go after one of my girls? What if they find me?

I'd have to wait until I got home to investigate what Larry and Dave were talking about.

•   •   •

The five o'clock whistle finally blew and I rushed to get home. I didn't even stop to say hi to Ma on my way down to the cave. This was too important.

I thud down the steps, almost tripping myself. I rush to my computer and turn the damn thing on. After hearing the familiar chime and letting it warm up, it is finally ready to connect to the Internet.

The first name that comes to mind is Rebecca's. I type in her name. Nothing comes up. Thank God, I think to myself, but it isn't nearly over. I had been sloppy. I didn't record the full names of all of them. Out of the eleven, I can remember only six full names.

I pull my Polaroids off the wall, one for each girl. I punch in the names of the ones I remember. Patty Flores, nothing. Linda Baker, nothing. Marie Kennedy, nothing. So and so forth until it got to her. My girl. My soulmate. Madeline Montgomery.

I take a breath and I steady myself. I'm sure there was nothing on her. There had been nothing for the other girls, but Maddy was special. I type in each letter slowly and methodically making sure I spell it correctly.

"Journalist Seeks to Solve Montgomery Cold Case," is the first entry that came up.

There are details on some forum, but my heart is beating too fast for me to make sense of the words. I see a collection of links and I click on the first one. It takes me to a site where there are a few audio recordings and I press play.

I hear white noise before the voice of a young woman starts speaking. She says, "Hello everyone, I'm Dakota Kilroy and you're listening to ShadowCast. Since this is the first episode, let me tell you a bit about myself and the case I'm trying to solve. I'm an investigative journalist with over eight years of experience, starting with breaking a story on prostitution in the modeling world while I was studying journalism at NYU. Later, I was a lead journalist at The Village Inquirer in New York City. I'm now back in my hometown of Santa Monica, California investigating the cold case of the disappearance of fifteen-year-old Madeline "Maddy" Montgomery."

My stomach leaps into my throat and I want to throw up. It's shocking enough to hear her name uttered out loud after all these years. It's worse to hear it said by someone who was coming for me.

• • •

Dakota had hit a snag in her investigation. She was running out of options. She called the rehab center where Selena was staying, and no one would let her speak to her. Selena's friend, Tiffany was off social media and all other forms of online communication. The only trace of her was in a local newspaper clipping from 2001, when it was announced that she and the rest of the St. Philomena soccer team had won the state championship. Everything else was a dead lead.

Dakota had found Tiffany's parents in the yellow pages. They hadn't moved in the last twelve years. She was about to punch their home number into the phone when it rang. A number with a New York area code flashed across the screen.

Dakota answered. "Hello?

"Hey, babe it's me," said a man's voice.

"Seth? What are you doing calling me?" she whispered.

"Listen, I get that we're broken up and all, but I need you — I really need you right now," his voice was both fast and slurred.

"I'm not coming to visit," she told him. "I couldn't even if I wanted to. I'm in California."

"That's not what I need. I need money. I'm in a real jam here," he said.

"How could you need money? You're in rehab. Your insurance and parents are covering the cost," she said.

"I had to get out. That place is too restrictive, babe. You would have hated it. I couldn't stand another day," he told her.

Dakota put her head down and held her forehead. "Seth, are you using again?"

"Yeah." His voice had quieted down. "I just need one more fix and I'll quit for good this time."

"Goddamn it. No, I'm not giving you any money. Go back to rehab and stay there until you've completed the treatment." Disappointment rose in her like stomach acid after a bad meal.

"Please, baby," he begged.

"I have nothing to give. I haven't had a job in three months. I'm living with my parents. I don't even have an allowance like I'm some middle schooler. I can't," she said.

"Fine," he said in a huff and hung up the phone.

Dakota cupped her face in her hands. She couldn't believe what Seth had turned into. Before she could process what just happened, her phone vibrated again. Another New York area number flashed on the screen.

"Listen, I told you I'm not giving you any money," she yelled into the speaker.

"Excuse me, ma'am. I'm not asking you for money," said a woman in a tight and professional tone.

"Oh God, I'm so sorry. I thought you were someone else," Dakota explained.

"That's all right, ma'am. I'm calling from Emory and Flynn Pharmaceuticals. Mr. Emory would like to schedule a meeting with you next week."

"I'm sorry, who is Mr. Emory and what is this about?" Dakota wrinkled her brow in confusion.

"Sean Emory is the CEO of our company and he'd like to meet with you to discuss sponsoring your show, *ShadowCast*," the woman said.

"Oh, okay. I wasn't expecting this. Sure, I'll meet with him," she said.

"Great, how's Monday at 12 pm at the Chez du Mer?" the woman asked.

"That works for me, I guess."

"Great, Mr. Emory will see you then."

• • •

Monday arrived but Dakota had already decided she would not like Mr. Emory and she would not take him up on his proposal to sponsor the show. She had looked him up online and had already pegged down exactly what type of man he was.

In his business headshot, he beamed at the camera with gelled back sandy hair and intense green-brown eyes. He appeared to be about forty years old and was too attractive for Dakota to even look at his photo for more than a few seconds without flushing.

I won't let his appearance fool me, thought Dakota. She pegged him for a preppy, entitled, smooth-talking captain of industry who spent his free time dating an endless line of empty-headed and cosmetically enhanced women.

She was certain he'd be a typical rude businessman like so many pinstriped suit-wearing men who would steal cabs away from her or trample over her feet on the subway platform near the financial district of New York.

Besides not liking him for the image he presented, she didn't think it was right to put drug commercials on her podcast.

Dakota pulled up to the hotel with these notions in mind. She handed the keys to a valet who refused to let Dakota park the car herself and she went inside. Before she entered, she straightened the white button-down shirt she had borrowed from Cassidy who was now too big to fit into her pre-pregnancy clothes.

The way her mother and sisters fussed over her appearance before this meeting made Dakota feel like she was getting ready for prom, not a business lunch. The women picked out a tattoo-concealing outfit of form-fitting black trousers, a white shirt, and a cream-white leather jacket that Capri brought over from her house. She lent it to Dakota freely, save for the various instructions on what foods she wasn't allowed to eat while wearing the jacket for fear of stains. That meant Dakota's favorite combination of pasta and red wine was out of the question.

Cassidy did her makeup, which was much to Dakota's liking except for some magenta lipstick she wiped off in the car. Debi spent nearly forty minutes getting Dakota's stringy hair to flow into gentle curls that hung down by her shoulders. Of course, she had to put in her itchy contact lenses and leave her glasses at home. With her new appearance, she felt like she belonged in Southern California for the first time in her life.

Dakota walked through the white and teal lobby and entered the vast restaurant with eight-foot-tall windows that looked out onto the sapphire blue sea. She gazed across the room to see Sean Emory sitting at a small white marble table, staring out the nearby window.

He looked different from his professional photos. He was even more handsome, arrestingly so, like he had stepped out of an old film. But he wasn't sitting stiffly at the table in a double-breasted navy suit like she imagined he would be. He was leaning back in his chair, in light slacks and a plaid button-down. His hair was longer than it was in his picture. It gave him a boyish and playful energy.

Dakota had walked all the way to his table without him noticing her.

"Mr. Emory?" she asked, doubting herself for a minute.

"Yes," he looked right at her and smiled. Dakota felt herself smile in return but stopped herself.

"Dakota Kilroy?" he asked.

She nodded.

"Please, sit down," he motioned toward the turquoise chair across from him.

Once seated, she said, "Mr. Emory, your assistant said you wanted to discuss—"

"Please, call me Sean," he interrupted. "And let's get to business in a minute. What'll you be having?" he nudged the menu towards her. "Care for some white?" he asked as he waived a waiter over and placed an order for the best Pinot Grigio they had.

"I have to say this is not what I was expecting," he said as the waiter walked away.

"What do you mean?" Dakota looked up from her menu, where she was looking for a meal she could order that wouldn't put her sisters' clothes at risk of staining.

"Well, there aren't any photos of you online that went along with your work. Your Facebook, even your profile picture, is private. Smart girl. So by your resume, I was expecting a stern authoritarian type, like a Janet Napolitano. But after listening to you, I imagined a cute and frail girl with that sweet voice of yourself. I definitely wasn't expecting a supermodel."

"Oh Mr. Emory, haven't you learned by now?" she said, closing her menu.

He leaned in.

"Flattery gets you nowhere," she quipped.

He let out a booming laugh. "I told you, call me Sean. And that hasn't been my experience. But anyway, it's true. You've got your movie-star blow-out, couture clothes, not to mention you're — what? — at least six feet tall and gorgeous."

"Five foot ten," she replied. "And I've always felt a bit gangly. I don't normally dress like this. My sisters did my look for the day. They actually are models though."

"Really? Wait. Kilroy. Are your sisters the Kilroy twins?"

"Yes, actually they are."

He smacked his hands together and laughed. "Playboy models and a hardened investigator all in one family."

"They did one spread, that hardly qualifies them as Playboy models. They were mostly cheerleaders before they got married. But," she realized she had been caught off guard. It surprised her how disarming Sean was. "This isn't about my sisters."

"No, it's not. But why don't we order before we get down to the brass tacks?" he said.

As soon as the waiter took their orders, Sean said, "So my executive assistant told you I wanted to sponsor the show and—"

"Yes, that's what I wanted to talk with you about," said Dakota, not wanting to give him the chance to state his case. "I'm not comfortable publicly endorsing a pharmaceutical company. I'm not a doctor and I don't think ads for prescription drugs are ethical. Plus, the nature of the podcast is so sensitive. I just don't think it would work."

He smiled. "Well, if you'd let me get a word in, I was going to say I want to sponsor it privately. That means no commercials or promos or anything like that. I'm usually a very skilled negotiator but with this, I'm laying my cards out. This case intrigues me. I'm dying to know what happened to Maddy, and I think it's quite noble that you're trying to solve this thing all on your own for no pay. I'll give you anything you ask for. Name your price."

Dakota raised her eyebrows in surprise.

"Seriously. The only thing I ask for in return is to be with you every step of the way. So I can be there as you interview potential leads, dig around through old files, put clues together and eventually solve the case." He looked excited like a kid just before he opened gifts on his birthday.

"Wait, you're willing to pay me some wild sum of money so you can work with me, unbeknownst to the public, as I solve this missing person's case? Why would you want to do that?" she asked.

"I told you, I got really into the case after listening to the first few episodes. I want to be there as it happens. I find it thrilling," he explained.

"I appreciate your enthusiasm, but this isn't just some adrenaline junkie sport. This is a real person with a real life that went missing. A person who meant the world to me. Can you be a part of my investigation while respecting Maddy and not treating the case the way people rubberneck at a car accident on the highway?" she asked him.

His face grew ashen and his body tensed. "Yes. I'll be the most respectful person you've ever met. Seriously, I do feel the pain of Maddy's family. I won't take this lightly. I just want to help."

"Okay," she said.

"You haven't given me a number," he said.

"What?" asked Dakota, thinking he had asked her out and she didn't even notice it.

"Your price," he said. "What was your annual salary at your last job?"

"$45,000," she said.

He pulled a checkbook out of his back pocket and scribbled in it. "Here's a check for sixty thousand. You can work for me on this case for over a year if you have to. I'll cover any other expenses, as well."

Dakota stared down at the check. "This is too much. I can't accept this."

"Dakota, please. I own the majority of a company worth over 7 billion dollars. I'll be fine. Take the money." He winked at her.

Dakota's mind flashed to her awful interview at the *Santa Monica Bulletin*. That would be her future if she didn't get an income soon.

"Okay, I'll accept this," she said, her heart racing. "Tomorrow, we need to get down to work."

• • •

"I see you've come prepared," said Dakota, as she sat down next to Sean. He had put a binder full of newspaper clippings and notebook scribbles on the table at the coffee shop.

"I would have never guessed you were a true crime aficionado," Dakota continued.

He put on a pair of reading glasses that didn't do anything to hide the flawless architecture of his face.

"Yes, yes I am," he said with a less-than-humorous expression as he pulled items out of the binder and tossed them over to Dakota's side of the table.

"Really? Well, when we have downtime, I'd love to get your opinion on other cold cases, especially the Zodiac," she said.

"I'm not really into horoscopes," he said, barely looking up from the papers in front of him.

"The Zodiac Killer. One of the most notorious uncaught serial killers of all time. What true crime fan doesn't know about him?" she asked.

"Oh, I'm not really into serial killers, just missing persons." His voice shook a little as if he didn't really believe what he was saying.

"Hmmm." Dakota sighed as she picked up the items he had tossed over to her and straightened them in a neat pile.

"I'm surprised you don't have anything with you," said Sean with a scowl, the lightheartedness Dakota had experienced in their meeting yesterday had faded.

"I do, it's all on here." Dakota held up her laptop and showed him a database of newspaper articles all on Maddy's disappearance.

"Good," he smiled a little.

Dakota scrolled through the twenty-six articles in total that were published about Maddy. "Most of these articles are basically the same. 'Missing Girl Not Found,' 'Local Girl Missing, No Leads,' 'No Leads in Montgomery Case.' It's frustrating."

Sean put two articles on top of Dakota's keyboard. "What about these searches? It says the police searched twice, once alone, once with volunteers. Is there anything in your system about what they found, if anything? What I have here is vague."

"They did three searches, one with police personnel, two with volunteers," said Dakota without looking into the database.

Sean paused to sip his coffee before turning back to her with a crinkled brow. "How do you know?"

"I was there for both," she told him.

Dakota remembered those days as some of the most painful times in her life. Standing less than an arm's reach away from the people walking on either side of her. They were all decorated in bright orange visibility vests. She moved in step with these strangers through the overgrown field with tall grass coming up to her hips, lodging pollen particles and sharp spurs into the fabric of her jeans. She still could smell the sweet fertile scent of earth and feel the stems of dead plants crumble beneath her feet as she pressed on. She could still hear a man's voice call out from several yards away and see his arm shoot up in the air like a firecracker on the Fourth of July. He had found something, and a sickening feeling rose in her chest as she was certain she was about to see the body of her best friend, her only real friend, rotting away in the field behind their school.

But it wasn't Maddy, just some bones from a long-dead animal. She searched again with the group of police and concerned citizens at a park that was a known spot for body-dumping. Her parents told her not to go, but their voices only rang in her ears like she was underwater. Police warned her about the psychological damage finding her friend might cause, but she just stared at them, flat-faced and empty. After a few uncomfortable seconds, they conceded and let her join the search party.

"I didn't know," said Sean.

"The police searched the night she went missing with dogs and flashlights. In the morning, school was closed, and they asked for community volunteers and I offered to search the school grounds. No one really pushed back against me being there. But I think they saw me as an asset. I know Maddy's appearance and behavior. I knew the school and the wild, untamed grounds that surrounded it, so no one objected. I searched the public park with them a week later, once again, nothing," she told him in a voice that hid her emotions.

"Are there records of the searches?" said Sean.

"Yes." She pulled up a few articles that detailed the searches.

Sean's bottle green eyes darted over the words in the article. They confirmed her story. The police reports in the article listed animal bones, a girl's shoe, and backpack being found. Both clothing items were later confirmed not to belong to Maddy.

"See, nothing of interest," she took her computer back from Sean's grasp. "Well, unless they're hiding something."

"What do you mean?" he asked.

"No one has seen the actual police files on this. They are all with Detective Muldowney and he won't let me look at them, that's for sure."

"Have you asked?" asked Sean, with a hint of condescension.

"Of course, I did," Dakota defended herself. "Saw him last week. He basically gave me a pat on the head, told me not to worry about it, and that he'd solve the case."

"He's had twelve years to solve it!" yelled Sean. His voice made a few other patrons at the coffee house jump.

"Sorry," he said to them and they all turned back to their iPhones, laptops, or newspapers.

"I agree," said Dakota. "If he gave us a chance to see the files, we could get somewhere."

Sean stroked his chin while staring at the screen of the laptop. "How well do you know him?"

"I've known the Muldowney family since I was a child. He's got a wife and three kids. They all attended catechism with my sisters and me at St. Philomena's church, but he couldn't afford to send them to the school so they went to public."

"What are his kids like now?" asked Sean.

"Well, the two older sons both joined the military, but according to the gossip my mother told me a few weeks ago, Samantha, his youngest, got herself into trouble. She spent most of her first semester at Stanford partying and it looks like she's going to fail out," she said.

"I bet that's gonna cost her dad a pretty penny," he said with a half laugh. "Can you get him on the phone?"

Dakota pulled out her phone and pressed the detective's contact information.

The phone rang.

"Dakota, I was just about to call you. How could you investigate this case so publicly without even talking to me first?" Anger gargled in the old detective's voice. "And you didn't even ask the family either? Have you no respect for—"

Dakota stopped him. "Detective, there's someone who wants to speak with you," she said and handed the phone to Sean.

"Hey, Detective Muldowney, how are you on this lovely Santa Monica morning?" asked Sean, the charm was back on and it was radiating out of every word he spoke.

Dakota could hear the retired cop trip over his words through the muffled speaker. "Um, I'm fine, I guess. Who is this?"

"I'm Sean Emory, CEO of Emory and Flynn Pharmaceuticals and the sponsor of *ShadowCast*, Dakota's show," said Sean.

"So you're the one making this investigation possible." Detective Muldowney's voice spiked with agitation. "Listen here, I have got a lot of choice words for you."

"Did I mention that my alma mater is Stanford?" Sean asked.

"No," replied Muldowney, his tone turning from irritation to confusion.

"And I'm a yearly donor with a sizable contribution. I hear your daughter, Samantha, is having a bit of trouble there," Sean continued.

"How did you find out about that?" asked Muldowney.

Sean stretched his feet out, his back leaning against the chair. He kept the phone pressed to one side of his face while his other arm stretched out and rested on the back of Dakota's chair. "One phone call and she is re-enrolled for the next semester, no questions asked."

"And why would you do that?" he asked.

"Simple. I'd do it for anyone who'd let Dakota and me take a look at the files on the Montgomery case. Your daughter might be causing you over $40,000 if I don't step in here," he grinned.

Sean could hear the gray bristles on Muldowney's unkempt mustache rustle as he moved the phone from one side of his face to the other.

"Forty grand for a few files seems like a pretty good deal," said Sean, growing impatient.

"I can't let you have them." Muldowney's voice was hoarse. "It's unethical."

"I'm sorry you feel that way. Tell Samantha good luck from us." Sean moved the phone away from his ear.

"Wait, wait," the detective called out. "I won't give the files over to you, but I'll let you make copies and I keep the originals," he said.

Sean smiled. "Sounds like a deal to me. Dakota and I will come by shortly and after the copies are made, I'll make that call. See you soon." Sean hung up the phone.

"Wow, that was impressive," said Dakota with raised eyebrows of both respect and suspicion.

"Whatever it takes to get the job done," he looked over at the binder in front of him and sighed. "Sometimes, the more you look at something the more distorted it gets. But can I ask you something?"

"Sure," said Dakota.

"As Maddy's best friend, what does your gut say? Who would have hurt Maddy? Was it that Connor guy?"

"No," Dakota shook her head. "I tracked down his arrest record last night. He was in jail overnight when Maddy went missing. He's clear."

"Then who?" asked Sean, moving closer.

"Well, I think…" Dakota started.

"No. No thinking. Just say the first name that comes to the top of your head. Go!" he commanded.

"Selena," she blurted out.

Sean asked, "Who is she again?"

"She was a bully at school. She picked on Maddy because she was so much smaller than everyone else. But anyway, I recently found an entry from my diary, dated two days before Maddy disappeared. Selena and her friend, Tiffany, threatened Maddy in front of me. They even set something on fire in front of us and said if Maddy didn't do as they said, she'd leave school in a body bag."

Dakota felt an acidic burn of hate rise in her stomach. She wanted to beat the living shit out of Selena.

"The thing is," she continued, forcing the violent daydreams out of her head. "I didn't remember this incident until after moving back home this winter. At the time, everyone was so frantic, and I was so numb from the whole thing, Selena must have slipped my mind. Plus, she was allegedly home sick that night. I told Muldowney about this, but he practically laughed it off."

Sean scowled, the soft lines around his mouth became deeper. "You've got to be kidding me. That is a serious lead and he just dismissed it like it was nothing. Where is this Selena now?"

"Rehab, court-appointed. No visitors at all. Only calls from family are allowed. I've tried calling several times and they just hang up on me."

"We've got to talk to her. We have to see her," he said.

"Good luck," said Dakota, throwing her hands up in the air.

Sean clenched his jaw, looking more determined than ever. "I'll figure out something. After we make this visit to Muldowney's, I'll hunt her down."

•   •   •

Dakota and Sean pulled up to the detective's home. It was a gray ranch home with patchy sod on the front lawn. The house was situated far from the beach and the luxury homes that dotted the neighborhoods of Santa Monica.

Sean pounded on the door, but no one answered. "He stood us up!"

"No, I didn't," a voice said from behind them. The detective was leaning out the window of his old Chevy Monte Carlo, while smoking a cigarette. With one last puff, he tossed the butt on the ground and got out the car.

He handed a beige folder over to Dakota. "I drove to Kinkos while you two were doing God knows what. I didn't want to wait around and watch you two work a copy machine."

"How can I trust that you copied everything from your original file?" asked Sean.

Detective Muldowney jiggled the key in his front door and opened it. "Come inside and you can compare the copies with the originals."

At the kitchen table, Dakota laid out the freshly copied papers that the detective had shoved in a weathered blue folder. The detective opened his folder of the originals and compared them, piece by piece. After the trio verified that all the material from the first file was present in the second, Sean pulled out his phone and tapped a number on the screen.

"Jimmie, my man, how have you been?" said Sean.

Dakota and Muldowney heard a faint male voice on the other end but couldn't make out the words.

"So glad to hear it," Sean continued. "Listen, I was wondering if you could help a buddy of mine out. My friend's daughter, Samantha Muldowney, may be facing academic probation or even expulsion, but I was wondering if you might reconsider and let her come back for the spring semester. You know what the first semester can be like. I'm sure she'll turn it around this time."

There was a pause.

Then Sean said. "That's right. M-U-L-D-O-W-N-E-Y. Thanks so much, man, I really appreciate it. Next time I'm up there, let's hit the driving range. Great, thanks, Jim."

He hung up the phone and said with a smug smile, "All taken care of. But the semester starts next Tuesday, so you better call Samantha and get things squared away for her return."

ShadowCast

Muldowney stared at him in awe. "Wow, thank you so much, Mr. Emory. You're really helping us out," the detective stepped forward and shook his hand. "But I trust that those files will be kept private and will only be used for investigative purposes. Not to post around the Internet or sell them to a newspaper."

"They're just for us," Sean confirmed.

"I won't let anything happen to them," Dakota said.

The detective just gave her a nod that seemed to say, "it's not *you* who I'm worried about."

Chapter 7

I turn off that horrendous radio show. I reach for the plastic waste bin under my desk and wretch. Nothing comes out. I steady myself and wipe the sweat from my palms on my jeans.

My eyesight is blurry and my head feels like it weighs a thousand pounds, but I force myself to concentrate. I click the little half cycle at the top of the browser to reload the page. There it is in black and white, her name: Madeline Montgomery. And some bitch was looking for her. It's been over twelve years — why can't she let sleeping dogs lie?

I hit play on the episode again and dig my fingernails into the cushioned arm rests of my office chair as I hear the voice of the investigator once more:

"You may be wondering how I know all this about Maddy. That is because I'm not just an investigative journalist, I was Maddy's best friend in high school. Her disappearance still haunts me to this day. Like all the people who were close to Maddy at the time she went missing, I'm constantly bothered by questions about where she is, what happened to her, and if she is still alive. People have told me to make my peace with it and move on. But I can't. That's not what a best friend would do. Twelve years later, I'm finally putting my skills to good use to find out what really happened."

I pause the recording again. Anger rises in my veins. This Dakota woman isn't going to give up, I can feel it. Not if she has a personal connection to the case. Plus, she's one of those career types, those women who think they are as tough as a man just because they act like one. I can't imagine what my sweet angel would have been doing being friends with a ball-buster like that.

But I can't think about Maddy right now. Not only can I simply not bare it, but I have a much larger task in front of me.

ShadowCast

I pack up the Buick for my yearly pilgrimage to Vegas. I don't bring much, just a cooler full of sandwiches and a change of clothes in case I need it. Of course, I have about two hundred bucks in cash with me just in case the gambling bug bites. I'm planning on driving there, dropping off that damn letter, playing a few rounds of blackjack and turning right back around.

• • •

It's barely past six in the morning and the sun is just piercing the horizon. I slam the trunk down and feel eyes on me. I turn around and I see Ma in her long flowing blue nightgown staring at me from the porch.

"Yeah, Ma?" I ask, knowing she's got something to say.

"Don't mind me," she snaps. "I'm just going to be sitting alone all Saturday while my idiot son runs an errand he should have taken care of weeks ago."

"It's not going to be that long, I promise," I say in a sweet voice. "I'll probably be home for a late dinner."

"It's just that every time you do this, I—" her voice trails off and I can see tiny pools of tears in her eyes.

"What is it?" I come closer to her and gently rub her back.

In low whisper she says, "Every time you go, I just think they're gonna catch you and take you away from me."

"Oh Ma, no one is going to catch me, not after this many years." My mind flashed back to the sound of Dakota's voice filling my ears and making me nauseated. It's best I don't tell her about that. I'm sure it'd give her a stroke.

"Okay, just be careful," she tells me as I hug her goodbye.

Several hours later, I can see the lights of Vegas poking out of the flat desert landscape. It always made me marvel how you could still see those lights from such a distance even in the broad daylight.

For a moment, I feel better knowing a craps table and a whiskey lie ahead of me. But my mood only sours when I remember the real reason I'm here. Goddamn, I mutter to myself. One bad mistake back in 1969 and I'm still paying for it.

• • •

I drive through all the flash and glitz of the strip and find the little post office on the outskirts of town where I always send the letters. I pull out what I wrote back at home and glance over it. My handwriting looks just like a woman's. At first, it took me forever to get it right — those exaggerated loops and perfect Ks and Rs of her cursive handwriting. Thankfully, Rebecca left a bunch of diaries behind for me to learn from. When it first happened, Ma had me staying up until dawn practicing my writing until it looked just like hers. Now, it's second nature to me, I flip between my usual scribble to elegant cursive in the blink of an eye.

My letter is no different from last year. I talk about the adventures she gets into, owning a night club in Vegas. The strippers and show girls who get into fights, the drunk patrons who try to fight the bouncers who are twice their size, and the celebrities who make covert appearances while they're in town. All of this is, of course, a lie but none of the gray-haired ladies that Ma lets read the letter when it arrives seem to notice.

I fold the pieces of paper and put them in a stamped and addressed envelope.

The dry desert air hits me in the face as I get out of the car. I walk across the asphalt and drop the letter into the blue mailbox and release a heavy sigh. As I sit back down in the driver's seat, I see a sign with red and orange lights that spell out 'CASINO' in my rearview mirror. A couple of slots couldn't hurt.

It's several hours later when I finally notice that the sun has almost disappeared behind the distant mountains, giving the world a golden-brown glow. I can't believe I lost track of time. Once the cards started flipping, and I started winning — and then losing and then winning again, I lost all sense of time and space. Gambling and women, they'll be the death of me.

My eyesight isn't what it used to be and soon it will be too dark for me to see right. It's not safe for me to drive four hours straight in the pitch-black desert.

Down the strip and over several blocks, I find a motel with a neon blue sign that tells me there is a vacancy. At the counter, there is a blond with a full figure. She is wearing a bright pink blouse that is tucked into a skin-tight leopard-print skirt. Her hair is done up into victory curls, but the lines on her face and the stains on her teeth tell me she is far too weathered to be the pin up model she is imitating.

For a moment, I think that this is what Rebecca would have ended up looking like if she had lived.

"Good evening, sir. Need a room?" she says in an accent that was more at home in Minnesota than Nevada.

I nod. "Yes, just for the night."

"That'll be $90," she tells me.

I reach into my pocket and realize I only won about $40 back from my time at the casino.

"I don't have that much in cash," I say.

"We take Visa and MasterCard." She looks hopeful. I can tell she doesn't want to lose a customer.

"Ma doesn't like it when I use credit."

She laughs with a snort. "You let your mother tell you what to do? Aren't you a little too old for that?"

My face feels hot even in the air-conditioned lobby.

"It's not a big deal, just run it." I hand over the red plastic card with my name on it, she rings me up and hands me a key to room number 12. Once inside my room, I brace myself. I'll have to tell Ma.

The phone rings three times and she answers, "Who is this?"

"It's me. I got caught up with things here and I booked a room for the night," I confess.

"Edward, how could you? You were supposed to be home from work hours ago," she shouts into the phone.

"Ma, we've been over this. I'm Freddy, your son. Edward was your husband. He's not here anymore, but we just happen to sound alike." I shake my head. I hate hearing her get like this.

"Stop it, Ed. Freddy's just a little boy. He can't sound like you. Quit trying to play a trick on me. Anyway, Rebecca has a recital for her dance class next weekend and I wanted to make sure you were home for it," she continues in the same scolding tone.

"Ma, it's not Edward. It's Freddy, I swear. Look around you. It's 2012, not the 1960s," I say, not knowing how to explain this to her.

"What are you trying to pull?" she asks.

"Look in the mirror," I shout. This is too painful for me to listen to.

"Edward, would you stop this?" she hisses.

I slam my fist down on the nightstand. "Just do it, Ma."

"What happened? How did I? Why am I so old?" She lets out a little cry. "It was just yesterday when the kids were in school and..."

"It seems like yesterday, but it's not. It's your brain playing tricks on you," I say in a calm voice.

There was a pause.

"Hello?" I ask.

Nothing.

"Hello? Ma? Answer me!" I shout.

"What? Who is this?" she asks me.

"It's Freddy."

"Why the hell aren't you home, I've been worried sick."

I take a deep breath. I don't have the energy to explain to her that I just told her where I was. "I have to stay over. I ran out of time and booked a room," I say. "The drive isn't as easy as it used to be. You're not the only one getting old. I need to rest, but I'll head back first thing."

•　　•　　•

In the car the next morning, I hook my phone up to the stereo system. As soon as I hit play on the pre-downloaded episodes of ShadowCast, Dakota's voice surrounds me.

I want to turn it off. I want to scream. I want to cry. But most of all, I want to kill her. I want to slit her throat and watch the life run out of her eyes. After all these years, I can't let her be my undoing.

As I drive, the episodes continue. I heard the voices of the people who claim they knew my angel, but they didn't appreciate her like I did. She didn't belong to any of them but me. Dakota has no right to take her from me and give her to her parents. If she really belonged to them, they would have kept a better eye on her in the first place. No, she's staying with me so I can visit her and talk to her anytime I want.

I force myself to put my anger aside. "Stick to the facts," I say to myself out loud as I drive through a flat barren highway road. She has no idea. She keeps thinking it's someone from school. She's so far off my trail, she isn't even on the same planet.

I tell this to myself to calm my nerves and to reassure myself that my secrets are safe from Dakota, the world, and even Ma to some extent. I mean she doesn't know all of it. But the secrets, the memories of them are burning in my brain.

Is there anything I can do to keep this bitch away from me? To keep her from even considering someone like me taking Maddy? I consider moving Maddy, or finding a better place for all my pictures and souvenirs. Hell, I might even convince Ma to move to a new house.

I'm so lost in thought trying to be one step ahead of this nosy slut, I don't notice my car pulling to one side and leading me off the road entirely. I try to steady it and get it back on the road, but it's too late. My car ducks and bobs as it slows down on the rough desert floor. I clench the emergency break and get out of the car to see that the left rear tire is completely shredded.

"Shit!" I shout in the empty desert. I open up the trunk to find that I do have a spare, but I left the car jack at work. I had to bring it in to help Dave with an issue with his fuel line last week and I forgot to take it back.

I limp along the mostly empty road until I see a small town rising in the distance and a beckoning gas station sign high in the air.

Inside the stale-smelling gas station, I'm able to buy the jack I need. I'm flustered and overwhelmed as I pull the car behind the store. I crank the lug nuts off my ruined tire and heave the spare out of the trunk.

Just as I'm getting ready to screw it into place, the sound of a feminine laugh catches my ears.

ShadowCast

It's a blond girl. I can't tell where she even came from, but she couldn't be more than seventeen years old. She has softly curled hair that bounces as she moves. She's wearing a tight green tank top and jean shorts that show off long legs I just want to run my tongue up and down.

Lust. It's bubbling up again. I'm consumed by it. No, I have to walk away.

I quicken my pace and finish securing the tire to my car. I'm about to throw the jack in the back of my trunk when I hear her say, "Hey, do you have a smoke?"

She has a lighter in her hands.

"No, I don't," I tell her, trying not to look at her in the face.

"Are you sure?" she comes closer.

"Yeah, but I don't have any on me," I say. "Why don't you go in and get a pack?"

"Can't. I'm only sixteen," she says. "But I'll pay you extra if you go and get me a pack." She gives me a pouty look.

"I can't." I turn away from her.

"Please," she calls out in a baby voice.

She got me. I'll do anything she asks. "Fine."

I return with a pack of Camels in my hand.

"Why don't you smoke in the car with me for a bit. It'll keep you cool from the sun," I say to her, keeping my voice from shaking.

She shrugs and follows me to the car.

Inside, she lights up and lets soft gray smoke trickle out of her pink mouth and out the cracked window.

Just as she relaxes, I lock the doors.

She lets out a scream and tugs at the handle.

"Don't worry, honey. This won't take long," I tell her as I reach for her neck.

Less than two minutes later, she's out cold. Behind the store, no one can see me so I drag her limp body into my trunk. I slam the lid down and drive the rest of the way home in silence.

Chapter 8

"What the fuck are you doing in here?" asked Selena. Her dark eyes glared straight ahead, trying but failing to intimidate her interviewer.

Dakota didn't answer; she was going to let Selena get her anger out first.

"I was told, 'No visitors, no visitors' from the second I got in here," Selena went on. "And then, what do they do? Allow you in because you have some rich sugar daddy. What the fuck do you even want to talk to me about, anyway?" She dashed her fist against the table in front of them.

The high school bully didn't look how Dakota remembered her. Her slick-back ponytail was replaced by a main of frizzy hair. The naturally long and bony build of her face was even more pronounced with a smattering of pockmarks healing across her cheeks.

"Do you remember Maddy?" Dakota finally asked in a cool voice.

The mention of Maddy's name caused Selena's anger to disappear like a match blown out by the wind. She went from looking like a Doberman about to attack to a lap dog that looked guilty of peeing in the house. "Yeah, that little girl, the smart one. Man, she was annoying. Whatever happened to her?" she asked.

"She was never found," Dakota replied.

"Weird." Selena gave a shrug and adjusted her ill-fitting sweatshirt.

"Yes, it is weird." Dakota had enough of playing it cool. "So weird that twelve years later, no one has any idea where she is. That's why I'm here. To find out what happened to her. I'm asking everyone who knew her if they could tell me what they remember from the time she disappeared. That includes you."

Selena didn't give a response.

"And it would be even more helpful if you agreed to let me record this," Dakota said.

"No way, I'm not answering anything. I'm not stupid. I want a lawyer." Selena crossed her arms and looked at the wall across the room as if rows of 'Just Say No to Drugs' posters from the 80s were more interesting than talking to Dakota.

Dakota took a deep breath. "I'm not a cop and this isn't an official police investigation, so you don't need a lawyer. You don't have to talk to me at all. Just say the word and I'll leave, but I think it's best that we talk."

"Why's that?" Selena wrinkled her brow.

"It may seem a little more suspicious that you didn't voluntarily give me an interview. People out there know that you didn't like Maddy and now you're one of the few people I've talked to who is refusing an interview. They will draw their own conclusions," Dakota said.

Selena didn't answer, but Dakota could tell that her tough attitude was fading.

"Look, I just want to ask you what you remember from December 2000." Dakota pulled out her phone with the attached microphone and placed it on the second-hand coffee table that stood between them in the rehab center's common room.

Selena rolled her eyes. "Fine, fine. Ask me whatever and record it for all I care. I didn't do anything."

Dakota pressed record, but before she could ask her first question, Selena blurted out, "I'm not gonna lie, I didn't like Maddy. She was always showing everybody up. She was the smartest, the prettiest, the best singer and the best musician in our class. And she was two years younger. There was nothing left for the rest of us. She may not have been that popular to hang around with, but it seemed like everybody wanted to be like her."

"Okay," Dakota steadied herself. "Just for clarity's sake, this is Dakota Kilroy and I'm speaking with Selena Diaz inside a rehab facility where Ms. Diaz is currently being treated. Today is February 2, 2012. All right, so you didn't like her, is that why you threatened her?"

Selena straightened up. "When did I threaten her?"

"Two days before she disappeared, you came and cornered the two of us in the library. Tiffany, your then best friend, lit a piece of paper on fire and threw it at us. Then, you said that if Maddy agreed to do your homework for the rest of the next semester, you would tell your brother to go out with her. Since you knew she had a crush on him, you thought she would give in. But when she didn't outright agree, you said — and I'm quoting directly here — 'I'll make sure you leave school in a body bag'," Dakota told her.

Selena's eyes widen. "Look, that's just how I talk. I go big. But I don't mean it. I wasn't actually going to hurt her, I just wanted to get her to do what I said. But none of that matters anyway. Because I didn't do it."

"Do you have any proof of those claims?" Dakota asked.

Selena smiled. "Yeah, kinda. I wanted to tell the cops about it, but my mom said to keep quiet. My grandmother wasn't exactly here legally and the last thing she wanted was the police stopping by my house. But it's fine now, she got her papers."

"So what is it then?" asked Dakota, inching the phone closer to Selena to make sure the recording would be clear.

"I remember I was sick," Selena began. "Like really sick. And I was upset. I wanted to be in the pageant, but now I couldn't go. I had a high fever and my mom called the doctor. I think he kept the office open late for us, so as soon as she came home from work, she drove me to see him. I was in the passenger seat and looking out the window, trying to take my mind off feeling like shit. We were passing the school and there Maddy was, up ahead walking towards the school dressed in an angel costume. I remembered it made me mad because I wanted to be the soloist for the pageant, but Maddy got it instead. So, being sick and seeing her in that costume about to sing the song I wanted to sing really pissed me off — I mean so much so that I can still remember exactly how it felt, even to this day."

Dakota let out a huff. Selena had to be lying. "That doesn't make sense with the timeline Maddy's mother gave us," she told her.

"What you mean?" asked Selena.

"Mrs. Montgomery said she dropped Maddy off right around 5:30 that evening and she watched Maddy walk through the school gates towards the auditorium. That was the last time anyone saw her alive or dead."

Selena let out a sharp laugh. "I don't know what her mother's deal is but she's lying. I know what I saw, I know how mad it made me feel. She didn't drop Maddy off."

Dakota stopped the recording.

"So soon?" asked Selena. "I thought we were just getting started."

"You swear to God or whatever you believe in that you saw Maddy walking on the street that night?" Dakota leaned forward and looked deep into Selena's eyes for any hint of dishonesty.

"I swear," Selena put one hand on her heart and the other up towards heaven. "I can admit I've lied a lot in the past, but this time I mean it for real. I saw her clear as day walking on the sidewalk about three blocks away from the school. Didn't she live down the street, anyway?" Selena asked.

"She did. About five blocks from the school." Dakota said with her mind racing.

"See, it's more than possible she decided to walk to school instead of getting a ride with her mom," Selena said, almost a little too proud of herself.

Dakota had a fine-tuned bullshit meter, but Selena's story didn't set it off. "I can't tell you why, but I believe you," she said in a low voice.

Selena threw her hands up in the air. "Finally, someone."

"Listen," Dakota began. "I'm sorry for what you're going through. My ex is going through the same thing. Those opioid drugs really can—"

Selena cut her off. "Well, you moved on quick."

"Oh Sean," Dakota realized she must have seen him in the lobby when they arrived. "That's my business partner. We aren't together," she explained.

Selena was no longer amused by the situation. "Right, right. Well, if you don't have anything else for me, can I go?"

"Yes," said Dakota.

Selena stood up, but Dakota stopped her. "But just one question. Where's Tiffany?"

"Ha! Haven't heard?" Selena laughed.

Dakota shook her head. "No, I just got back into town."

"Oh right, you were a big city girl for a while," sneered Selena. "If you had stayed around, you'd have found out that Tiffany is now what you'd call an escort."

Dakota was surprised. "Really?"

"Yep. So good luck trying to track her down." Selena laughed again as she exited the room.

•　　•　　•

Sean was waiting outside, leaning on the side of the car when Dakota left the rehab center. Dakota could sense the eagerness in his posture. He wanted an answer, but she still didn't have one.

She shook her head. "It wasn't her."

Sean took a deep breath. But instead of being disappointed, as Dakota had expected, he seemed relieved.

"This is getting to be a lot for me. I need to take a break from this stuff. Why don't we do something, just the two of us?" he proposed.

"We can't just take a break. There is a lot more work to do," Dakota said.

"I know, but I've learned in my advanced age," he joked, "that you have to step away from your projects once in a while or they will eat you alive."

Dakota nodded and thought of Seth. "That's true."

He moved his body closer to Dakota. "So, let's go somewhere fun. What's there to do around here?"

"There's surfing and swimming, if you like that sort of thing," she started. "I don't. There's the pier which is fun if you're like seven years old. There's the mall and the shopping centers if you're into conspicuous consumption."

"Man, you're such a Debbie Downer," he grinned at her.

"*Debby Downer?*" Dakota teased. "What are you from the 50s? No one says that anymore."

Before Sean had a chance to defend his phrasing, she went on. "But Selena said something that could really change the outcome of—?"

"I can't listen to this anymore right now," he said. "I'm sorry. I knew someone who went missing a long time ago and it just brings up some bad feelings for me. I want us to continue, but let's take some time to relax," he explained.

"Maybe," said Dakota, gritting her teeth. She hated taking breaks, especially when she might be making progress on a case.

"I don't come to California very often. I just want to enjoy being here in the warm sun, with a great view of the ocean and a beautiful woman to show me around."

"Oh brother," she rolled her eyes.

He looked at her straight on. "What? Is that such a crime for me to think you're nice to look at? You can try to hide it with your baggy shirts, worn-out jeans, and lesbian shoes."

"Hey, that's offensive." Dakota poked him in the chest in a way that was both playful and mean-spirited at once. "You have no idea what kind of social pressures the fashion industry puts on women and—"

He put his hands up as if he was surrendering in battle. "All right, all right. Calm down. I'm just saying you're putting a wall up. You're trying to hide your natural beauty from the world, and I think you shouldn't."

"Why? Because you want some arm candy bimbo to show you around California?" Dakota was flustered. She wanted to hate everything he was saying, but she could feel her cheeks reddening as he complimented her.

"See, that's it." Sean began. "You think any woman who is remotely attractive or embraces her beauty is a bimbo. And that's not right. You can be all the things that you are: intelligent, fierce, loyal, and be attractive. It doesn't take your independence away."

Dakota scoffed. "How do you know I'm loyal? For God's sake, I'm about ready to give back that check you gave me."

"You won't do that and it's because you're loyal. To Maddy." He placed his hand on the spot where her left cheek met her jawline. "It's been 12 years since she went missing. Most people don't care about their high school friends after graduation, but you're out here fighting tooth and nail to find her years after the fact. That's true loyalty."

Dakota moved away from his grasp and cleared her throat. "Okay, we can take a break, but just for today."

• • •

Dakota and Sean found themselves on the sand-strewn planks of the famous Santa Monica Pier. Sean grabbed her by the hand and pulled her past pockets of tourists and concession stands to the end of the boardwalk.

He leaned his arms over the railing and said, "Would you look at that!"

To Sean's credit, he was right — it was a beautiful view. The ocean stretched out a bright sapphire blue before them. Soft white waves lapped at the shoreline. This California winter day was warm, and the sky was clear, save for the occasional fluffy white cloud.

Sean looked down at her. "Aren't you hot in that thing?"

He was referring to her second favorite beat-up sweatshirt. It was a thick red hoodie that read "New York Fire Department" on it. However, the stick-on letters for the "F" in "Fire" and "P" in "Department" had almost completely worn off with the others following suit.

"A little," she replied.

"I can't comprehend how you'd leave the house in that thing," he said.

"Hey, I love this sweatshirt. The proceeds were donated to 9/11 first responders," she told him.

"Well, that's great and all, but why don't we find you something a little more weather-appropriate and well, that's not falling apart." He started towards the gift shop.

He turned around and said, "Stay there, let me surprise you."

She protested, but all he did was wave at her and proceed to enter the store. A few minutes later, he returns with a plastic bag in hand. She opened his present to see a white tank top with shiny rhinestones that spell out "I Heart California" with the heart spelled into the shape of a pink heart.

"You've got to be kidding me," Dakota laughed. "I'm not wearing that."

"Oh, come on, lighten up. It's a million degrees out, you can't stay out in that thing. Take it off and put this on."

Dakota looked around. "I can't."

"Why?" he asked.

"I'm not wearing anything under it."

"What? Really? Not even a bra?"

"Yes, a bra. But I can't just stand out in public with my top off," she said in a whisper.

He rolled his eyes. "It's a beach town, no one will notice. I just saw some chick in a thong bikini; I doubt anyone will notice your bra while you change."

"I don't want to get arrested for public indecency," she told him.

Sean looked around. There wasn't a cop in sight. "No one will see. Here. I'm tall, I'll cover you."

He spread out his arms so that the panels of his unzipped golf jacket created a make-shift curtain.

"Oh, all right. Close your eyes," she told him as she began to wrangle her arm out of one of her sweatshirt's sleeves.

"As you wish," he said, keeping his eyes closed.

Dakota dumped the sweatshirt on the ground and pulled the sparkly top out of the bag.

She had it halfway over her head, when she realized the plastic tag had gotten caught on the clip keeping her hair up.

"Crap," she muttered.

"You okay?" Sean asked.

"Yes, I guess." Dakota wrestled with clip. It was now lodged deeper in her hair and forming a knot making it impossible to let go of her hair and the tag that was attached to her shirt.

"Goddamn it, come on," she yelled at it.

He laughed.

"Let me help you," he said, looking through a crack in his closed eyelids.

"Fine," she said, letting him see her.

She glanced back to catch Sean staring at her, transfixed.

"What?" she asked. Then, she remembered he had not seen her tattoos before. Up until this point, she had worn sweaters and long pants that covered all of her body art from her collar bone to her ankles.

"I just was not expecting that." He let out an uncomfortable laugh.

He untangled her hair from the tag.

"Are you freaked out?" she asked, used to the disapproving glares of strangers.

"No, not at all. They're beautiful," he said. "But, that bra. It's falling apart. You need new clothes," he laughed.

"Hey," she said, pulling the shirt down over her gray bra that had underwire and padding leaking out the sides.

They stood there in silence for a moment before Dakota broke the tension. "You said you wanted to have fun today, right?"

He nodded.

"Well, dragging me away from the investigation to come here has earned you one ride on the roller coaster," she said, walking towards the yellow ride composed of twisting tracks.

"Oh," Sean's face drained of color. "Actually, I don't do well on those things or any amusement park ride, for that matter. I have motion sickness and a fear of heights."

"Too bad," she smiled and pulled him along.

At the other end of the pier, Dakota and Sean strapped themselves into the seats.

"Relax," she said. "This one is nothing, trust me. I've been on almost every extreme roller coaster in the country. I could take a nap on this one."

"If you say so," Sean said, as the brakes released on the coasters and they slowly ratcheted up the steep incline. Within seconds, they were jetting down the track and had dropped several feet over the bunny hills. Sean let out a piercing scream over every drop and twist. Dakota did all she could to keep herself from laughing at his terror on a ride that barely gave her a thrill.

"Now that wasn't so bad," Dakota said, as the ride screeched to a halt.

Sean got out and stood on shaky legs. "That's it. I'm getting a beer."

At the edge of the boardwalk, they leaned once again over the railings. The sun was beginning to set and cast a golden hue over the water. Dakota licked at a vanilla soft serve cone in between sips of Miller Lite, while Sean nursed his third beer.

"I'm so surprised you're such a baby about a roller coaster especially one so small. Look at me, I'm Sean Emory, captain of industry, armchair detective, and a total pansy," Dakota teased.

"That's not very nice," he replied.

"Sorry, you are just not what I expected," she said.

"Neither are you," he laughed.

Dakota took another swig of her beer before tossing it out. "Well, I got to be heading back. I want to get another episode out tonight."

"It can wait until tomorrow morning," he told her. "No need to burn the midnight oil."

"Well, I got to get back home anyway. There's nothing like the nightly 'Why don't you get a real job' from my parents before bed," she said with dread in her voice.

"Or you could just not go home." He inched closer to her.

"What do you mean? Like run away? I'm not ten years old, that won't work," she laughed.

"I mean my hotel is right off the beach there," he pointed. The Chez du Mer's soft yellow exterior jutted out onto the beach, less than two miles away. "It would just be convenient for you to stay over and we can get back to work first thing. Plus, you can avoid your parents for the night."

On any other day, Dakota would have said no. But with a slight buzz from the alcohol and a touch of adrenaline from the roller coaster electrifying her nervous system, she said, "All right."

They left the car parked near the boardwalk and walked down the warm sandy beach to his hotel. Halfway there, Sean reached out and held her hand. Curling it to his mouth, he kissed it. Her rational brain told her to pull away, but she couldn't will herself to let go.

In the room, she quickly texted Cassidy to ask her to tell their parents she would be away for the night and the next day. The last thing she needed was panicked parents calling the police when she didn't return home.

She moved over by the window and looked out to the sea. The sun was completely gone and a blanket of navy-blue sky with shining stars covered the sky. The flashing neon lights from the pier were visible from where she stood, reminding her of where they had just spent the day.

Sean moved next to her and studied the delicate lines on her face, her high cheekbones, small nose, and cinnamon-brown upturned eyes. He wasn't going to wait any longer. He guided her face closer and kissed her.

Dakota thought she would resist his advances, but she didn't want to. She gladly kissed him back, wrapping her arms around his neck.

He pulled away and smiled. "That's not what I thought would happen."

"What do you mean?"

"I thought you'd reject me and give me some lecture about professionalism."

"Trust me, I'm tempted to but, this just feels—" She leaned in and kissed him again.

"There's something I've been dying to do since the Pier," he said as he slid his hands under her shirt and undid her bra.

"Hey," she protested.

He lowered his hands and held her by the waist. "Don't worry. I'll be the perfect gentleman tonight. I don't believe in going too far on the first date, if you want to call this a date. But I just can't stand the idea of you wearing that thing you call a bra."

She shook her head and pulled the bra straps off her shoulders, down her arms, and handed him the ratty old undergarment.

He studied it with amazement. "I can't believe this thing hasn't disintegrated into the air by now."

"Stop it, it's not that bad." She pushed at his chest.

"Why don't we have a nightcap and get to sleep early," he suggested. "That way you can record early in the morning. I'll even run out to the car to get your laptop and microphone for you."

She agreed, and he proceeded to make a whiskey drink for the both of them from the minibar.

Before long, they curled up in the soft white bed and drifted to sleep.

Chapter 9

The sight of the glowing red numerals on the bedside clock made Dakota panic. Sleeping past seven in the morning was a sin in the Kilroy family. Her father would be livid if he found out she slept past ten, even if today was a Saturday.

She crawled out of the bed still in the tacky 'I Heart California' shirt from the day before. Room service had brought a full continental breakfast for the both of them. On the coffee table, Sean had already set up her laptop and microphone for a day of recording and editing. To her right, on one of the white armchairs sat a purple box with a black ribbon around it.

Her name was scribbled across the card that was tucked under the ribbon. She lifted the lid to see three bras. One white, one in black lace and another in soft blue. She looked at the label. They all were in her size.

The bathroom door opened and Sean stood there with a towel wrapped around his waist just below his softly contoured abdominal muscles pointed into a V.

"Do you like them?" he asked.

"Yes, of course. That was very sweet of you, it's just that... I'm not sure. I mean, we just met. You're financing my show and now you're buying me lingerie?" Dakota held her face, not sure how to react.

"Look," he said as he pulled on a t-shirt over his chest. "I don't want you to think I'm trying to buy your affection or that I'm a pathetic guy for falling for a girl who is fifteen years younger than him, but I'm crazy about you. And to risk scaring you away, I have to tell you that I think I'm falling in love with you."

Her eyes widened. "Really? With me? When did that happen?"

"The moment I saw you that first day," he confessed.

Dakota was taken aback. She'd never attracted a man like this before, especially one who treated her so well.

"Do you not feel the same?" he asked, his face falling.

"I mean, it takes me a while," she explained.

"Of course," he replied, looking down at his feet.

"But I do like you. More than I should. Can we just see where this goes without rushing anything or using scary words like 'love'?" she asked him, coming closer and taking his hand.

He nodded and kissed her. "Absolutely. We'll play it by ear."

●　　　●　　　●

After finishing her breakfast, Dakota turned on her computer, uploaded the recording of Selena's interview and placed it into her editing system. Once the audio file sounded as clean as possible, she recorded her intro:

"Welcome back to another episode of *ShadowCast*. This is an episode I've long been waiting for. Today, we're talking about Maddy's high school bully, Selena Diaz.

"Selena seemed to have an issue with Maddy the moment she came to St. Philomena's. As you will hear shortly in her interview, Selena was jealous of Maddy being so smart since Maddy skipped two grades and won a scholarship to attend the elite private school. Additionally, Maddy was a gifted musician and singer. Selena, whose parents are influential in the world of Latin music, dreamed of being a singer as well. This caused her to resent Maddy for having a superior musical gift with the violin, piano, and vocals. This resentment manifested itself into constant name-calling, threats, mean pranks, and occasional physical attacks at the hands of Selena and her best friend, Tiffany Kowalski. As I mentioned earlier on the show, Selena threatened Maddy two days before she disappeared. Through some digging, I was able to locate Selena in a rehab program. Selena has been struggling with addiction for the last five years. After driving while intoxicated, a judge ordered Selena to spend ninety days in a facility that will go unnamed. I was able to speak with her. Here is our conversation."

Dakota paused the recording and began to edit it for quality.

Sean smiled. "You know, I was a classical guitarist. It's one of the ways I got into Stanford. I was in their musical program for all four years to keep my scholarship while I was pre-med. I'm not surprised Maddy had a knack for string instruments too."

"What does that have to do with anything?" Dakota looked up from her laptop.

Sean broke his gaze with Dakota and walked across the room to pour himself another cup of coffee. "Oh, nothing. I'm just drawn to certain people, and it often turns out they're string musicians too. It's one of those strange coincidences."

"Well," said Dakota. "I hate to burst your bubble, but I can't even play *Chopsticks* on the piano, so we don't have that in common."

"I won't hold it against you," he said in a sweet tone.

Dakota placed the interview recording into the file editor. She let it play and when the cursor passed the end of the file, she began recording again, this time for the outro:

"I apologize for abruptly stopping the recording with Selena. I'm sure many of you listeners out there would have wanted me to continue, but what Selena was insinuating shocked me. Everyone, including myself and law enforcement, took Mrs. Montgomery's word as truth. No one would have thought she would lie about the whereabouts of her only daughter on the night she disappeared. But my gut tells me that what Selena said was true. As someone who spent every school day with Selena Diaz from the third grade to senior year of high school, I feel like I know her well enough to tell when she is lying. And she isn't.

"I haven't been perfectly honest with you listeners. I did have brief contact with the Montgomery's. They came to my house and told me they feel hurt by me starting this investigation without speaking with them first. For that, I'll admit, I was wrong and I do apologize. I jumped in head-first to this podcast because I want to get answers about Maddy's whereabouts after all these years. I didn't want to wait another day to speak to the family, but I should have and for that I'm sorry. However, after speaking with them, they did agree to give me their blessing to continue the investigation but would not allow me to interview them. After hearing what Selena believes to have seen that night, I think it's time I speak with the family again.

"Before we wrap up for the day, there is another lead. Tiffany, Selena's friend. I have often feared she would enact violence against Maddy per Selena's orders, whether they are direct or indirect. I sometimes find myself speculating whether Tiffany took it upon herself to threaten or harm Maddy to please Selena. After I stopped the recording, Selena informed me that Tiffany is now a high-end call girl. I'm not sure if I'll be able to find her, but I hope to track her down for an interview. That's all I have for you now. I'll be posting a photo of Tiffany from my high school yearbook on the podcast's website in case you want to see if you've ever come across her. Once again, if you have any tips on where Maddy might be or if you just want to share your theories, please email me at the address provided in the show notes. Until next time, thank you for listening."

Dakota stopped the recording and took a sip of water from the glass on the table. She looked up to see Sean, leaning against the back wall, with his arms crossed and his face burning red.

"Why didn't you tell me?" he asked.

"Tell you what?" she replied, startled by his sudden change in mood.

"That Selena saw Maddy on the street? That Jackie lied?" he said.

"I tried, remember?" said Dakota, standing up. "I was about to tell you by the car, but you're the one who insisted we take a break." She stood in front of him, arms crossed mimicking his position.

"I can't believe she did that." He turned and slammed his fists into the counter of the small kitchen in his room.

Sean continued, "And then she lies about it to the cops, to you, to everyone. She says she saw her walk into school, but she fucking lied. If she told the truth, the police could have found her. Or at least they could have asked people if they saw her walking on the streets. I mean she was in a costume; it would have been hard to miss. There is a chance someone saw her get taken. Then we could have had a description of a vehicle or even a description of the perpetrator himself. But no, she had to look like the good mother to everyone else. That was more important to her than finding her daughter."

"Wow, hon, calm down." Dakota stroked his back. "Trust me, if this turns out to be true, I'll be just as upset as you are, but we can't confirm either story right now."

"It's true, I know it," he said.

He paused before saying. "Post the episode."

"I haven't edited the ending yet. I'm afraid it will sound too breathy," she said.

"Post the episode. I want her to feel the embarrassment as her façade as the perfect parent, the helpless victim, comes crashing down," said Sean.

Dakota didn't object. She was mad at Jackie too. She walked back to the computer, compressed the file and uploaded it for the world to hear.

A few moments later, Sean turned around. The redness had drained from his face and he looked like himself again. Sean scooped Dakota up in his arms and sat with her on the couch.

"I'm sorry for being so angry before. I hope you don't think it was directed at you," he told her.

"No, I don't," she nuzzled her head onto his chest.

"Good. I just don't like when people lie when the stakes are so high."

She nodded, and he kissed her again.

"You know," he started. "You called me 'hon' for the first time a moment ago."

"Oh," Dakota whispered. She had never let a term of endearment slip out so casually before.

"Are you not comfortable with us seeing each other or something?" he asked, looking down at her, but still keeping her held close.

Dakota was hit by a pang of nausea. Thoughts of Seth made her doubt her own instincts as both an investigator and as a woman. "You see, the last time I got involved with someone I was working on an investigation with, things didn't end so well," she said.

"Yes, you mentioned that. But what does that mean exactly?" he asked.

Dakota grimaced.

He stroked her cheek. "It's okay, you can tell me."

"I was with this guy, Seth, for over two years back in New York," she began. "He was another investigative journalist at *The Village Inquirer*. About a year ago, our boss assigned us this case to look into whether drug cartels were cutting their drugs with fentanyl which is a—"

"I know," said Sean, his years in pharmaceuticals made him no stranger to the addictive power of those types of prescriptions.

"Right," said Dakota. "Well, Seth is the type of guy who goes into something full force. He never does something halfway. It made him a great investigator, but when dealing with such dangerous substances, it was a problem. The plan was that he would get in on the ground level. He knew a guy who knew a guy who was in the mob running drugs. They let him in, and he was going to report back to me what they were doing. He found himself tempted from time to time to try the product and one time, curiosity got the better of him. Anyway, he got hooked and continued using even after we wrapped up our report. He started to ignore my calls, our boss's calls and spent more time with his new 'friends' than at work."

Dakota's voice became somber. "One day, I tracked him down. He was in a back alley in Brooklyn. I saw him buy drugs off another guy. This confirmed my suspicions. The dealer saw me looking and pulled a knife. Seth defended me and fought the guy off, but the commotion caught the eye of some police officers who were driving through. The dealer ran off and I was still semi-hidden behind the corner of a building, but they caught Seth with one hundred dollars' worth of heroin on him. He's lucky because he got into a program for rehab to avoid jail time, but it didn't stick. The last time I heard anything about him was over a week ago. He busted out and was begging me for money." Dakota wanted to cry but blinked back the tears.

"Did you send him any?" asked Sean.

"No, but that's not the issue," Dakota explained. "I'm afraid the investigation will cause problems for us, the way it caused problems for me and Seth. Not that there is anything here you could get addicted to, but we could get in too deep and become too involved. It could ruin the investigation and how we feel about each other."

"This investigation won't cause problems for us, I promise. If anything, it might bring us closer together. I'm not Seth. I'm not going to leave you for drugs or missing girls or anything." He brushed her hair away from her face and kissed her on the forehead.

She smiled at him. "Does today count as our second date?"

"Um maybe?"

"There was a meal and a present. That seems like a date to me."

"I guess it does. Why do you ask?" he asked.

"Because if it's no longer the first date then," she looked over to the bed.

"Right," he smiled. "I thought you'd never ask."

Two hours later, Dakota was naked, wrapped in a sheet and beyond exhausted. Sean emerged from the next room, redressed in an old Stanford shirt and a pair of shorts. "Wanna head down to the beach for a little while?"

"I'm gonna need a minute," she moaned.

"Never had it that good before?" he asked.

She gave him a silly look, but omitted her answer — even though it was yes.

"Why don't you get yourself together and go back home. I'm sure your family is worried," he said. "I can wait in the car until you're ready to go."

"But I want to stay here." She rolled to the other side of the bed.

"And I want you to, but you're gonna need a change of clothes and your laptop charger if you wanna keep working on this stuff," he said.

Thoughts of the investigation spiked her adrenaline once again and zapped her out of her stupor.

"You're right." Dakota groaned. "I got to get home."

• • •

Dakota pulled up to her house, but before she even turned the engine off, someone was pounding their fists on the driver's side window.

Both Sean and Dakota jumped.

The man stood back. Dakota recognized him as Connor Freisinger.

"What the hell?" she yelled at him.

Sean got out of the car and said, "What are you doing?"

"That bitch ruined my goddamn life," he screamed.

"Calm down, man. What are you talking about?" asked Sean.

He stepped back and motioned for Dakota to leave the vehicle. She opened the door and peered out, expecting Connor to attack her, but he didn't.

Out of the car, she asked, "Connor, what are you doing here?"

"You haven't noticed what your little true crime groupies have been doing to me?" Snake-like veins were swelling in his forehead.

Dakota shrugged, "To be honest, I haven't checked my email or any of the comments in the last two days. I was busy with other interviews."

"It would be smart of you to check on them more often." He clenched his fists.

"Slow down, Connor. What happened?" Dakota demanded, not bothered by his anger.

"Well, it seems like these people, these fucking strangers from the Internet, think I'm guilty. That being in jail the night she went missing isn't good enough. They think I'm some loser who could never get girls, so when Maddy rejected me, I killed her. And that's not true, none of it. I'll have you know I lost my virginity at twelve to a neighbor girl — thank you very much. I *can* get girls," he stated.

Sean and Dakota recoiled in disgust from this piece of personal information.

"And of course, I didn't kill her or take her or do anything with her," he continued.

"Connor, I believe you. And even in that episode, I told them, I was no longer considering you as a potential suspect. I really don't believe you could hurt Maddy," she said.

He shouted as he broke down in tears. "I loved her. I really did. But now, my reputation is destroyed. I'll have to close my business. I'll lose my house, my car, my everything. I'll probably end up on the street. You've ruined me."

Alarmed by the sounds of the argument, Ken came outside to see his daughter between two men he didn't recognize, and one of them was screaming at her. Ken dipped his head inside and pulled out his favorite nine iron from the golf bag he left by the door.

He walked across the cul-de-sac to where a man dressed in army fatigues and a black t-shirt was yelling at his daughter. He heard the man scream, "You ruined me," at her.

The man lunged forward about to reach his hands around Dakota's throat, when Ken swung the club back and brought it down on the man's face.

Connor fell to his knees yelping in pain.

"Stay the hell away from my daughter," Ken yelled at the cowering man.

"Dad," gasped Dakota.

"You freak, you just busted in my face." Connor rolled on the ground, holding the left side of his face.

"I'll bust more than your face if you ever speak to my daughter again," said Ken. "Now, get the hell out of here and don't you think of coming back."

Connor forced himself to stand. "Okay, okay. Fine, I'll leave. Just never contact me again and keep my name out of it," he said to Dakota.

Connor rushed down the street to where he had parked his Jeep and sped off.

"Dad, you didn't have to do that," said Dakota.

"Yes, I did. And it seems like your friend here wasn't going to do the noble thing and defend a lady," Ken said, while eyeballing Sean.

"I was going to defend her, you just didn't give me a chance," said Sean, coming around the other side of the car.

"Who is this guy, anyway?" Ken asked Dakota.

"This is Sean Emory, he's the man who's sponsoring my show." Dakota turned to Sean. "And this is my dad, Ken Kilroy."

Sean stuck his hand out and Ken reluctantly gave it a quick shake.

Ken smirked. "It's a good thing you two are here then. We've got a situation on our hands that only you can fix."

Ken led Dakota and Sean into his house. Inside, Dakota was surprised to find her mother sitting down with Mr. and Mrs. Montgomery.

Mrs. Montgomery leapt to her feet. "How dare you? What the hell gives you any right to talk about me the way you did? Isn't it enough you're looking into the case? Do you have to drag my name through the mud in the process?"

She was about to fire more questions at Dakota when she looked past her shoulder and saw Sean.

"What in the world?" she asked, staring at him.

"Hi, Jackie, how've ya been?" Sean asked her.

The expression on Mrs. Montgomery's face was a mixture of surprise, hatred, and disgust. Sean looked more like a kid who got caught stealing money out of his mom's purse.

"What's going on here? Do you two know each other?" Dakota demanded.

"Darn right we do. Dakota, meet Sean, Maddy's biological father," she said.

Dakota slowly turned her head back to look at Sean. "You're what?"

He put his hands up, as if bracing from impact. "Listen, I can explain."

"Explain what? That you're too smart and too cool to have stuck by your woman and your child," Mr. Montgomery chimed in. "I understand relationships don't always work out, but to just ignore your daughter like that. It's downright irresponsible."

"Yes, I know. I know. I feel bad enough as it is," said Sean.

Mrs. Montgomery shook her head. "I never thought I'd see you again, and here you are. Wait," she paused. "What are you even doing here?"

"He's the sponsor for my show." Dakota felt a rush of shame spike through her body.

"So that's your plan. You wait twelve years after our daughter disappears to team up with her investigator friend, so you can paint me as some negligent parent. I'd say you're far more negligent than I ever could be," yelled Jackie.

"I wasn't there for my kid and I realize what a mistake that was. I'm sorry for not helping out more," said Sean.

"I swore if I ever met you, I'd be kind and understanding. I'd do what the Lord says and forgive, but I'm afraid I can't," continued Mr. Montgomery. "I can't stand men like you. The kind that use women for what they want and move on."

"Now wait a minute here. I'll take the blame for being a dead-beat dad, but that's not what happened. Jackie, why don't you tell your husband the truth about the night Maddy was conceived."

"The truth, what truth?" Mrs. Montgomery rolled her eyes.

"How you took advantage of me?"

Just as the words left Sean's mouth, a hush fell over the room.

"Oh please? That's not what happened!" Jackie scoffed.

"Yes, it was. I remember it perfectly. It was at Joey Miller's party. I was a major stoner back then and you knew that. I'd hit the bong pretty hard that night, too hard. So I went to go lay down in Joey's room. You came in and asked if I wanted a blow job. I said yes and after you got going on that, you got on top of me. I tried to get you off me, but you told me to relax and enjoy it. I was so dizzy and out of it, I couldn't do much to get you off me. And I could tell you sober, because your pastor daddy would have smelled it on you or made you take a pee test, but you needed to rebel and there was nothing he could do to stop you from having sex. Let's be clear about this, if a man did what you did to me, he'd be thrown in jail."

Jackie was stunned, her face was bright red with embarrassment. She called out, "Robert, we need to go!"

Dakota blocked the couple from leaving. "No, I need you to tell me the truth."

"Haven't you had enough truth-telling for one day?" Jackie tried to push Dakota out of their way.

"No," Dakota insisted. "I need to know if what Selena said about Maddy walking to school alone that night is true and I need to record it."

Everyone in the room stared at Dakota.

"You two can talk about what happened the night Maddy was conceived later. I won't mention it on the air, but all of this doesn't take away from the fact that she is still missing. I need to hear it from you, Mrs. Montgomery, what really happened the night she went missing," Dakota said.

"Fine." Jackie took a deep breath and released her anger with it. "I'll talk to you, but I don't want him around when I do."

Dakota nodded and took Mrs. Montgomery out to the backyard. They sat down at the table the Kilroys used for outdoor gatherings. Jackie wouldn't look Dakota in the eyes as she started the recording:

"This is Dakota Kilroy speaking with Jackie Montgomery, Maddy's mother, on February 3rd, 2012. Jackie is prepared to comment on the claims made by Selena Diaz about how Maddy got to the school pageant on the night of December 7, 2000." Dakota turned to Jackie. "Mrs. Montgomery, please tell me what really happened that night."

"You see, it wasn't a good day," the woman began. Her voice was low and tentative.

"I'm sorry, but can you please speak up, the mic may not be able to hear you," Dakota said.

Jackie cleared her throat and spoke again with a louder voice. "I was having a bad day. Things at work were really stressful. The boys were young at the time, six and two years old. Anthony had gotten into a fight at school that day and I had to leave work early to deal with him. On top of that, Michael was in the midst of his terrible twos. At home, he refused to have any of his dinner, flinging his pasta across the floor and screaming at the top of his lungs. Anthony was in his room pouting because he thought he was unfairly punished by the teachers for fighting with another boy. I knew it was impossible for me to get the both of them buckled into the car to drive Maddy the five blocks to school. I asked if Maddy was willing to walk by herself. She said yes, but she wasn't comfortable changing at school in the backstage area with the other girls. I told her to just put on her costume at home and walk over. It was only five blocks. No one would notice her. And that's what she did. I remember it. Five thirty-eight was on the clock when she walked out the door, never to come back." Jackie's voice broke.

"Why did you tell a different story to the police?" asked Dakota.

"I didn't want them to think what the world already is thinking: that I was a bad mother or that it was my fault she disappeared. So I made it up. At the time, I thought she was just hiding somewhere, too embarrassed to admit that stage fright had gotten the better of her to sing the solo. I didn't think the details of what I told the police would have been so important because I thought she would come back to us within a few minutes or even an hour or two. But the hours passed, and the days went by, she was nowhere to be found. I realized it'd look like I had something to hide if I went back on what I had told them, so I stuck with my story. I feel so awful and ashamed." She buried her head in her hands and cried.

Dakota had no patience for Jackie's tears; not after her lying, not after what she did to Sean. "How did your parents and your husband, Maddy's stepfather, feel about her?"

Jackie wiped her eyes with the sleeve on her faded blue cardigan. "Robert loved her like she was his own. It didn't matter that they weren't biologically related. It didn't even matter to him that he was black and she was white: she was his daughter and he was her father. He never indicated any resentment towards her, ever, if that's what you're implying."

"What about your parents and Robert's parents?" Dakota asked.

"Both of Robert's parents died before we married. And when it comes to my parents," she paused, to let out a quiet sob. "Well, let's just say they were less than thrilled about the whole thing when I announced I was pregnant at seventeen and that the father had no intention of marrying me. Dad was humiliated. He thought no one in his congregation would ever listen to his sermons again if they found out his own daughter had fallen from grace.

"But I turned it around. I became the perfect reformed sinner. I threw away all of my 'skanky' clothes and dressed modestly like the Bible said. I focused all my attention on raising my daughter and keeping other women from making the same mistake. I gave lecture after lecture at that church about the perils of being a young, unwed mother. That's how I met Robert. My father wanted to make the church more welcoming to minorities, so he reached out to Robert who worked nights after his day job helping young men turn away from drugs and crime at a local community center. He started to teach men's Bible study at the church, and we fell in love and got married. I thought all of this redeemed me in my father's eyes but—" Jackie stopped and stared out into the distance.

"What?" asked Dakota.

"I feel like my father was still ashamed of me and by extension, Maddy. She was a living reminder of his failure as a parent and his daughter's sin. He loved her, but I couldn't help but sense that he loved Anthony and Michael more because I had them with my husband. Sometimes, I thought it was because they were boys, but I don't think that's it. I don't think he could ever let it go all the way," said Jackie.

"Thank you, Mrs. Montgomery. That's all I need." Dakota stopped the recording.

Jackie stood up. "May I leave now?" She asked with venom in her voice.

"Yes." Dakota nodded.

As soon as she was gone, Sean appeared in front of Dakota at the table.

"Why the hell didn't you tell me?" she snapped at him. "Did you purposefully come out here to have sex with your daughter's best friend?"

"No, I came out here to find out what happened to my daughter. I wasn't expecting to feel this way," he said.

She stood up and paced around the green lawn outside her home.

"You swear this wasn't your plan?" she asked.

He came up to her, stopping her in her tracks.

"It most certainly was not." He brushed her hair away from her face.

ShadowCast

Dakota wanted to lean in and feel his warm chest against her body. She wanted to kiss him and declare this complicated situation wouldn't get in the way of their relationship. But she couldn't. It would go against her integrity as a journalist and as a person.

"I don't know about this," she said, turning on her heels and leaving him alone in the backyard.

Chapter 10

They say the number thirteen is unlucky, but I don't think killing my thirteenth victim will be any unluckier than killing my first.

The trouble is I swore to myself and to Ma that I was done forever. She was sick of cleaning up the mess my sinful urges created. I couldn't bear to tell Ma that I'd broken my promise to her so I kept the girl in my cave for the last seven days without her noticing.

Thankfully, this girl wasn't a screamer. She was quiet enough for me to leave her tied up without a rag taped to her mouth. On top of that, Ma wouldn't notice any extra food going missing for the first two days because I don't feed them until the third. It keeps them submissive. And once they see a big plate of roast beef, steamed vegetables, and a warm buttery biscuit coming their way, they don't put up a fight when I want to do things to them.

This one's name is Cheyenne. She isn't as fiery of a catch as I thought a rebel teen girl like her would be. The first night I ordered her out of her jean shorts and green tank top and had her put on a black bra and corset that had garter belt attachments for the fishnet stockings I like. After she was dressed, I told her that if she didn't want me to hurt her, she should just be a good girl and let me do what I wanted to. If she protested or made it difficult for me, she would get a beating of a lifetime.

Tears filled her eyes, but she agreed. On the bed, she spread her legs when I commanded and let me inside. I wanted to show off how much of a man I was to her. I wanted to rock her world and give her an orgasm like she never had before. But it was too good for me to last. I lost control after two minutes.

The next day, I could last longer but the more I got going the less I cared about what she thought of me. She wasn't going to survive this, so what did it matter if she thought I was a *stud in bed or not. I got more aggressive, barely noticing the person on the other end. She could have been Cheyenne, Marie, Patty, or Rebecca. It didn't matter.*

This couldn't go on much longer. Ma was growing suspicious of me constantly wanting leftovers from dinner every night this week. It was time to say goodbye to Cheyenne.

Tonight is the night. One more ride and she would be put to sleep forever. I walk over to the cave and open the metal door. She's tied with rope on a cot. She's naked, but I left her with a blanket over her body. I untie her and say, "I need you to wear this tonight."

She looks at me blankly.

Out of a ziplock bag, I toss her an orange and yellow crochet bikini. It's musty and old, but I can't bear to wash it or replace it.

I untie her and watch as she pulls the bottoms up around her slender hip bones then strap the triangles of the bikini top around her tits. She dashes her blond hair back and stands before me. I take my Polaroid camera out and snap a few shots of her.

"Lay down," I tell her and she does.

I take two more pictures. Can't waste this film. They don't make this stuff like they used to.

"I'm going to have sex with you again, but I'm going to ask you to say things to me while it happens," I instruct her.

"What things?" she asks.

"Say, 'Freddy, stop!' Call me a 'sick little boy,' and say, 'you're bad and dirty'."

"Why?" she asks me.

"Because I said so," I yell.

She cowers back.

I smile. I don't want her to be too scared. That would ruin it.

"Relax, I'm sorry for yelling. Just say those things and try to push me off. Don't actually push me, just pretend like you don't want it."

We look at each other for a second, both knowing that she indeed does not want it, but that didn't really matter. She lays down on the bed and waits for me. I climb on top of her and try to kiss her. She moves my head away and says 'Freddy, stop!'

I grin at her. "Good girl."

She slaps at my chest, "Stop it, you sick little boy."

I lay my weight down on top of her and yank the bikini bottom off.

"More," I tell her.

She struggles against me and says, "You're a bad boy, this is so dirty."

That really gets me going.

"What am I?" I ask her.

"A sick, bad, dirty boy, Freddy," she whispers into my ear. In that moment, her voice sounds just like Rebecca's sultry voice, her skin feels like Rebecca's buttery-soft flesh, and I can't help but finish.

"Rebecca, yes!" I shout.

She looks at me confused, but doesn't ask who Rebecca is.

"Wow, you're such a good girl," I tell her, as I put my pants back on. "It's too bad I can't keep you any longer."

"I can leave?" she asks with excitement bubbling up in her voice.

"Oh no, honey. It's time for us to say goodbye, but you'll never leave here," I explain.

Realizing what I was implying, she rushes at me screaming. She tackles me to the ground and tries to choke me. I push her off me and she crawls out of the cave into the living area of the basement.

I don't let her get far.

In the corner of the room, there is a shovel. It's still fresh from the grave I dug for her last night in preparation. Just as she gets to her feet and screams at me once more, I smack her in the jaw with the shovel.

She falls, trembling in pain. I smack her three more times, each whack radiating throughout the basement. By the time I'm done, part of her skull is crushed flat. Her blood, brains, and hair are smeared across the tile floor and my muddy shovel.

The door to the basement creaks opens, and I brace for Ma's shrieking. She must have heard the struggle.

Instead she has a steady and cool tone. "You promised me that after Madeline, this would stop."

"It did," I say.

"It was bad enough I caught you with your sister, but you've made me clean up your mess time and time again. I'm an old woman now. I can't help you anymore."

"Ma, you're right. And I was good for a long time. A real long time. I see so much temptation around me every day, but I don't give in. But I saw her and I just couldn't help myself." I shrug.

She looks at Cheyenne's smashed head and recoils in disgust. "Well you're going to have to help yourself from now on, and you're going to have to deal with burying the girl alone. I'm too frail to lift a body and scrub the floors on my hands and knees. For heaven's sake, the doctor is afraid of me fracturing a hip in the shower. Lord knows what will happen to me while cleaning up after another one of your incidents."

"I'll take care of it myself. You just go upstairs and rest." I lightly pat her on the back and guide her up the steps and out of the basement.

I sigh. I have so much work ahead of me. After I bury Cheyenne, I scrub the floors and bleach every surface she touched. Hours later, I join Ma upstairs. She's sitting on the fluffy floral-patterned couch with her knitting needles in her hands.

"I never understood why you were this way," she says to me. "I blame your father. If he spent more time at home than with those whores he was seeing on the side, you might have turned out normal."

"Maybe, if you spent more time fucking Dad, he wouldn't have needed those whores in the first place and he wouldn't have left us."

"What did you just say to me?" she hisses.

"You heard me," I say this confidently. I can't let her think I'm afraid to tell her what I've been thinking this whole time. "Your idea that sex is only for procreation is wrong — that we should just ignore our desires. It drove Dad crazy and that's why he left."

"That is what God intended it for," she insists.

"God or no God, it's the truth. You made me feel ashamed of my sex drive. I didn't know what to think about it other than it was wrong. You made me think all attractive women were slutty bitches who deserved Hell for tempting men. So that's what I did. I gave them Hell. Now, sex, punishment, and death are all the same to me. I can't have one without the other. So I must keep doing this. I want to stop but I can't. I try for so long, but then when something stressful happens like this Dakota thing, I have no other way of relieving it."

She glares at me, "What Dakota thing?"

Crap. I forgot I wasn't going to tell her about it.

"There's this investigative journalist named Dakota Kilroy. She started a podcast which is like a new type of radio show, where she is looking into the disappearance of Madeline." I let out a deep breath.

Ma's face turns gray. It's like looking into the face of Medusa herself. "Investigating how?"

"She's going through a list of potential witnesses and suspects to see what they remember from the night she went missing," I explain.

"How much does she know?" Ma asks.

"Not much," I say. "The official police report says Madeline's mother dropped her off at the school which is a lie. It doesn't seem like Dakota knows any different. So far, she investigated a few teachers and students. It's getting some traction on the online forums, but no one has even suggested a stranger yet. They assume if she was dropped off at school, it had to have been someone she knew or someone who had access to the school grounds that took her."

"What about the parents? Has she talked to them?"

"All she said was that Maddy's mom and stepdad gave permission for her to investigate, but they refused to be recorded for an interview."

"Stepdad?" Ma looked at me with a spark in her eyes.

"Yes, remember she told us that. Her mother wouldn't tell her who her real father was."

"What a slut," snaps Ma. "Bet she didn't even know his name."

"I don't know how this Dakota woman is going to find anything to close her case. She's just going to keep hitting dead leads," I say.

Ma gives me a slight smile. "Not if we help her out."

"What do you mean? You want us to lead her to me?" My heart beats fast at the thought of my mother wanting to turn me in.

"Heavens no!" She holds up a hand and waves me off. "I mean, take some of those sick souvenirs you keep and plant them around her parents' house."

I stare at her dumbfounded.

"Yes, I know about them," she laughs with a snort. "Your dirty Polaroids with the girls dressed up in Rebecca's old swimsuit. The locks of their hair or the panties they were wearing. The newspaper clippings about police being unable to find the missing girls. I've seen them all including Maddy's bloodied angel wings."

"You weren't supposed to see them," I whisper.

"Of course not, but you work such long hours and I get bored. So I clean up a bit downstairs for you and I found your mementos even after I told you to burn all the evidence after each girl. But no, you had to get all sentimental. But that's okay. I don't blame you. At least, not right now. We can use those photos and Maddy's clothes to frame her stepfather."

I'm embarrassed about my souvenirs. It stings me in the chest. I want to scream at her for going down into my cave, even after I told her never do that. But I can't bring myself to be angry with her, especially when this is all my fault.

"How would I frame him?" I ask.

"Put two and two together. Everyone knows stepfathers are more likely than real fathers to abuse their kids. Make it look like he raped and killed Madeline. Just put her clothes and

one of those photos in a closet somewhere and get the police to show up there. And as soon as they do, he's going away for murder." She claps her hands.

"How do I get them there?" I ask.

"Oh, I can't come up with everything, Freddy. You'll figure out a way."

* * * *

I feel sick to my stomach, pulling out of my driveway this morning. Maddy's angel wings from the night I took her are sitting in my trunk wrapped in a black trash bag. Inside, I also have my pictures of her.

Now I never had sex with her. It was different between us. She was my soulmate and we were waiting for marriage. But as the future husband, I was entitled to some previews of what I'd be getting on the wedding night. So, I dressed her up in see-through nighties, white corsets, and lace panties and had her take some photos.

I laugh to myself a little. Any stepfather with those photos in his possession would definitely get sold down the river.

I pull up in front of their house on Shadow Lane. I see the stark white church in the back of the lot and the gray house that stands next to it. This area looks too bleak for Southern California. There is an air of gloom that hangs over the place.

Then I see him, the reason for the gloom, Pastor Shaw. Ma used to go to his church before she switched to a new one closer to home. I remember her dragging me in there as a teenage boy to hear his sermons about the hellfire that would be waiting for me if I didn't repent and surrender to Jesus at that very moment.

Unfortunately, it didn't do me any good. I found the whole thing to be a silly theatrical production. But either way, Pastor Shaw had a heaviness about him. He was older now, but the intensity in his broad-shouldered stance could still strike fear in my heart.

He and the wife are leaving their house and getting in the car. Neither of them notice me.

There are no cars parked outside Maddy's parents' house. Everyone must have been gone to work or school for the day. This is my time to strike, but I don't think it's safe to put all my eggs in one basket. I want to hurt the fire and brimstone pastor as well.

I get out of the car and dash past the church to the pastor's house with the trash bag in my hand. I might as well bring down the man who wasted so many of my Sunday mornings with his idiotic preaching while I'm here.

The street is quiet at this time of day. Barely any cars on the side street. I doubt anyone will see me — and if they do, no one will notice. The old couple foolishly left the backdoor unlocked. A little too much faith in the protectiveness of God can be unwise.

Inside, I sneak upstairs and into the master bedroom. The room is painted a deep navy-blue. It's not deep and beautiful the way the ocean is blue. It's simply dark and heavy. The bed has a black and gray comforter over it and two brown nightstands on either side.

I can tell which side belongs to the pastor instantly. The wife's side is full of pictures of her family; it's overflowing with little glass frames. But the pastor's side is empty, except for a small gold statue of a crucified Jesus.

I creep over and open the little drawer. It squeaks and I freeze, forgetting I'm in the home alone. Inside, there are old receipts and a few birthday cards from the years prior. I lift up a few cards and nestle the photos of his granddaughter inside.

Once out of their house, I walk a few yards to Maddy's old place. It's just as small and shabby. The wooden paneling is falling off the back, and the paint has cracked from the sun. Their backdoor is locked, but it's nothing I can't jimmy free with a credit card. A few moments later, I'm inside the Montgomery house.

I race upstairs and find the parents' bedroom. Under the bed, there are a few dusty suitcases that look like they haven't been used since WHAM was in concert. I unzip the largest one and I take her wings out of the bag and hold them to my chest. If I close my eyes, I can still smell her sweet scent and it feels like I'm hugging her for real. I force myself to place them in the suitcase, zip them up into the darkness and tuck it back under the bed.

I leave the master bedroom and head for the stairs. Across the hall, a pastel purple room catches my eye.

It's her room. The family hasn't changed it in the twelve years she's been gone.

I walk into it and I burst into tears. "I miss you so much," I call out as if her ghost still lingers there. I run my hand across her white lacey bed sheets, then I lay down and rub what was left of her scent on me. I open a drawer in her dresser. It's her panty drawer. I pull out a pair of light green hipster-cut underwear and slide it into my pocket. I simply can't help myself.

On the dresser, there are pictures of her with her friends. Well, one friend. A tall willowy brunette. This must be Dakota. I lift up the photo and hold it closer to my face. She's pretty, but nothing like Maddy. I study the face and I learn her light brown eyes, her small nose, and sharp jawline. I need to know what she looks like.

I hear yelling outside and freeze. It sounds like teenage boys getting into an argument. I peer out the window of Maddy's room that looks out over the front lawn. A teenage boy with medium brown skin and wavy hair is sitting on his bike, out front of the house. Another boy who is blond with freckles pulls up his bike next to the first boy. This must be her brother, Anthony and his friend.

I listen to their conversation.

"Mrs. Abrams is gonna shit bricks when she notices we skipped," calls out Anthony. His blond friend high fives him. "Senior skip day!"

ShadowCast

"Dude, the official senior skip day isn't until May," laughs Anthony.

"Whatever, any excuse to ditch that place," says his freckly friend.

They ditch their bikes out front and walk towards the front door. I rush down the steps and out the backdoor just as I hear Anthony put his keys in the lock.

I stay flat up against the wall of the back of their house for a few minutes. I don't hear or see them anymore, so I make a break for it. I speed walk past the church, down the sidewalk and get into my car.

I take panicked breaths once I'm behind the wheel. That was close, but it will just be a matter of time before they find what I left behind.

Chapter 11

Dakota had spent the night curled up in her childhood bed on top of her red and black flannel blanket with her mind racing.

"I can't believe I slept my best friend's father," she murmured to herself in a tone of self-flagellation. Her stomach ached at the thought.

It wasn't the fact that Sean was biologically related to Maddy that bothered her. Since he hadn't been a part of Maddy's life, Dakota didn't see him in the same sexless way she viewed most of her childhood friends' fathers. He didn't drive her home from sleepovers in pleated pants and wicker belts, making awkward small talk about school like her other friends' dads did. She had trouble seeing him as a relative of Maddy's, especially since she inherited the dark hair, small frame, and pale complexion of her mother. It seemed like a biological impossibility that the tall, tan, sandy-haired Sean could be her father.

What bothered her about the situation was Sean's lies. Not only did he omit this crucial detail, he could have compromised the integrity of the investigation. The best friend and father of the missing girl sleeping together while they attempted to solve the case wouldn't look good to the police or the public. And if any word got out, it might cause people to disregard her efforts completely.

Hours later, Dakota's restless mind finally surrendered to sleep. But before the sun had even risen, a hand reached out of the darkness and grabbed her shoulder.

She woke up with a jolt to see her mother, wrapped in a light blue robe standing over her.

"What is it, Mom?" she asked.

"I was told not to tell you this, but I'm going to anyway," Debi started.

"Tell me what?" Dakota sat up on the bed and reached for her brown-framed glasses on the nightstand.

With her eyesight restored, she could see the look of concern on her mother's face.

"They found something. The police have been called and they..." Debi trailed off.

"What did they find? A body?" Dakota's heart dropped at the idea.

"No, they didn't say what exactly happened. But Mrs. Shaw found something in the pastor's possession that made it look like he did something to Maddy. She called the police on him. They took him away and now their house, the church and Maddy's old house are being searched. If I were you, I'd get dressed and get over there. Muldowney will probably be there too, he might tell you what's going on." Debi pulled out a pair of Dakota's jeans from her dresser and a long sleeve black shirt and handed them to her daughter. "Get dressed and hurry."

Dakota quickly changed out of her pajamas and into the clothes her mother handed her. She rapidly brushed her teeth, with the rough bristles scraping her gums and haphazardly washed her face with a bar of soap. She walked down the stairs with her bag in one hand and the other forcing her tangled hair into a ponytail.

Debi was downstairs with a pot of coffee already brewed. She poured coffee with a spot of cream into a travel mug and handed it to Dakota along with the keys to her car. "Go," she said. "Today, you might finally get your answers."

Dakota nodded. She had not seen her mother act this serious in years.

In the car, she pulled out her cellphone and dialed Sean. After four long rings, a sleepy voice answered, "Hello?"

"It's me, Dakota," she said, not sure how to address him.

"I know," he laughed.

"They found something at the Shaw residence. The pastor is in custody. The police are there now. I'll see if I can find anything out. You can come meet me there if you want," she offered.

"Are you sure you want to see me?" he asked.

"This isn't about us today. It's about Maddy. We could find her today, and you should be there for that."

"I'll be right there."

Dakota parked the car down the block. From around the corner, she could already see the red and blue lights casting disordered shadows over the neighborhood. The sirens were off, but the presence of first responders could still be heard through the static on their walkie-talkies and the chatter between officers.

She walked up the sidewalk to where the area was taped off with yellow caution tape.

"Ma'am, please step back," said a young officer who was standing on the right side of the tape.

"It's okay, let her in," said Muldowney, stepping out of the darkness and into the flashing lights.

The young officer lifted the tape and let Dakota step through.

"That's surprising. I thought you'd have told me to fuck off," she said to him.

He chuckled. "No, I'd never say that to you. And not just because your rich friend helped me out. I understand why you've been trying to so hard to get to bottom of this."

Dakota was surprised. "Thanks, that means a lot."

"Even though you're one big pain in the ass," he laughed and nudged her with the end of his elbow.

He walked over to another officer who was older, with a round pot belly and a deep-set smirk on his face.

"Gerald, show the girl," Muldowney said.

"Are you sure? Didn't she know her?" he asked.

"Yes," answered Muldowney, before turning to Dakota. "What we're about to see might be disturbing, but it shows that Maddy was kept alive for at least several months after her disappearance." Gerald handed Dakota three plastic bags. Each one contained a Polaroid snapshot of Maddy.

In the first one, she is standing up against a gray cinderblock wall in her angel costume. Muldowney turned it over and showed her the writing on the back. It said, "Madeline M. Dec 8, 2000."

The second photo showed Maddy sitting on a bed with her legs tucked to the side in a see-through white nightie. "Madeline. March 23, 2001" was scribbled on the back in the same chaotic handwriting.

The last photo was the most disturbing. Maddy was dressed in a white corset and panty set. The corset had a garter belt that connected to white stockings.

Her hand was handcuffed to a water pipe against the same gray wall as the first picture. But worst of all, she was wearing a wedding veil.

"Madeline. June 6, 2001." Muldowney read aloud. "That means she survived at least six months in captivity."

"Where did you get these?" she asked him.

Muldowney let out a sigh. "Mrs. Shaw, Maddy's grandmother was organizing things before bed last night when she went to fish out a few receipts needed for a refund on a sweater she purchased for her husband. She found these photos stored in the drawer of the pastor's nightstand. She didn't even ask her husband about them. She understood what they meant, and she called 911 right away."

"Can I get a copy of the call?" asked Dakota.

"It will be made public in about a week's time," Muldowney explained. "But we are trying to find out where these photos were taken. Come with me." He motioned for Dakota to follow.

He walked with her through the taped-up front door of the Shaw house.

"There is no wall that matches the gray background from the photo. All the walls in this house are drywall and are painted a shade of blue. There is no basement in this house either. At the church, there are white walls that look like the one in the second photo, but no gray cinderblock or brick anywhere. If he took her, she was held in a separate location, and I need to know where that was."

"There's a basement in Maddy's house," Dakota said.

"We're having men search it now," he said.

"You got a warrant for the Montgomery House?" she asked.

"Well, Pastor Shaw owns the land and the house, and the warrant is for any property he owns," explained Muldowney.

In front of her, Dakota saw police officers ducking in and out of the Montgomery house. "Can we check out the basement?"

Muldowney nodded.

Inside, both the police detective and the journalist were disappointed. The basement was barely finished. The walls were part concrete and part wooden slats and beams. They looked nothing like the wall from the photo.

"Maybe, they redid it?" asked Dakota. "And replaced the cinderblock with this?"

Muldowney inspected the walls. The wood looked rotted, and the concrete was cracked and crumbling. "No. This looks like it hasn't been touched since the '90s."

An officer with a thick red beard poked his head into the basement. "You're going to need to see this." He motioned for the two of them to follow him.

Up on the second story, an open suitcase lay in the middle of the Montgomery's master bedroom. A different officer stood back, circling the suitcase taking pictures.

Muldowney and Dakota peered inside. And Dakota's hand flew over her mouth to hide her gasp.

It was a pair of angel wings. They were made from cloth, wire, and synthetic feathers. The edges were slightly yellowing, but the top of the feathers was stained red with blood.

"Tell Gerald to get those pictures up here," Muldowney barked at the ginger-bearded officer.

Moments later, the heavy-set officer rushed up the stairs with the evidence in hand. Muldowney took the photo of Maddy in her angel costume that was taken on December 8, 2000. He compared the wings on her back to the ones in the suitcase.

"Looks like they're the same ones," he said.

"All right," a voice said behind them. It was an African American woman in a navy-blue pantsuit. "Everybody out. We need to secure this building to make sure we aren't tampering with any evidence."

She turned to Muldowney. "I understand that you were the lead on this case many years ago, but I've been assigned this case and only active members of the police force are allowed on the premises."

Muldowney opened his mouth to protest but knew he didn't have a good argument for being here.

"Fine, we'll leave." Muldowney slapped the baggies containing the photos into her hand and walked past her.

"Wait," she said. "Are you Dakota Kilroy?"

"Yes," Dakota answered.

"You submitted film the night Madeline Montgomery went missing, didn't you?" she asked.

Dakota nodded.

"Can I review the footage with you again?"

"Of course."

• • •

Once outside the house, the woman asked, "Do you need a ride? I can take you."

"No, I have a car. I'll meet you at the station, Detective. I'm sorry I didn't get your name," said Dakota.

"Detective Brook Carter," she reached her hand out and shook it.

Just as Dakota turned to walk towards her car, she saw Sean approaching her.

"Who's that?" asked Detective Carter.

"Sean Emory. He's Maddy's biological father."

"Then I'm going to need to question him, too." She turned towards Sean and walked up to him.

"Excuse me, sir. I'm Detective Carter. Are you Madeline Montgomery's father?"

"Yes, by blood. I didn't raise her," he explained.

"Would you please come to the station with me? I'd like to ask you some questions."

Sean nodded and said, "I won't be speaking to the police unless I have a lawyer present, and neither will Dakota."

"Sean," Dakota yelled in protest.

"That is your right, sir. But you are not under arrest, we just have a few questions," she said.

"I understand that, but why is Dakota being questioned?" He crossed his arms and stared down at the detective.

"She recorded the school play which your daughter was supposed to be a part of. The Shaws were in the audience and I want to see if I can learn anything from the footage with Dakota," she explained.

"We'll both talk after I call a lawyer," said Sean, looping his arm around Dakota's waist and pulled her away.

"What in the hell are you doing?" she asked, after Sean dragged her down the block.

"Making sure they don't arrest either of us for kidnapping," he said.

"What are you talking about?" She wrangled free of his grasp. "They want our help. They won't be looking at us as suspects. At this point, it looks like it was her own sick grandfather who did something horrible to her," Dakota said.

"Yes, that's what it seems. But trust me, cops have a way of twisting your words around and making you look guilty. That's the last thing we need. Let me call my lawyer back in New York and ask if he can recommend someone from the LA branch of the firm. Let's go in together with someone by our side. Don't worry, I'll pay for the both of us." Sean gave Dakota the same look she used to give Maddy when someone was trying to bully her. It was a look of fierce protection and Dakota didn't like it.

"You don't have to do that. I'm not your girlfriend or anything," she said.

"You're not?" His voice quietened.

"Uh, no? First of all, we only spent two days together, and we never talked about being together for real. On top of that, you lied to me and hid the fact you were only paying me to investigate this case because you're the estranged father of the missing girl." Dakota struck him against his chest.

He grabbed her fist and pulled her in. "Listen, I'm sorry. I never meant to lie to you. I just wasn't sure when would have been the best time to tell you. I didn't want to ruin what we have."

"We don't have anything." Dakota pulled away from him. She got in her car and drove off leaving him standing alone on the sidewalk.

•   •   •

Dakota found herself inside a conference room at the police station. It was warmer in atmosphere than it was when she was last called in to this station, twelve years ago. The table was made out of wood and not cold metal. The chairs had cushions on them, and their room actually had windows that let in sunlight.

Detective Carter had an officer wheel in a pushcart containing a television with a built-in VCR. Next to Dakota sat her lawyer. Sean had paid for legal counsel for her anyway. The man was boring-looking with skin the shade of oatmeal, and a flabby gut hanging over his suit pants. She had already forgotten his first and last name. His only purpose was to advise her on her answers and intervene when the police were pushing too hard.

Detective Carter opened the case file, which Muldowney must have surrendered to her.

"So, it says on December 7, 2000, you were in charge of taking photos and filming the Christmas pageant at St. Philomena's. Walk me through what you remember from that day," she requested.

"It was a typical school day," Dakota began. "We got out of class around three in the afternoon like always and we'd normally all go home. But since it was the night of the pageant anyone involved was supposed to return there around 5:30 for last minute prep. I was on the school newspaper and the yearbook. It was a small team: just one teacher and three students writing everything. Since the other students on staff weren't very good at technical stuff, I was asked to record the event."

"What time did you get to campus for the pageant?" asked the detective.

"Around 6:30 pm, a half hour before the pageant was about to start," Dakota answered. "I set up the video camera. It was on a tripod at the back. Once I hit record at the start of the play, I could take my seat in the front row to take pictures without worrying about it. I got a seat on the front left side so I could get good pictures of everybody in the show."

"Did you see Maddy at all before? Backstage or anything like that?" she asked.

"No, why would I?" Dakota shrugged.

Detective Carter narrowed her eyes in on Dakota and she realized the detective had not been made aware of Mrs. Montgomery's confession.

"Oh." Dakota reached out and took a sip of water from the glass the police had provided. "You don't know. You're still operating on the old timeline."

"What old timeline?" asked Detective Carter, with a hint of frustration in her voice.

"I have it on tape that Mrs. Montgomery lied to the police. She did not drop Maddy off at school and watch her walk onto the school grounds like she claims she did. She was too overwhelmed by her other children to drive Maddy to school. Instead, she asked Maddy to walk from her house to the school. I also have it on record that Selena Diaz, another student from St. Philomena's saw Maddy in her angel costume on the street, making her way towards the school that day. It's from that moment that no one ever saw or heard from Maddy again," said Dakota.

The detective leaned forward in her chair. "You're telling me that her mother has been lying to the police the whole time?"

"Yes," Dakota nodded.

"Can I have a copy of this recording?" Detective Carter asked.

"It's on the Internet. I have a podcast called *ShadowCast* about Maddy's case. I thought you knew," Dakota said with a smirk.

"No, I did not," she said.

Dakota let out a laugh, punctuated by a snort. The lack of communication in the local police force was so poor it was comical.

"You find this amusing?" asked the detective.

"Only a little," she said.

Detective Carter frowned and straightened her navy blazer over her white button-down shirt. "Before I investigate your claims about Mrs. Montgomery's statement. I'd like to review the camera footage you filmed for the school which we've had in evidence for the last 12 years."

"Go ahead." Dakota waved her arm out, motioning the woman to continue.

Her dull-faced lawyer shot her a look, indicating she should turn down the snark.

The detective grabbed the remote off the pushcart and hit play. On-screen, a teenage Dakota stared into the camera as she fiddled with the buttons on the side. The camera blurred and zoomed in and out, before focusing on the stage behind Dakota's head and neck. Young Dakota walked around to the other side of the camera and an audible "good" was heard, as she realized the camera was focused properly. The teenage Dakota onscreen walked to the front of the auditorium and sat in a hard plastic chair in the front row.

Detective Carter fast-forwarded through the empty minutes until the Maddy's parents arrived. They were on time, two minutes before the show was due to start. The room went dark and Mrs. Pruitt took the stage to a round of applause. She began speaking about the spirit of Christmas and how much work the kids in the pageant had done to make sure the performance would be a success.

The music started up and kids ran on stage in their elf costumes. They performed a little skit about how Santa makes toys in his workshop. Just as the second skit about Ebenezer Scrooge was about to start, a man walked past the camera. His face was cold and serious. It was Pastor Shaw. The old man found Jackie and Robert and sat next to them in the seats they had reserved.

Carter stopped the recording. "Interesting. He was late. About fifteen minutes. I'd have to ask him why that was. Where was Mrs. Shaw at this time?"

"She was babysitting Maddy's younger brothers. They were usually too hyper to sit through a pageant," said Dakota. "Do you think fifteen minutes is long enough for him to have taken her?"

"It's certainly possible," The stern-faced woman said. "Thank you for your time, Ms. Kilroy. You've been a big help." The detective stood up and left the room with the case file in hand.

Dakota and her lawyer were let out of the interview room moments later.

Outside, Sean was standing next to her car, waiting for her. When he saw her approaching, he stood up straight and greeted her with a look of relief. "Good, you're out. Was Tony helpful?"

"Who?" she asked.

"The attorney," he said.

"Right. A little, yeah. What did they ask you?" she asked him.

"I provided them with documentation that proved where I was for all of Maddy's childhood and where I was when she went missing. They had Jackie confirm earlier that I was the biological father. It was fast. They must have figured out real quick I didn't have the opportunity or the desire to kidnap the daughter I hadn't seen in fourteen years," he said.

"Good." She half-smiled at him.

"Listen, it might be best for me to go home for a while," he said.

"Oh." Dakota didn't want him to go. She was mad at him for keeping such an important thing from her, but the idea of him not being around left a feeling of emptiness within her.

"Don't worry," he put a hand on her shoulder and stroked her arm, before pulling his hand away. "Keep the money and I'll still help you with anything you need. But it looks like I've only made things worse between us. Please call me if anything happens."

She nodded.

He leaned forward and kissed her on the forehead. She closed her eyes.

"I'm sorry, for all of this," he said.

"It's okay," she told him.

They looked at each other for a moment before Sean pulled himself away from Dakota's gaze. He got into his town car and headed off towards the airport.

Chapter 12

I booked a room in a hotel. It's more expensive than the hotels that I normally stay at but a girl like this doesn't work cheap motels. I have to make sure I don't scare her off. Plus, I went to the casino again last week. I was riding the high from framing the angry old pastor and that stepfather for Maddy's disappearance and I headed straight to the blackjack tables. Having Maddy's undergarment in my pocket must have worked like a good luck charm because I kept winning and winning. I turn my luck over to the slots and Bam! I hit with the jackpot — 12 thousand dollars.

What should I do with this cash? That's what I was thinking after the teller paid me out. Then, an episode of ShadowCast came to mind. Selena. That druggie bitch who used to bully my poor dear Madeline mentioned her friend was an escort. Tiffany.

I did some digging around. I asked a few guys who were rich clients at the shop. You know, the kind who bring their Porsche 911 in for custom work. One of them gave me a number for a madam. Most of them seemed surprised I was interested, but they just patted me on the shoulder and told me to enjoy myself. After I got the woman on the phone to believe I wasn't a cop, I asked for pictures of the girls she was offering and low and behold, there was Tiffany. She still looked like the high school beauty queen she was back then in the yearbook photo Dakota posted online. The only difference was she was wearing more makeup and was calling herself, Holly.

Now, I'm in this hotel room in downtown LA. It's one those tall towering buildings made of glass. The room has a killer view of the city. Not to mention a plush California king-size bed. There's a soft knock at the door. I rush to answer it. In front of me, there is a tall woman with a slender build. She has a warm complexion with golden hair and bright blue eyes. She's one of the most beautiful women I've ever seen even though she was a little older than the girls I normally like. I want her instantly.

"Hi, I'm Holly," she says in a light and airy voice.

"Is that a Breakfast at Tiffany's reference?" I ask her.

"How did you know?" she smiles. She's wearing a tight black satin dress. She sits down on the bed and the slit on the side of her dress reveals thigh-high stocking trimmed with black lace.

I force myself to look away from her body — this is strictly business, Freddy.

"Because not only are you an escort like Holly Golightly, your real name is Tiffany," I explain to her.

She freezes.

"Don't worry, I'm not a cop." I laugh a little, trying to lighten the mood.

"A P.I.?" she asks.

I shake my head no.

"A stalker then?" She looks spooked, like she's about to make a run for the door.

"No, no, no. None of that. Relax. Please, I'm not going to tell anyone." I wave my hands in the air as if I'm surrendering in battle.

"Okay, so how do you know my real name?" she asks, her tone defensive.

I lean in and lower my voice. "Do you remember a Madeline or a Maddy from your high school?"

"Yes," she snaps.

"Did you not like her?"

"My friends and I hated her," she says. "She was a little show-off. Little miss perfect. Could do no wrong. All the boys had crushes on her but she walked around, acting — more like pretending, she didn't notice. Why do you ask?"

"I'm going to ask you to say something to the police about her," I say.

"It's not so easy for someone like me to go to the police." There's a look of bemused frustration in her eyes. I bet she thinks I'm an idiot.

"When you say you have information on the murder of a teenage girl, they will forget all about what you do for a living." I smile. That will convince her I'm serious.

She crosses her arms over her chest. "Why would I say anything? I don't know what happened to her."

I reach into my pocket and pull out my wad of cash. "Twelve grand. All yours."

Her eyes widen.

I cut the stack in half. "Six now, six later. All you have to do is walk into a police station and tell them exactly what I tell you to say."

"And what's that?" She raises her eyebrows at me but turns her attention back to the cash.

I clear my throat and begin. "You saw Maddy on the night of the pageant, December 7, 2000, around 5:30pm. You saw her get into a car, an old black pickup, to be exact. Say you saw her stepfather, Robert Montgomery and her grandfather, Pastor Shaw in the truck. Pastor Shaw was driving. They stopped on the road where Maddy was walking in her angel costume. Her stepfather got out of the car and grabbed Maddy by the wrist. She yelled at him to get away from her, but he scooped her up, threw her in the back seat and they took off. Tell them you didn't say anything at the time because you thought that Maddy was just in trouble for trying to walk to school alone. And that you also thought her mother, Jackie was telling the truth about seeing her daughter get to school that evening — which turned out to be a lie."

"I don't remember anything about her family. What do these two men look like?" Tiffany asks.

"Her stepfather is black. He's got short curly hair and a small goatee with medium brown skin, but deep wrinkles in his forehead and around his mouth. He's got kind of a square face and a boxy build. The grandfather is a bit slenderer. He's got pale, almost gray looking skin. Back in 2000, he had brown hair that was turning gray, it's now all silver. He's very stern and mean-looking," I tell her.

"Okay, I'll do it for the money, but if I get popped, you have to bail me out and get me a lawyer. A good one." She glares at me.

"Agreed." I stick out my hand and she shakes it.

.   •   •

After spending over 16 hours at the police station, Tiffany was released from questioning and returned to the hotel to meet me.

When I let her in, she was beaming from ear to ear. "I did exactly what you said. They ate it right up. Looks like those two might have been wanting to sleep with their stepdaughter and granddaughter for a long time. The cops asked if I was willing to testify in court and I said yes. I assume that's what you wanted me to say?"

"Yes, of course, and if you do get called, I'll give you my number, so we can practice what to say," I offer.

"So why do you care so much about those two getting locked up?" she asks.

"You have to promise you won't freak out." My stomach is in knots.

"You can't freak me out, honey, not after the things I've seen and done in this line of work." She pats me on the shoulder and laughs.

"Well, you have to agree to mutually assured destruction, before I tell you what I did and give you the rest of the money," I say.

"You mean like dropping bombs on each other?" she asks.

"Kinda. You see, you're a criminal so I can rat on you, and I'm a criminal and you can rat on me. But if we agree not to rat on each other, I can tell you." I smile at her, trying to look as friendly as I can.

She nods. "Fine by me."

"I care about those men going away for Maddy's murder because I'm the one who actually killed her." The words flutter out of my mouth and into the ether. I feel a weight lift from my body. It feels good to confess.

She stares at me for a moment like her brain is trying to compute what I just said. Her face lightens. She bites her lip and leans forward.

I duck out of the way, fearing she's trying to attack me for killing her classmate.

"What's the matter with you?" she asks. "I was trying to kiss you."

"Kiss me? For what?" I ask.

"For killing that bitch," she giggles. "You can't imagine much grief that girl caused me. I mean, she was nice enough, but at home my parents wouldn't stop talking about how impressive Maddy was. They'd always ask why I couldn't be as smart as her or as dedicated to playing a musical instrument as her or dress conservatively as she did. I'm not stupid or anything, but I'm not gifted like her. I don't like practicing, so I gave up the piano at age eleven. Plus, I like being sexual. I love showing off my body and giving men pleasure and men giving me pleasure. I don't want to be like her and no one would ever just let me be myself."

"I'm sorry they were like that. My Ma is real hard on me too. That's why I'm like this." With a shaking hand, I reach up and brush a loose strand of hair out of her face.

"Like what?" she asks.

"Can't get girls on my own," I admit, but this time I felt more shame than relief.

"You're not so bad. You're kinda handsome in your own way."

"No, you're just saying that."

"I'm not, And to prove I'm not, I'm gonna give you a good time. For free."

I blush. "I've never... I mean, are you sure?"

"Yes, don't worry. I'm not technically an escort right now. You paid me to go to the police, you're not paying me for what I'm willing to do to you right now." She drags me by the collar of my shirt over to the bed and pushes me down on the mattress.

•   •   •

I think I'm in love again, for the second time. The first time was with Maddy, now it's with Tiffany — a girl that hates Maddy. Normally, I would be very mad at someone who spoke of my Madeline in such a way, but after what she did to me last night, the girl can say whatever she wants. She can call Ma a fat pig for all I care if she'll keep touching me like that.

I think this is it. She's the one. After we finished up last night. I asked her out on a date. A proper date. Dinner and a movie. And not as an escort. Just as Tiffany. And she said yes. I can't believe my luck. Looks like things might turn out okay for ol' Freddy after all.

I'm beyond excited and nervous. It feels like my stomach is doing flips inside my gut and my hands are constantly covered in a layer of sweat, even though I wipe them on my pant legs every few minutes. I'm outside in the car, parked down the street from her apartment like she told me. I'm using the LeSabre tonight, hoping my classic car would impress her.

A few minutes pass and I see her silhouette approaching the car from behind me. She then slides across the bench seat, kisses me and says, "Hi baby, did you miss me?" before lightly grazing my crotch with her hand.

"Oh did I," I say. That was stupid. I bet that made me sound like a dork.

"Where are ya taking me tonight?" she asks in a melodic voice. Man, she is perfect.

"The Steak House on Green Street," I respond.

"Oh," she coos. "I've always wanted to go there."

"Well, tonight's your lucky night. Get anything you want, the whole thing is on me," I say.

"Thanks, baby." She curls up next to me as I drive, rubbing her lavender-scented perfumed skin against my blazer.

She is in a marigold wrap dress that goes down to the floor. But there's a slit up the side of the thigh that reveals one long tan leg with a pair of strappy high-heeled sandals.

Maybe this was too good to be true. She could be playing me. I heard of call girls and strippers doing this to men. Pretending to be into them just to get money, fancy dinners, and attention.

"Babe, you're sure you're not working tonight? That it's just us, for real? Like I'm not a client, just a man you're dating?" I need the reassurance.

"Yes babe, of course. I like you a lot. Remember what I did with you in that hotel room?" She asks, batting her long eyelashes at me.

"Yeah, I sure do," I laugh. "To be honest, I'm still sore."

"Well, I didn't charge you for that. And I'm not charging you for this or anything else that happens tonight. This is just us. I'm not Holly tonight. I'm Tiffany and I'm all yours." She wraps her arms around me and places her head on my shoulder.

"Okay, sorry. I just doubt that a girl as pretty as you would like a guy like me," I murmur.

"Oh, stop it," she lightly slaps my shoulder.

I believe her. For better or for worse, I believe her.

Dinner flew by. We made chit chat about movies, the weather, and LA traffic. She never said a negative thing about me and didn't complain about any of my habits mother said were disgusting. She didn't care that I doubled dipped my fries, forgot to put my napkin in my lap or used the wrong fork for the salad. Maybe I wasn't as repulsive to women as I had thought.

When the dessert menu came and Tiffany suggested that we share the chocolate lava cake, I was afraid she would judge the sloppy way I eat, but she didn't. She even fed me forkfuls of the dessert, getting the chocolate sauce on my face. Afterwards, she cleaned up my skin with her napkin saying, "Whatever I don't get now, I'll lick off later."

I paid for the bill by just handing the waiter my credit card. I didn't care what tonight cost, it was worth it.

Now, at the end of the date, I'm getting nervous again. But she quells my fears with one simple question:

"Are you ready to go back to my place?" she asks.

"Of course," I tell her.

I'm now inside her quaint studio with one large bed at the farthest wall of the apartment. To the side, there is a small kitchenette and a bathroom. In front of the bed was a wall-mounted small flat screen with a desk and a laptop on it. It looks brand new.

"Oh, is that one of the new MacBooks? I really wish I could get one," I say, rushing over to it.

"Yeah, it is. I just got it."

I'm closing the lid of the laptop when she says, "Don't. It's updating and closing it will cause it to malfunction."

I lift the lid back up. "Sorry."

"All right now," she says, pulling at the strings of her dress. "Take off your clothes and get on that bed."

The first time we had sex I had kept my shirt and boxers on. But now, the thought of her seeing my doughy physique made me want to run home to Ma.

"Come on, don't be shy," she says.

I stand there paralyzed with embarrassment.

"I'll go first." She unties her dress completely and pulls it off. Underneath she has a matching bra and panties with a light pink floral pattern. It made her look younger like — she was seventeen or eighteen instead of twenty-eight.

My lust for her overpowers my embarrassment, as I began tearing off my clothes. She comes closer to me, kisses me and pulls at my belt. Soon I was naked, on my back in her bed. She lay partly on top of me with my erection in her hand.

"I bet your mom doesn't like you doing this," she teases.

My face flushes. *"No, no, she does not. She says sex is only for making children."*

Tiffany laughs. *"What a sad life that must be. Here, let's make her mad together."* She gets on top of me and I'm in heaven once again.

I feel safe, wanted, and masculine for the first time in my life. Afterwards, I'm propped up on one of her many fluffy throw pillows, still naked but not embarrassed anymore. She's snuggled up right next to me.

"You know what I want to hear about," she says.

"What?" I ask.

"What you did with Maddy?" she asks.

"Oh no, hon. That will only make you jealous or upset." I kiss her on the forehead.

"No, it won't. I hated her. I don't care what happened to her. I don't care if she had you because I have you now." She pulls me close and rests her head on my chest.

I give in. *"Fine, but it's rather embarrassing."*

"Oh please, stop it. Just tell me what happened." She twirls my chest hair with her slender fingers.

I look into her beautiful blue eyes and melt. I'd tell her anything she wanted me to.

"I saw her a few weeks before she went missing — before I took her — I mean," I start. *"We stopped by Ma's church where Maddy's grandfather happens to be the pastor. I was in the car, waiting for Ma to come out, when I see Maddy come skipping along from her house to the doors of the church. She's about to enter when she runs into Ma and a few of the older ladies from the church. They stop her and chat with her for a minute. I can't hear what they're saying but they're all smiling at each other. I'm love-struck. Don't get jealous babe, but I was."* I check to make sure she isn't seething with envy. But she only smiles at me and I continue.

"She was the most gorgeous creature I had ever seen with that dark hair and those intense eyes. She had porcelain skin with a light splash of golden-brown freckles across her nose and cheeks. She didn't even look like she was from this planet. When Ma got back in the car, I was afraid she had noticed me staring and knew what I was always thinking when I saw beautiful youthful girls. But instead, she said, 'Freddy, that's the type of girl you should have met when you were younger. The pastor's granddaughter is the most polite young woman I've ever met. I hear she's nothing short of genius. A child prodigy on the violin. Might even get into

Julliard. Can you imagine if you had met a girl like her, got married, had four or five children with her? It would have been perfect. You know, you're not getting any younger. It's about time you put all this foolishness to rest, marry a nice Christian girl, have a family, finally move out of your mother's home.' She gave me that look which meant she was annoyed with me."

Tiffany pulls me in close and lets out a sigh. "Then, what happened?"

I clear my throat. "Well, um, I spent the next few weeks daydreaming about her. I knew Ma meant I should have married a girl like her when I was in my twenties or I should find someone my age now. But I couldn't help but feel like if I got Madeline to agree to marry me, Ma would finally be proud of me. So I was driving home from work one night, December 7th to be exact, and there she was. Dressed as an angel to boot. I took it as a sign from God. She was meant to be my wife. I pulled over and asked if she wanted a ride. She told me she was fine, but I said I knew her granddad, which was partly true, and she got in. But I didn't drop her off a few blocks down the road like she asked. I took her straight home, through the backdoor and into my basement. The cave, I call it, it's where I keep all the girls."

"Other girls?" Tiffany asks, her voice is meek and demure. I'm sure she must feel threatened.

"Oh honey, yes, but don't worry. I'm beyond that now. Now, that I have you." I stroke her hair and that calms her down.

"Okay, so what happened to Maddy when you got home? Did you kill her right away like she deserves?" she asks.

"No, no." I shake my head. "She was scared, but she didn't scream or fight back much. I only had to hit her once to get her to listen to me. It drew blood and got on her clothes but at least she settled down. She just asked me to let her go. I said I couldn't do that right now. But you see, I was nicer to her than the others. I wasn't going to use her for my fun and dump her. I wanted to be with her for the rest of my life. It must hurt to hear babe, but it was true at the time."

Tiffany is looking away from me. This must be tough for her to listen to this. I need to just spit it out.

"I brought her food. I gave her many outfits to wear and let her read as many books as I could find in the house. It wasn't after several weeks that Ma got wise to what I'd done. She was angry but she backed up my plan, like she always does. She wanted me to get married to Maddy and give her grandkids, tons of grandkids. We planned to get married that June. June 25th, to be exact. I still remember the date. Ma had found a pastor from a small church in the desert who was willing to perform the ceremony. After the wedding, we planned to move away, somewhere up North in the woods in Oregon. We'd have a cabin, live off the land, and she'd give me five children, at least. Three boys and two girls. I didn't do anything to her while we waited for our wedding night. Ma said my bride had to be a virgin on her wedding day.

"But one night about a week before the wedding, she was clearing the dishes for us and overheard us discussing Ma's plan about moving across state lines. She started panicking and screaming about how we're never going to let her go and how she missed her mom and just wanted to go home. I said that she couldn't do that, that she belonged to me now. She threw a dinner plate at me and ran out the backyard. I rushed after her. She was about to get to the end of our yard and hop the fence to get into the neighbor's property when I caught up to her. I pulled her down to the ground and muffled her screams with my hand. I wanted to wrangle her and bring her back into the house. She was about to get the spanking of a lifetime, I can tell you that. But I couldn't quite get a hold of her. I knew there was no bringing her back inside and there was no letting go of her. Her hollering was going to alert the neighbors, so I grabbed her by the head. I kissed it as she still fought against me. I said, "Goodbye, my sweet girl. Just remember when you get to heaven that you'll be waiting for me." And then, I twisted her neck in one fast motion. I heard a snap. Her body twitched and then stopped moving. I buried her behind the greenhouse where the rest of the girls are. But I buried her in a shallower grave, so I could be closer to her whenever I went outside. And that's it, baby doll, that's how I killed her. I hope you aren't feeling jealous."

Tiffany cuddles closer to me and says "I'm not jealous. You learned that girl wasn't the one for you. She was stubborn and didn't appreciate you. I have even more reason to hate her."

"You really feel that way?" I ask.

"Of course, honey," she says.

"Can we get married?" I blurt out.

"Really? I'd love to, Freddy," she smiles. "But, I'm not exactly the young Christian virgin your mother would approve of."

"Oh, I don't care about what she thinks anymore. You're the one for me," I say.

"But, I don't want to live in the same house as her. We can't get married until you move out and find a place for us," Tiffany demands.

"Of course," I tell her. "Those are my first duties as your future husband. I'll start looking for a house and a ring."

I hold her close and we drift off to sleep.

Chapter 13

Detective Carter sat down across the desk from Dakota. She had once again been asked to speak with the police about Maddy's disappearance.

"This is rather unorthodox for me to bring you in here like this," the detective began. "And it's even more unusual for me to admit that someone else is ahead of me on an investigation. Now, I mean no disrespect to Detective Muldowney, but I doubt he had his bases covered back then. He should have looked at the case from different angles. He should have pressed the mother harder, perhaps she would have confessed that she didn't give an accurate statement. But the last time I spoke to you, I have to admit, you impressed me. You knew far more about these people than any cop on the case ever did. Granted you were friends of the missing girl, but you clearly have a talent for this that very few people will ever have," she said.

"Thank you, Detective, that means a lot to me," said Dakota, forcing her face to remain neutral in expression when all she wanted to do was gloat.

"So, we have evidence that is pointing us at Robert Montgomery and Calvin Shaw. Yet, there's something in my gut that tells me something's amiss here, and I'd like your two cents on the matter," Detective Carter explained.

"Of course, happy to help." Dakota motioned for the detective to continue.

Detective Carter put up a finger. "But first, I am going to need you to agree to keep the details of what you see and what we discuss today entirely confidential. None of this can go on your radio show. You can't tell your friends or family about this."

"I'll keep everything to myself," said Dakota.

Detective Carter stood up and left the room. She came back a moment later with a plastic bin. Inside the bin, she pulled out four plastic bags, one large, and three small.

She handed the large bag to Dakota. It continued the pair of bloody angel wings that matched the costume Maddy was wearing that night.

"Yes, I saw these when I was with Muldowney. It's horrifying," she said.

"And these," she continued. "Are these photographs that Muldowney showed you?"

"Yes, I've seen them too, right before you arrived on the scene."

"I know it's hard to look at these. But I need you to look again and see if you notice anything about them that strikes you as odd."

"Odd? It's not *odd* that she's tied up in lingerie in what looks like an underground cell?" she said before stopping herself. "I'm sorry, I didn't mean—"

"I understand," said Detective Carter. "Just try your best."

Dakota flipped the Polaroids over. She saw the scribbled handwriting in magic marker. "Oh, here's something. Several things actually."

"What is it?" Carter leaned forward.

"Well, first of all, it's weird that her stepfather or grandfather would call her Madeline. Everyone called her Maddy. And I mean everyone. I don't think I heard her family call her by her full name once. Even if they did something this perverted, I can't see them writing her name as Madeline. And on top of that, the letter M denotes her last name. Why would a kidnapper or killer take a photo of his victim who is a family member and make a note of her last name? If you're her stepfather or grandfather, you don't need to write down her last name or last initial. It's like this is part of a larger collection of photographs where the perpetrator would want to make sure he remembered his victims, which is why he'd use their last initial."

The detective looked displeased. "That is an interesting point, but that probably won't hold up in court. For all we know, they wrote it that way so it would look like someone else took the photo."

"All three photos were in Pastor Shaw's house, correct?" asked Dakota.

"Yes, in his nightstand," she said.

"Assuming he's the one who took the photo, this isn't his handwriting. I've seen it several times. Since Maddy's parents had to work double shifts and long hours to make ends meet, they weren't always around to sign report cards, permission slips, and other school things. She often had her grandfather sign these forms in their place. I remember he had a very distinct way of writing: It's perfect, almost as if he had a typewriter to write it for him. He used to harp on Maddy and me if he saw us completing our homework in anything less than perfect penmanship. This is sloppy and uneven. He'd never write like this." Dakota said.

"What about Robert Montgomery?" asked Detective Carter.

"I don't remember. I didn't interact with him a lot, but I have a feeling this isn't his writing either. You should ask for handwriting samples from both men and see if they match," she said.

• • • •

The next morning, Dakota was making herself oatmeal in the microwave when her mother came in from her morning walk.

"For you," said Debi, handing Dakota an envelope from the mail pile.

It was torn and bent, and her old address had been plastered over and forwarded. At the top, she noticed something that made her spine run cold. The return address said, "New York State Department of Corrections."

She tore into the envelope. She was hoping it was a confession. Maybe the real kidnapper and probable murderer of Maddy had been busted for another crime and was rotting away in some jail cell. Maybe he heard about the show and was writing a confession. It was strange that it was coming from New York state, but a lot could have happened in twelve years. He could have moved from Southern California, committed another crime, and got busted for it in New York. She unfolded the letter, praying to read an explanation for what happened on that night.

Dear Dakota,

I want to start by telling you that I'm so sorry for what I put you through.

Her heart stopped. This didn't sound like a letter from Maddy's kidnapper. She read on.

I always loved you and I will always love you. After we last spoke, I got desperate. I had to use again. It was like my veins were on fire and the only thing that would make it stop was shooting up again. I busted out of rehab, but I told you about that already. And I didn't have any cash on me for a score, so I found a led pipe behind a construction site and I used it to rob a gas station. But the cops found me a few blocks away. They booked me and charged me. I took a plea deal so now I'm facing three to six years in the big house. I detoxed in here. The first week was the worst week of my life. I still don't feel right, but at least I'm clean. I just wanted to tell you I'm sorry for what I've done and for ruining the best relationship I ever had. I hope you're doing well and that everything works out for you.

Love,
Seth.

A deep breath lifted Dakota's chest. It wasn't the jailhouse confession she was looking for, but it was the confession she needed. In all the chaos of investigating Maddy's case and her strange romance with Sean, she had forgotten about Seth, the relic of the life she once had in New York. This letter was proof it was over now. There was no turning back. She had to find the truth about Maddy. That's what God or fate — or whatever dictated the rules of the universe — wanted her to do and that's why she had been driven to come to California.

Her cell phone vibrated on the kitchen table, shocking her out of her mournful stupor. She answered the call. It was Detective Carter.

"Hello Dakota, I wanted to thank you for coming in and helping out. There's been a new development," the woman's voice said.

"What is it?"

"A classmate of yours whose name I cannot release came in and gave us a statement. They claim they saw Robert Montgomery and Calvin Shaw forcing Maddy into Mr. Montgomery's truck the night she went missing," the detective said, in an emotionless tone of voice.

"Oh my God. Why did this witness wait so long?" Dakota's voice was shaking. Maybe her idea about a stranger with a collection of photos was wrong. It could have been the two men Maddy trusted most in the world, after all. *No, It can't be*, she thought.

"The witness said they assumed Maddy was in trouble and they were pulling her in the car to reprimand her. It wasn't until the witness heard about their arrests on the evening news that they realized the gravity of what they saw. While I agree that the writing on the photograph is out of place for a perpetrator who knew his victim, it looks like we have no choice now but to go forward with filing a case against these two men. Thank you for your help," she said.

"You're welcome," said Dakota, as her mouth fell open and the detective hung up.

"You look shocked, what happened?" asked Debi, who came downstairs with Ken.

"Someone saw Mr. Montgomery and Pastor Shaw shove Maddy into a truck the night she went missing and they just came forward with a statement. The police are going to press kidnapping charges against them," she said.

"I can't believe they would do that to their own child and grandchild," said Ken, his face fuming with rage.

"But," said Dakota, in a small voice.

"What?" her mother asked.

"I know I should go with what the evidence is telling us, but I can't shake the feeling that someone else is responsible."

"Why?" asked Ken.

"It's a long story, and I can't really talk about the evidence they showed me, but I just got the sense it was someone who didn't know her. Someone far more dangerous."

Chapter 14

"Welcome back to *ShadowCast*," said Dakota into her microphone. "I'm your host Dakota Kilroy. Today, I have a very short episode for you. I was not able to interview anyone else because, as of last night, two people are in police custody for the kidnapping and potential murder of Maddy Montgomery. Since this case has now been reopened, the police have instructed me to keep the details brief as to not interfere with the ongoing investigation.

"What I can tell you is that evidence has been found in the possession of two people who knew Maddy well. It proves Maddy was kept alive for at least several months after she went missing and was held somewhere that was not on the property in which her family resides. Also, bloodstained clothing has been found that is believed to have belonged to Maddy. Police are still questioning the two individuals in custody to find out more information. As of right now, we still have no solid proof that will tell us whether Maddy was murdered, but it's highly unlikely that she survived. Thank you everyone for listening and I'll keep you posted as the investigation continues."

Dakota ended her recording and posted it to the site without even editing the sound quality. She didn't care anymore. She covered her mouth and cried. Her eyes poured tears down her face and snot bubbled from her nose. She cleaned herself up with a tissue, only to cry even more.

Her mind was filled with images of her best friend, handcuffed to a pipe somewhere, forced to dress up in sexy outfits, before her grandfather and stepfather had their way with her. And the worst part is that it went on for a while — she wasn't killed swiftly. She had to suffer through the fear and abuse for months, kept some place she had never been before, in a dark cold room. How could they do that? To their own daughter and granddaughter? *What monsters*, she thought. *This couldn't be true.*

She was about to shut down her computer and get something to eat downstairs, hoping some leftover pizza would take her mind off her best friend's horrible fate, when she heard a ping.

She clicked on her browser and saw she was still logged into her email account. A new email had just been sent with the subject line, "I think I saw her," written at the top.

Dakota clicked opened the email. It read:

Hi there Dakota,

My name is Steve and I think I saw your friend Maddy the night she disappeared. I'd love to tell you more. Here's my phone number, call me anytime.

She looked at the number. It had a Texas area code, but she decided to call anyway.

"Steve speaking, how can I help ya?" A man with a warm southern accent answered the phone.

"Hi Steve, this is Dakota. I just got your email," she said.

"Boy howdy, that was fast." He let out a chuckle.

"Yes, well, it got my attention," she continued. "Do you want to tell me what you saw?"

"Yeah, I do." He hesitated. "But first, are you recording our call? I don't want to be on the Internet especially the way people started ripping into that Connor guy. Plus, I'm not completely sure if what I saw was really her."

"I'm not recording this. I just want to hear what you have to say, and then we can figure out what to do about it from there," Dakota reassured him.

"Okay, great," he said. "Well, I'm a truck driver based in Dallas right now. But from '89 to '03 I lived in Riverside and used to run deliveries for a catering business in the Santa Monica area for most of my time living there. And I always remembered this weird thing I saw," he said.

"What was that?" Dakota asked.

"I remember it was right around sunset. You could still see everything, but it was getting dark, and it was definitely around Christmas time because I was making deliveries to office Christmas parties like crazy. Anyway, I was driving through Santa Monica, in that small industrial part of town and I see a girl dressed up like an angel. And I thought it was weird. I was stopped at a red light, but up ahead and to the right side of the road, there she was. She had her back turned, so I didn't see her face, but I did see the white dress, wings, and halo on top of her head. I remember that because it really stood out against her long dark hair. Well, she's walking along, and this car pulls up. It's a 1970 Buick LeSabre with a golden body and a black rooftop. In perfect condition. I mean, it looked like it rolled off the lot two days ago. I'm sure that it was the exact year, make, and model because my brother restores classic cars and I help him out from time to time to make extra cash. And I swear, I've never seen a LeSabre like that in such good condition."

Steve stopped to take a breath. There was silence for a moment and then a cough. Dakota knew he just stopped to take a drag from a cigarette.

"Anyway," he continued, his voice slightly more hoarse than before, "just as the light turned green and I drove up past them, I saw the passenger side door open from the inside and the girl in the angel outfit peer in and say something to the driver. I looked back in my rearview mirror, but a truck got in my way; by the time it drove past me, both the car and the girl were no longer there."

Dakota's pulse quickened. Her hunch was right. It hadn't been Robert and Pastor Shaw, after all. "This is great, Steve, you really have something there. Would you call the police tip line and ask if you can leave your statement with Detective Carter?"

"Oh, um, the police?" he stammered.

"Yes, is that a problem?" she asked.

"I mean, I'm just not a fan — plus I've got a record and I'm afraid they'll dismiss me when they see my rap sheet."

"What were you in for?"

"Well, back in the early 80s, I had a bit of a drinking problem. I was young and stupid. I started getting in trouble for minor things like disturbing the peace or public intoxication. But one night, this guy at my favorite bar in downtown LA started running his mouth and he was just pissing me off so we got into a scuffle, but I ended up breaking his jaw and putting him in a coma. They put me away for felony assault and battery from '84 to '88," Steve confessed.

"Have you been arrested since?" Dakota asked.

"No ma'am," said Steve, almost boastful. "I've been clean and sober since then and stayed out of trouble. I'm a family man now, even got my first grandbaby on the way."

"Well, I doubt the police will see your past record from almost 30 years ago as a problem. If you want, I'll tell the detective about your tip and give her your number to follow up with you. Does that work?" Dakota offered.

"Um, okay, that's better. Thanks for listening to me."

"No problem. Have a nice night, Steve."

She ended the call, only to dial Detective Carter right away to relay the information she was just given. The grumbling detective said she would look into it, but Dakota sensed she didn't want to follow any other leads that wouldn't convict Mr. Montgomery and Pastor Shaw.

Dakota realized she had to work this angle alone. She pulled up her database of newspaper articles and started looking up the description of the car. At first, there were a bunch of hits, but they had nothing to do with any crime. Finally, she typed in "1970 Buick LeSabre" and "abducted" and the results cleared up.

One article from the Desert Dispatch popped up. Dakota blinked twice. The article was published last week. She read the article with her eyes carefully studying each word:

"Barstow girl, Cheyenne Jones, was reported missing yesterday on February 4, 2012. She is sixteen years old and was last seen at the Shell station on Main Avenue. A cashier who was working at the Shell station at the time said he saw Cheyenne go outside for a cigarette. Later, he saw her talking to someone inside a vintage Buick LeSabre. The young man says that the car looked old but was in good condition. It was gold with a black roof. He saw Cheyenne get in the passenger seat and a few moments later the car was gone. The young man reports that he didn't think this was odd. He assumed that Cheyenne knew the driver. However, when she didn't return home that evening, her parents called the police and the young cashier issued his statement."

The article closed with a tip line number for any information about the girl. Above the article was a picture of Cheyenne. She was slender, blond, and pretty with her sun-kissed skin and big smile.

Two teen girls go missing and they both were last seen getting into this particular vintage car. Dakota knew this wasn't a coincidence.

•　　•　　•

There was a pounding on the door. It was the middle of the day and Dakota was home alone. Who the hell could that be? The police? Connor? The man with the LeSabre?

She opened the door to see a tall and gorgeous woman standing before her. The woman was in jeans and a t-shirt with a large duffel bag in her hands. She pushed past Dakota and came inside the house.

"Hey, what the hell are you doing?" Dakota grabbed the woman by the arm.

"Shut the door," she demanded.

Dakota did what she said, fearing this was a robbery.

"From the outside, it looks like we're rich, but we don't have any cash in the house or pills or anything else you want," Dakota said.

The woman rolled her eyes. "I'm not here to rob you, Dakota. It's me, Tiffany. Tiffany Kowalski from high school," she said.

"Tiffany?" Dakota could now place the face. "What are you doing here?"

"I don't have a lot of time," she explained. "But I met Maddy's killer and I have his confession on video." She pulled a black flash drive out her pocket and handed it to Dakota.

"What? You spoke to Maddy's stepfather or grandfather?" Dakota asked.

"No. They didn't do it. It's a long story but let me explain." Worry hung around the edges of Tiffany's pale blue eyes. Dakota motioned to the kitchen chairs for them to take a seat.

Tiffany sat down and brushed her long caramel-blond hair out of her face. "His name is Freddy King," she said.

"I don't know him," Dakota said.

"You wouldn't," Tiffany continued. "He's an older man who abducted Maddy on the night she went missing. His very controlling and abusive mother attended to Pastor Shaw's church, and that's how he saw Maddy. He became obsessed with her and eventually kidnapped her so she would become his bride. It's a weird and horrible story."

Tiffany began speaking at a hurried pace while glancing around the house. She looked terrified. "All of this is on video, on the flash drive. But I need to tell you, he's been listening to your show. He's been messing with the investigation to throw you and the cops off his trail. He heard the episode where you interviewed Selena and you mention I was an escort. Well, good-old Freddy contacted every escort agency he could find until he got to me. He paid me 12 grand to give a false statement to the police about seeing Mr. Montgomery and Pastor Shaw kidnap Maddy. When I returned from the police station to get the rest of my payout, he told me he's the one who really killed Maddy. I was shocked, but I knew I couldn't show it.

"I didn't want to blow my chances of getting him to confess on tape. So I lied. I told him that I thought it was hot that he killed Maddy because she was my rival at school. I had sex with him to get him to trust me, and then I said I wanted to be his girlfriend. After our first date, I took him back to an apartment I rented. I filmed him with the camera on the new laptop I bought with his money; after we had sex and he was in that comfortable relaxed state, I got him talking. He told me everything. And I'm sorry, but she's dead. He snapped her neck when she tried to escape. She's buried in his backyard."

This was the first time anyone had confirmed what Dakota had feared all these years. Maddy was dead.

Dakota's throat clamped shut. Her lungs refused to let air in or out. Her mind flashed back to a day over, twelve years ago, when Selena had tripped her during gym class and the hard linoleum floor knocked the wind out of her. She had been dizzy and felt faint, like she was going to die on her back in the middle of the school gym. Maddy had come up to her. She was so small, her school-issued gym clothes hung off her tiny frame. She pulled Dakota off the floor and patted her back until she could breathe again.

But Maddy wasn't there now to make Dakota feel better.

Tiffany leaned in. "Are you all right?"

Dakota forced herself to take a breath.

"Yeah," she said. "I have to see for myself."

Dakota's laptop was on the table. She jammed the flash drive into the USB port.

"I'm sorry, it's very graphic," Tiffany began, turning her face away. "It's the only way I could have gotten him to talk. You may judge me for it, but I've done worse things with worse men."

Dakota looked her in the eyes. "I don't judge you, Tiffany. I applaud you, you're much braver than I ever could have been. He could have killed you at any point during this, but you got him to trust you. That's amazing." Dakota reached out and squeezed Tiffany's hand.

The video player loaded on the screen. Tiffany sped up the video until it reached the part when Freddy was about to confess.

Dakota watched the recording. Tiffany was lying on the chest of an out-of-shape fifty-something-year-old man with tufts of black body hair sprouting from his torso. He had salt and pepper hair that looked like it hadn't been trimmed in months with a matching scruffy beard.

"That's Freddy?" Dakota asked in a low tone.

Tiffany nodded.

The two women listened in perfect silence as this man confessed to the murder of Maddy Montgomery and alluded to the murder of other women.

"We got him," Dakota said to herself. "We got the monster."

Dakota heard Tiffany let out a sharp cry.

"What is it?" she asked her old classmate.

"I have to run," Tiffany said, dabbing her eyes with her ring finger. "As soon as you go to the police with this, he'll come after me. He might kill me"

Dakota grabbed her hand again and held it tight. "No, stay here. The police will protect you."

"They won't protect a whore," Tiffany said.

Dakota shook her head. "They will, and even if they don't, I'll protect you."

Tiffany wiggled her hand from Dakota's grasp. "No, my bags are packed. I need to leave right away. I'm driving to Sedona to start a new life."

"I can't make you stay, but please don't hesitate to call me if you need anything," said Dakota, as she stood with Tiffany and walked towards the door.

She embraced Dakota. "I'm so sorry about Maddy. I really am."

Dakota nodded. "Thank you. For everything. Stay safe," said Dakota as she watched Tiffany walk out her front door.

•　　　•　　　•

Dakota wanted to cry. Dakota wanted to scream and kick and pull Freddy King's eyes out. But she couldn't. She was far too rational for that.

Stomping up the stairs, she rushed into her parent's bedroom. The room hid a safe behind a painting of the beach which hung on the wall opposite her parent's bed. She punched in the code she had known since she was a teenager and nestled the flash drive among a collection of legal documents and pricey jewelry.

This was the best place for it until she could figure out what to do. Should she play it on her show? Should she take it to the police? She wasn't sure. On one hand, she knew it was the right thing to do to give the evidence to the cops, but she could see Detective Carter's disapproving glance already. The cold-faced woman would do nothing but doubt Dakota. "Oh, a prostitute gave this to you?" she'd probably say with a snide look.

Dakota couldn't run the risk of turning over her only piece of evidence of the man who killed Maddy without being sure something would be done about it.

There was a shudder and a loud wincing noise. It was the garage door opening and shaking the whole house, meaning her parents were home. Tomorrow was the twin's birthday and they were throwing a huge birthday bash, as always.

"Koty, where are you? Come help," called her mother.

Dakota came downstairs to see Debi placing plastic-covered trays of finger sandwiches and hors d'oeuvres on the kitchen table.

"Can you put these in the fridge?" she asked, as Ken came in with an armful of grocery bags.

Dakota followed her mother's orders and loaded the wide stainless-steel refrigerator with platefuls of birthday party food. Ken bent over and placed several new bottles on the wine rack.

"Koty, can you hand me that Merlot?" Ken asked.

But Dakota was too lost in her own mind to process what her father was saying. All she could focus on was Freddy, and how she would bring him to justice.

"Koty, the Merlot," her father said again.

"Right," she said to him. She grabbed the bottle and handed it to him, but she couldn't make her mind focus. She dropped the bottle just out of Ken's grasp and it shattered on the ground.

"Oh, no. I'm so sorry." Dakota pulled some paper towels from a roll and knelt down to clean up the red liquid.

"You all right, kiddo?" he asked. "I haven't seen you space out like that before."

"It's just the case," she began.

"Oh Koty," Ken stopped her. "Can we give it a rest for a few days? I understand how important it is to you, but it's starting to be too much for us. Let the police handle it."

"Fine." Dakota let out a heavy sigh.

"Oh shoot," moaned Debi, coming in with more groceries. "We forgot to pick up the custom cake at the bakery on the way home. Now I have to go all the way back."

"I'll go." Dakota needed to get out of the house. The new information on Maddy's killer was weighing on her and if she couldn't tell her parents, she needed to get out and focus on something else while she made up her mind about what to do.

"Thanks, hun." Debi tossed her the keys. "It's at the bakery near the grocery store. The order is under my name."

Dakota took off in her mother's car and soon arrived at the large strip mall's parking lot. It was crowded. Cars zipped in and out of spots while parents loaded the trunk of their cars with groceries, ignoring their children screaming in their booster seats.

Dakota got out of the car and headed towards the SunnySide Bakery which was located in the strip mall next to the grocery store and a Happy Nails salon. She heard the honking of a horn and someone yelling. An old woman with long gray hair had been almost hit by a blue SUV. She looked lost and scared, almost like she didn't even know what year it was.

Dakota rushed up to her. "Excuse me, ma'am, are you okay?"

The old woman shook her head. "I forgot what kind of car I drive. I don't remember where it is or how to get home!"

"Can you click the car keys?" asked Dakota.

The old woman opened her hand to show a single key on a ring. It was small and silver with "GM" stamped on the side. Dakota realized that the model of her car was too old to have remote locking.

"That's okay. Do you remember your address?" Dakota asked her.

"Yes, 1366 Steeper Ave." The old woman smiled, proud of herself for remembering.

"That's not too far. Why don't I drop you off at home and someone else can come and get your car later?" Dakota offered.

"Thank you, dear," a look of relief washed over the woman's face. "That's awfully nice of you. I hope it won't be a big trouble."

"No trouble at all," said Dakota, guiding the woman to her Mercedes.

She pulled out of the parking lot and headed out on the main road.

"What's your name, dear?" the woman asked.

"Dakota."

"Oh, what an unusual name."

"Yes. My parents named me after where I was conceived. They were in South Dakota with my dad on a golf tournament. My old sisters — they're twins, well they named one of them Capri after Capri in Italy, where my parents had their honeymoon... It's actually their birthday tomorrow. I was on my way to get their cake before I ran into you."

"Happy birthday to your sisters! I'm Lillian by the way. I have two kids myself. My eldest, Rebecca, was named after the woman in the Bible. And my youngest, he was named after a war-buddy of my husband."

Dakota nodded and there was a minute of awkward silence, while they waited at a red light.

Lillian started up again. "What do you do for a living? I know you young girls nowadays all have jobs. It wasn't like that in my day. I only ever worked part-time as a religious education teacher."

Dakota answered. "I'm an investigative journalist. I'm currently looking into the disappearance of my best friend. She went missing twelve years ago."

"Oh, that's so sad," said Lillian.

A few moments later, Dakota pulled up next to a brown two-story house. It looked out of place, like it should be on the coast of Maine instead of in Southern California.

"Here you are, Lillian." Dakota got out and opened the passenger side door for her. She took the woman by the elbow and walked her to her door.

Lillian jiggled a large gold key into the door's deadbolt and it opened. "Why don't you come in for a moment? I have homemade lemonade in the fridge."

"I'm not sure if I can," said Dakota.

"Please? Just till my son gets home. I'm so lonely and confused these days," she said.

Dakota felt pity for the old woman. "All right," she said and entered the house.

Inside, Lillian poured Dakota a glass of lemonade at the kitchen table. She then turned to the wall phone and dialed a number. She returned and said, "My son is going to the store and he'll drive it home with a spare key he has."

"See, no harm, no foul," said Dakota.

The old woman threw her hands up in the air. "It's this damn memory of mine. It keeps turning off and on like a spigot I have no control over."

Lillian sat down at the dining room table. A half-played game of solitaire was laid out in front of her.

"I do crossword puzzles, study the Bible, and play these card games to exercise my brain. But it doesn't seem to help," she said, with a little laugh. "Especially since I can never finish a game. This darn deck of cards is missing the Ace of Hearts."

Dakota balled her hands into fists.

"What did you say?" she asked the woman.

Lillian picked up the King of Hearts. "One of the cards is missing from the pack. I only keep them because they are so beautiful."

She turned the card over to show Dakota the backside.

Staring back at her was the face of the witchy be-jeweled woman who gazed into a crystal ball. It was the same face that was tattooed on her chest, and the same face that was on the Ace of Hearts in her purse.

Dakota slipped her hand into her bag and fished out the card.

"This one?" she asked Lillian.

"Well, look at that. How have you ended up with what's been missing all these years?" she asked Dakota.

Lillian reached up, trying to pull the Ace of Hearts from her hand, but Dakota yanked it back.

"What is your son's name?" she asked her.

"Frederick," the woman replied.

"Full name." Dakota said, between her teeth.

"Frederick King," she said. "But we call him Freddy, for short. He should be here soon to check on me," she went on. "He only works a few blocks away at the auto shop."

Dakota sprang to her feet. "Thank you for the lemonade Mrs. King, but I have to go now."

"What about the card? I want to finish this game!" Lillian called after her.

"So do I, Mrs. King." Dakota said, as she pushed the front door open and headed towards her car parked down the street.

But she stopped in her tracks the second she saw the gold and black 1970s Buick LeSabre crawl up the street and park on Mrs. King's driveway.

A man came out of the car. He was short and round with shaggy gray-black hair that was pressed down under a baseball cap. He looked just like he did in Tiffany's video.

He walked to the door of his house, but before he entered, he turned around and stared at Dakota.

Dakota gave him a glance that said, "I'll be back."

He responded with a grimace that promised her this wasn't over.

Chapter 15

That insufferable bitch! How dare she come into my house when for the last two months she has been doing nothing but trying to ruin my life.

And don't think I don't know what she and that whore have been up to.

They think they were able to outsmart me, but they're wrong. Tiffany went to Dakota's house. I was there waiting outside Dakota's house. I was thinking about doing it, running into that big mansion she lives in and slitting her throat right there on the kitchen floor. Her parents would come home to see what happens when they raise nosy daughters. But something threw me off my game. It was Tiffany.

She pulled up to the house. She didn't notice me because I was sitting a few houses back in Ma's Toyota, but I knew her car and I knew her silhouette. She walked into the door and Dakota let her in.

Those two must have been working together from the start. How? I don't know, but I knew it was too good to be true. A gorgeous woman like that actually falling in love with me. I mean, what a fool I was! How could I think anything she said or did to me was real? She's a goddamn whore, for Christ's sake. How could I have trusted her?

I followed Tiffany after she left Dakota's house. I stayed on her tail for about twenty minutes until we got to a road where there was a red light. She must have checked her rearview mirror and saw my face.

Then the chase began, she hit the gas the second the light turned green and swerved onto the highway ramp. I got on the freeway too, following close behind her. I wanted to put the fear of God into her. I wanted her to know that there was no way she could betray me and live to tell about it.

She'd switch lanes without warning, but I'd quickly get behind her once again. She got off the freeway, only to take the next on-ramp and get back on.

But she wasn't losing me. I was right behind her again.

This continued for several more miles. I could tell she was freaking out, constantly looking behind her. I smiled knowing the panic I was causing that backstabbing bitch.

But then, the little slut did something strange. We were in the middle lane and she jutted over to the right lane and then straddled the line between the off-ramp and the freeway. I stayed right behind, focusing on her taillights until I look and see that the off-ramp was ending soon, forking off in a different direction. She wasn't slowing down or choosing one lane over the other.

This was a suicide mission. She was going to kill herself, I thought, because I knew that over the railing would be a three-story drop to the concrete ground below.

The divide was getting closer, I had a matter of seconds before we both would be going over the rail. I chickened out. I wasn't going to let this bitch kill me so I pulled off to the right and took the off-ramp down. I look back to see that at the last moment, she had pulled back onto the freeway and ditched me.

What a clever slut. If only she had put those brains to better use and found herself a proper job.

I made my way home, feeling hurt and cheated.

•　　•　　•

Ma was in a mood that day. I had tried to politely tell her since she's been having memory issues that it would be a good idea for her not to drive anymore. But no, she said. "Damn it, Freddy, you can't tell me what to do. You can't keep me here like one of those girls you imprison in the basement. You're not taking my freedom from me."

"It's just not safe. What if you get lost or cause an accident?" I protested.

She replied with, "I'm a safe driver. I have had only one fender bender in the 60 years I've been driving. I can't get lost if I'm going to the grocery store or to the post office. I've been there a thousand times, I'm sure I can find my way there and back. Quit babying me, Freddy."

I let the issue alone, maybe I'd just sell one of the cars which would force her to stay home during the day, I thought.

After my chase with Tiffany, I got a call. Ma forgot where she parked the car — or what the car even looked like, while she was at the grocery store so she asked some nice young lady for a ride home.

I come home to see that it's her, Dakota Kilroy, standing by her nice shiny Mercedes about to leave. How she pulled this off? I don't know.

Had she been following my mother, the way I had been watching her house and tailing Tiffany?

It didn't matter, the bitch had been in my house. She had spoken to my mother while she was having a fit of dementia, no less. Who knows the things she could confess when she's in that state?

This had gone on long enough. It was time to shut her up for good.

I just got inside the house after watching Dakota leave. Ma is standing at the sink, washing out a glass.

"Ma, what the hell were you thinking letting that woman in here?" I scream. I don't care if it makes her mad.

"Relax, Freddy. She's just some girl." She waves me away.

"No, she's not. Remember that woman I told you about. The one hosting a show about finding Maddy?" I ask.

"Not really." Ma shrugs.

"Well, that's her, Ma. Dakota Kilroy."

"I think she did mention something about solving a case," she says.

"What else did she say?" I press her.

"She told me she had to pick up a cake for her sister's birthday party. They are twins. Can you imagine?" she laughed.

"You shouldn't have let her in the house," I scold her.

Ma's voice gets higher and she lets out a little giggle. "Relax, Jacob. She seems harmless."

"Jacob?" I ask.

"Yes, now quit wasting time. Dad's gonna be home soon and if we don't have our chores done, he's gonna whoop our behinds," she says.

"No, that's not—" I try to explain.

"Quit making excuses, Jacob and start working," she pushes me out of her way.

Damn it. Her memory is going out again. She thinks I'm her brother and that she's back home on the farm in Indiana.

I didn't want to fight it. Not now. I didn't want to deal with the crying and the yelling that happen when she realizes where she is. I simply say, "Yes, Lillian. I'll get right to it."

I have to take care of this myself.

Downstairs, I get my supplies out of my cupboard. It's been a while since I had to use them. I got both Maddy and Cheyenne to get into my car perfectly willingly. But I have a feeling that the Kilroy twins will not be so easy.

I do a quick Internet search to find the address of Capri Kilroy, now Capri Cunningham. Her real estate developer husband helped design their house, so its address and pictures of the house are all over his website.

In no time I'm there, outside the sleek white party pad down by the beach. The garage is open. There's only one car in it. Her husband must not be home. I slowly pull my Toyota into the garage. So slow that it doesn't make a noise.

I open the door and stick my head inside. I don't see anything.

In the pocket of my large coat, I have duct tape, chloroform, and a torn cloth to use as a gag.

I'm in the kitchen. I look out over the island of granite countertops to see a wall of windows looking out to the sea. What a charming life!

I hear the tap of heels against the tiles. I duck back between the fridge and the door to the garage. Capri comes into sight. She's thumbing through a pile of mail that's been placed on the kitchen island near me.

One envelope falls to the floor and she bends over to get it. I spring into action. I grab her around the waist and shove a chloroform-soaked rag over her face.

She tries to scream and struggles against my grip only to go limp after a few seconds. I bind her feet and hands and place the cloth over her mouth with another piece of tape. I leave her on the floor for a moment. I close the garage door so that no one will see me lifting her body into my car.

I check her house and I find a white iPhone on the coffee table in the next room. I open it and scroll through the contacts in her phone until I see "Cassidy." There, I find her address written down on the screen. I memorize it.

I throw Capri in the trunk and shut the lid on her. Then, I drive as quickly as I can out of her neighborhood without arousing suspicion.

About twenty minutes later, I pull up outside Cassidy's home. I don't even take the time to process the level of opulence that her football player husband has provided for her. She's in the back of the house. No one else is home.

She's trimming roses from a garden out back and putting them in a vase. She turns and I see a large pregnant belly. I wasn't aware of this. Now she isn't going to fit in the trunk with her sister.

She turns back to the roses and I walk up behind her. She turns around and sees me, dropping the flower sheers. I lunge forward and grab her. I press the chloroform to her mouth, just like her sister, and wait for her to go down. I bind her hands and feet before I rush into the house. There on the sofa, there is a navy-blue blanket. I grab it and throw it over my shoulder. It takes all my might to drag her pregnant unconscious body into the back seat of my car. I cover her with the blanket to make it look like she's taking a nap and take off towards my house.

Once I get these girls locked in the cave, it's time to tell Dakota that if she ever wants to see her sisters alive again, she needs to stop her meddling.

• • •

Dakota was back at home with the cake in her hands. It was an ice cream cake and she was finding room for it in the freezer. But her mind was a mess. She had just seen her friend's killer, and she knew that he knew who she was.

"I can't believe it took you so long to pick up the cake," scolded her mother.

"Sorry Mom, I've got a lot on my mind. Plus, I had to help a little old lady who almost got hit by a car."

"I'm glad you're such a good Samaritan, but don't dillydally so much. Especially when we've got a party to throw," she said.

"I got it, Mom," said Dakota.

"That's odd," said Debi, looking down at her phone. "I just got this worried voicemail from Blake that he can't get a hold of Cassidy. She's not home like she would be." She looked down at her device again. "And Trevor's nanny just texted me. Capri won't answer the door."

Something was not right. Dakota knew it. Just then her phone buzzed. She answered it, assuming it was one of her sisters with an explanation for where they were.

"Hey," said a familiar voice.

"Sean?" Dakota asked, rushing out of the room to get some privacy.

"I miss you. A lot," he confessed. "This is the best connection I've had with a woman in years. I don't want to give up on that. I also don't want to give up on the investigation. Please give me a second chance."

"Look, Sean, I'm really happy to hear from you. But there's a lot going on right now," she said.

"Let me help," he said.

She took a deep breath. "I don't know how you can from the other side of the country."

"I'm actually only on the other side of your front door," he said. "I flew back. I had to see again."

Dakota opened the door and saw Sean standing out there with his phone pressed to his ear. His eyes lit up at the sight of her.

They both put their phones away and hugged each other. He stepped forward and kissed her. He looked down and said, "Sorry". He had stepped on a piece of paper. An envelope.

Dakota picked it up and pulled out a birthday card. It was white and pink with "Happy Birthday" written in gold sparkly letters.

"Oh, it must be for Capri and Cassidy. It's their birthday tomorrow," she told him.

She flipped it open to see who it was from. The note read:

Dear Dakota,

You need to stop what you are doing. Stop telling the police that you think they have it wrong. Stop recording your show. Take down all episodes of ShadowCast and delete all record of the show from ever existing. Destroy whatever evidence that whore gave to you. If you don't meet my demands in the next 24 hours, your sisters won't make it to their next birthday. No cops. Tell no one. I will call you from an unlisted number tomorrow morning to see if you are doing as I ask.

Your friend,

Freddy.

"Um, Dakota," said Sean, holding the envelope.

He reached in and pulled out a chunk of bloodied blond hair that had been pulled out by the roots.

Dakota's stomach twisted. "He has my sisters."

•   •   •

Dakota felt dizzy. The world was expanding and contracting before her eyes. She reached down and sat on the stoop outside her front door.

"While you were gone, I found the killer. The real one. It wasn't Robert or the pastor. It was a stranger. I think he's a serial killer," she said, in a breathless voice.

"Shit," said Sean.

Dakota continued. "Tiffany, the friend of Selena's, who is an escort, met Freddy. He hired her to give a false statement about seeing Maddy getting forced into a car by her stepfather and grandfather near the school. She later befriended him, he told her everything, and she got it on video. I have the recordings of his confession on flash drive in my parent's safe."

"Holy Hell." Sean rubbed his brow.

"His name is Freddy King. He lives with his mother at 1366 Steeper Ave. I talked to his mother yesterday; it's a long story but I confirmed Maddy had been to their house," she said.

"Jesus Christ, we need to go there and get your sisters back," he said.

"We have to wait until it's dark so we can sneak up to the house," she told him. "We can't tell my parents. They may freak out and call the cops."

Dakota rushed back inside. "Mom, Dad. I need to take off for a little bit."

"What for? You promised you'd help me decorate," said Debi.

"Sean's back," said Dakota.

"Oh, I like him," cooed Debi, "even if he's your friend's father."

"Well, that's what we need to talk about. We need to figure out some stuff in our relationship." Dakota stood by Sean at the front door as both her parents walked inside.

"Koty, I don't know," said Ken.

Debi poked her husband in the ribs and whispered loud enough for Dakota to still hear, "Ken, let her go. She could end up marrying a millionaire."

Her father turned around beaming. "You two go have fun. We'll be fine here."

Dakota pulled Sean by the arm outside and walked up to his rental car, a black BMW.

"Where are we going? Aren't we waiting until the night?" he asked.

"Yes, but first, we need to show up prepared."

Chapter 16

In a big box store, Sean and Dakota filled their shopping carts. They found all black outfits, flashlights, rope, duct tape, an ax, a hammer, and two stun guns. Sean also loaded two tool belts and a pair of bolt cutters into the cart.

The pudgy cashier gave them the side-eye as she rang up the strange assortment of items. Dakota watched her, waiting for her to call the manager over. Maybe they had a protocol for this, a silent alarm under the cash register that alerted the police when someone bought something suspicious.

Dakota shook her head. She was getting paranoid. *I guess that's what happens when a serial killer is holding your sisters hostage,* she thought.

At the cashier stall to their right, an old woman in a tight dress was purchasing a family-sized bag of skittles and a crossbow. A few rows down, a kid ran up to his mother, begging her to buy a carton of jellybean flavored milk. Nothing that Dakota and Sean were buying seemed particularly odd in *this* store.

As night came, Sean and Dakota grew silent. They were both festering with rage under the surface like a volcano before an eruption. They changed clothes in the back of the car, which Sean parked in a distant corner near the store where they had just purchased their supplies.

Sean strapped a tool belt around Dakota's waist, pulling it to the tightest notch.

"Man, you're skinny. Do you even eat?" he tried to sound jovial in tone, but the joke came out hollow.

"Sometimes when I get carried away on a case like this, I stop eating," she explained.

He fitted the belt with the ax, a stun gun, and a roll of duct tape. He then fastened his own belt around his waist and strapped in the other stun gun, the hammer, the bolt cutters, and the rope.

They drove the fifteen minutes to Freddy's house and parked several doors down. Dakota turned to Sean whose face was frozen with a look of both anger and dread.

"You don't have to do this. We don't have to. I can disobey the note and call the cops," she said.

"No, absolutely not," he snapped. He cleared this throat and started again. "Sorry. I can't risk him executing your sisters the second he hears sirens coming down the street. On top of that, I have to do this for Maddy. I wasn't there to raise her. I wasn't there to protect her from this cruel world. The only way I can absolve myself of that is if I go in there, free your sisters, and give Freddy what he's got coming to him."

"Wait, you're going to kill him?" Dakota grabbed him by the arm.

"Yes, isn't that what we've been preparing for all day?" he asked.

"I thought we were going to free my sisters, restrain Freddy and call the cops, so he can get served justice." She was surprised at Sean's sudden vigilante streak.

"No," he said. "He doesn't get a trial after he killed my daughter and possibly many more girls."

"I'm not sure, the confession tape didn't say exactly what happened to them," said Dakota.

"It doesn't matter. He's a no-good son of a bitch. If he gets arrested, there isn't a guarantee he'll get sentenced. He could hire a sleazy lawyer who will be able to convince a jury that his confession tape was just boasting to show off to a new girlfriend. Or they could take the insanity defense. They could claim your show prohibited him from getting a fair trial since everyone is starting to hear about it. A million things can go wrong in the legal system. Also, California doesn't have the death penalty. He won't get what he really deserves," said Sean, slamming his palms against the steering wheel.

"That's not for us to decide," said Dakota. "He took a life and potentially many others without warrant or justification. If we are going to live in a civilized society, we have to show him we're better than that. That we don't kill. So let's go in there, get Capri and Cassidy out and hog tie the bastard and wait for the cops to come and take him away."

"Fine," said Sean, taking a deep breath to diffuse the anger that rushed through his veins. He wouldn't stoop to Freddy's level after all.

Sean and Dakota slinked between houses, pausing behind trash cans and large ferns so their movement wouldn't be easily noticeable by neighbors or Freddy himself. Thankfully, the streetlights on this block were old and dull, and the one that loomed over Freddy's house was out entirely.

There was a gap between the detached garage and the fence on the farthest side of the King property. Dakota and Sean sucked in their stomachs and carefully wiggled their way through the tiny space.

Once through, they found themselves in a large backyard. It was clear from both the home's appearance and the size of the yard it was built long before Southern California was consumed by the urban sprawl that stacked homes close to one another.

In the center of the yard, there was a greenhouse with a large weeping willow dangling its soft branches over the transparent structure. Dakota and Sean pushed their bodies up against the side of Freddy's house, feeling the uneven shingles dig into their backs.

They looked up. Not a light was on.

The pair inched their way across the left side of the house and then put their back up against the rear wall. Dakota took a few steps forward but stopped dead in her tracks causing Sean to walk into her.

"What are you doing?" he whispered.

"Look." She pointed at the ground by their feet. At the bottom of the house, there was a small basement window. It shot an illuminating yellow light out against the patch of grass that lay in front of it.

"He could be down there. And if we walk across the window, he could see us and be waiting at the door," she whispered.

"Fuck," huffed Sean.

Dakota peered across the back of the house. In the middle of the backside of the home, there was an iron door at the bottom of a few steps, clearly leading down into the basement. Through the darkness, she could see a padlock was attached to the door's latch. Past the door, there was another small basement window, but there was no light radiating from it.

"You know what this means?" said Dakota.

"What?" Sean asked.

"We have to go out how we came in. Cross the front of the house, get into the back yard from the right side and approach the house that way because the other window's light is not on. So, if he is there and awake, he won't see us pass by that window."

"Okay, fine. Let's go" said Sean shuffling away.

The couple crossed the left side of the house and yard again. They squeezed through the space in the fence by the garage and tip-toed towards the front of the house.

Just as they were about to pass the first downstairs window, Dakota dropped to all fours. Sean copied her and they crawled past the first window, then the front door and then the last window on the right. As they stood up again, Sean peered into the window behind him and saw the soft flashing of multicolored lights.

It was a TV set, and it was casting the light across a sleeping old woman, who had fallen asleep on the couch with her knitting needles in her lap.

"That's his mom. The woman I met earlier," said Dakota.

Sean nodded, and the two continued to the other side of the house where they came across a wooden gate to the backyard.

Due to both Sean and Dakota's height, it wasn't a challenge for either of them to reach over the fence and unlatch the gate from the inside. Sean gently pulled the gate towards him and it let out a slight squeak.

"Shhh," hushed Dakota.

"What do we do? If I open it all the way, they might hear it."

"I got it," said Dakota, as she patted her pants down.

She pulled out a small tube of lip balm.

"What's that gonna do?" he asked.

"Just watch," she said.

She went up to the hinges of the gate and rubbed the waxy substance around the moving metal parts. Once she had finished, Sean moved the gate an inch further. It didn't make a sound. He gave Dakota a thumbs up and the two of them walked through the gate and closed it behind them.

Inside the yard, they pushed themselves up against the wall of the house. They took slow and deliberate steps even though each of them felt an adrenaline rush which begged them to move faster. They passed the dark basement window and made their way to the back door.

Sean pulled the bolt cutters that had been dangling from his side and fastened it around the lock in his hand. "This might make a noise, so be prepared in case we've alerted him to our presence."

Dakota nodded and reached for the stun gun that was at her side. Sean pressed the metallic mouth of the cutters together and they bit through the padlock with a crunch. Dakota slipped the lock off and threw it on the ground without making a sound.

They opened the metal door and entered a dark hallway. They kept the door open behind them in case they needed to run for it. After their eyes adjusted to the darkness, they noticed a smaller wooden door in front of them.

"Damn it," hissed Sean.

"No, it's okay. We can get in, but this time he'll know we're here for sure," she said.

"Fine, might as well get this over with," he said.

Dakota took out her ax and in one swoop, she knocked the doorknob off. It broke into two pieces and each nob fell on the ground at their respective sides of the door, each making a thud.

They pried the wooden door open and walked the three cinderblock steps down into the semi-sunken basement. They looked to their left. It was an open space with a large bed, a couch, and a bean bag chair. The chair and couch were set up to face a large television with gaming consoles attached to them.

To the right, a room was illuminated by a ceiling fan light, but most of the room was blocked by a wall that jutted out by the door. Dakota and Sean took two steps forward and craned their necks to peer behind the wall.

Dakota reached back and grabbed Sean's hand. It was him. Freddy.

He was sitting at his desk with his feet up. His bulky black headphones were plugged into his desktop computer and something on his iTunes was playing.

He sang aloud, "It was Summer of '69," in a poor impression of Bryan Adams' voice. Both Dakota and Sean took a breath. He hadn't heard them after all.

Creeping past Freddy, they tip-toed down the basement hallway until they found another door. It looked like one that you would find at an old prison.

They pushed against the door and it opened. On the right, they saw a gray cinderblock wall full of photos, scraps of clothing and newspaper clippings of missing girls.

Dakota swallowed hard and forced herself to turn away from the wall. Past this area, there was a narrow entryway.

Dakota rushed through it but stopped in her tracks.

Her pregnant sister, Cassidy was on a tiny cot. She was tied by her feet and hands to the bedframe with a gag in her mouth and a blindfold on. Beside her, Capri was handcuffed to a long metal pipe, with both hands behind her back, facing away from the door. She was gagged and blindfolded as well.

She gestured to Sean and motioned for him to use the bolt cutters to cut Capri's restraints. Dakota leaned over Cassidy and reached for the blindfold. Dried blood was caked onto the side of her face. She was the one who had her hair ripped out.

Her hands and feet were red and swollen from the tight restraints. Dakota tugged on her sister's blindfold causing Cassidy to try to scream through her gag.

"It's me, Koty. It's all right. Just stay quiet." She pulled the blindfold down and looked into her sister's frightened face.

A tear leaked out of her left eye as Cassidy realized she was being rescued. Dakota stopped and moved over to Capri. She was panicking; she mistook Sean's touch was that of her captor.

Dakota lifted the blindfold and looked at her other sister.

"Both of you, listen," she said in a low tone. "He's still here, wearing headphones and listening to music, so he can't hear us and we want it to stay that way. So don't scream, don't talk, don't do anything until we get you out of here."

Carpi nodded, her makeup was smeared, causing black and gold eye shadow to run down her face. Blood was caked on her head as well, from what looked like a blunt instrument.

Sean clamped the bolt cutters over the chain of the handcuffs. "Pull your hands apart to make the chain as taut as possible," he told Capri. She did what he asked, and the cutters snapped the cuffs in two.

Dakota had turned back to Cassidy. She pulled the rope from its knot and freed her right hand. Capri rose to her feet, and with Sean, worked to untie Cassidy's other arm and legs.

Dakota looked down at Capri's right hand. Her pinky and ring finger were swollen and curled down in an unnatural way.

"What happened?"

"He broke them because I was being insubordinate," she said, not taking her eyes off the restraint she was working with her eight good fingers.

"He said that if we didn't listen to him, he would keep me until I gave birth and then sell Isabelle on the black market," said Cassidy.

"We wouldn't let that happen," said Dakota, helping her pregnant sister sit up.

The four of them walked out of the cell, past the wall of photos and into the dark hallway.

There was a thump. They froze. It was the sound of Freddy putting down his headphones and getting out of his chair.

Dakota peered behind her. The staircase to the inside of the house was right next to them. She shoved Cassidy and Capri towards the staircase and said: "Run."

The two women began stomping up the staircase, right as Freddy turned the corner to see Dakota and Sean standing in front of him.

He smiled. "What do we have here?" He glanced behind them to see the backs of Cassidy and Capri heading up the staircase and through the door into his house.

"What have you done?" He lunged at the two of them.

Sean reached for his hammer and swung it at Freddy, hitting his right temple. Freddy staggered back and held his head. He leaned down while still facing forward and grabbed something. It was a tire iron and he swung it around like a batter stepping up to the plate.

Sean stepped back, expecting a retaliating blow from the unkempt man. Instead, Freddy swung at Dakota, yelling, "This is what you get for not minding your own business!"

Dakota tried to defend herself. She pulled the stun gun from her belt, but it slipped from her grasp and landed on the floor. The iron smacked the side of her head and she fell to the ground.

Sean leaned in to give Freddy another blow from the hammer only to feel something from behind push him forward and out of the way.

"You whore," an old woman's voice screamed. It was Lillian. She had caught Capri at the top of the stairs and had forced her to walk back down into the basement.

"I know what you've been up to," she continued.

Dakota looked up to see Lillian holding a frying pan over Capri's head. "How dare you sleep with my husband and think you have the right to come into my home?"

"I didn't," Capri stammered, brushing up against Sean and grabbing his arm.

Lillian caught sight of Freddy holding a tire iron. His face hung open in shock at what his mother was doing.

"And you," she said marching up to him. "How dare you ruin the sanctity of our marriage vows with a common whore, no less? I'm through with you, Edward!" She lifted the frying pan above her head and brought it down on Freddy's face.

He stumbled backward, with his nose spitting out blood. "Please, don't," he called after her.

She leaned over him and struck him two more times until he was on the ground and silent. Turning back to the three strangers who were staring at her. She exclaimed, "Don't judge me, this is a domestic issue. None of your concern."

"Lillian," began Dakota as she got to her feet. "I'm sorry to tell you this, but you're having a memory problem again. That is not your husband. I believe your husband has been gone for a long time now. That man is your son, Frederick."

Lillian scowled and opened her mouth to protest their claims, but she stopped herself. She noticed the bloodied frying pan in her hand and the unconscious Freddy on the floor.

"Oh my Lord, what did I do?" she dropped the pan with a thud and rushed to his side. She pushed her hand up to his neck and moved it around frantically.

"I don't get a pulse," she screamed.

"We're calling 911," said Dakota.

"No, not yet." She held up a hand.

"Why?" Dakota's eyes darted to Sean and Capri who were just as surprised at the old woman's actions as she was.

"I remember you. I remember you're trying to find out what happened to your friend." Lillian held her head in her hands and said, "I've had enough of this. It's time to tell the truth."

She stood up, bracing herself against the railing on the cinderblock stairway that led to the backyard.

The three of them crowded in closer to hear what the old woman had to say.

Dakota held out her hand and asked. "Mrs. King. Can I record this?"

"Yes, why not?" The old woman laughed. "It needs to come out after all these years."

Dakota attached her portable microphone to her phone and pressed record.

Lillian continued, "It all started when he was fourteen years old. I mean, before that, he was a bit of a strange child. Didn't have too many friends. Liked to talk to himself a lot. 'He's just a shy boy' is what they told me. I was desperately afraid he'd turn out like his father. A womanizing, no-good cheat. He left us when Freddy was seven and Becky was just about ten."

"Rebecca is your daughter, correct?" asked Dakota, remembering what the woman told her about naming her daughter after the biblical Rebecca.

"Yes, it all started with Rebecca," the old woman began. "When Freddy was fourteen, he was in a particular type of mood. He was very destructive, very angry and very sad. I knew it was because he couldn't get girls to notice him. It was the late '60s. Everyone was having sex in muddy fields and protesting the war. Rebecca was one of them. Man, she was a hellion. She was gone most nights of the week. "Crashing" at her friends' houses as she called it. I knew she was smoking reefer and screwing boys in the backs of their vans when she wasn't home. I couldn't blame the boys. She was a good-looking girl. Thin figure, pretty face, blond hair in that feathery style. That's the problem, her looks got even her brother to have a crush on her."

Lillian let out a heavy sigh, brushed her willowy hair out her face and continued. "It started small. She'd say Freddy would peep at her in the shower or while she was getting dressed. He always would deny it. I found her underwear in his drawers, but he said it was a mix up in the wash. But one day, I come home to hear a ruckus upstairs. Rebecca is screaming. Freddy is yelling something back. For a moment, I thought it was just a fight between siblings, but it sounded different. There was more screaming and thrashing and then a dreadful silence. I walked up the stairs with my heart in my throat. I pushed aside the door to Rebecca's room to find my Freddy, my son, with penis out, thrusting it inside his sister. But that wasn't the worst of it. I looked at her face and it was lifeless. Her neck bent down at a strange angle. I knew right there what he was doing. I stood there in silence with my mouth open. I wanted to scream, but the sound wouldn't come out."

The old woman hung her head down and sucked in a sob. "For the next few minutes, it was like I wasn't even in the room. I was watching myself from above just stand there as my son violated his dead sister's body. Because I couldn't make a noise or move, Freddy didn't know I was there. So he just kept at it until he was finished. I watched him put his bottoms back on; he turned around to see me standing there with a silent gasp plastered on my face. I was horrified at what I had seen. But I knew I would be even more horrified if the news of what had happened got out. I was already 'Poor Lillian' to the neighbors and other parents at school. Getting divorced back then was not as casual as it is now. It ruined your reputation especially when it gets out your man was after other women. And now, this! This would ruin me. I could live with being the sad divorcee, but I couldn't live with being the mother of a son who killed his sister and raped her dead body.

"So I swallowed my scream, forced it down real deep. I said to him, 'Now you listen, and listen good. I'm not going to let your sick behavior ruin my reputation and what's left of this family. I've had enough of you King men and your disgusting desires. So, this is what we're gonna do. We're gonna write a runaway note from Rebecca. She's been threatening to run away to Las Vegas to be a showgirl for a while, so let's just say that's what she did. Anyone who asks for her, show them the note. Then as soon as it's dark, we're gonna bury her in the yard." And that's what we did. For years, people thought my daughter was just a runaway. It might have caused some people to question my ability to parent, but at that time, almost every teenager on our block ran away at one time or another. Every year, we'd write a letter from Rebecca to us at Christmas time. Freddy, when he got his license the next year, would drive up to Vegas, dropped it in the post so it would have the correct postmark on it, in case anyone saw it. I'd show it to the neighbors and a few church friends every year. Tell them the strange things she was up to. That she did a show with Elvis in the crowd and she saw Frank Sinatra at a blackjack table. They ate it up. We kept it a secret for all of these years."

"But what about Maddy?" asked Sean, with rage in his eyes.

She put a finger up. "I'll get to that. You see, it continued. I hoped, after the incident with Rebecca, he would be so ashamed, so filled with self-hatred, he would never do such a thing again. But I was wrong. Five years later, I wake up in the middle of the night to see him digging another grave in the back yard. I ran out into the darkness, without shoes or a robe, to find the lifeless body of another young blond teen girl being lowered into the earth by my son.

"I begged him to stop killing. I threatened him with the police if he didn't. He said since I helped him bury Rebecca, I would go to jail with him for being an accomplice. I had to keep my mouth shut, or we'd both rot in jail for the rest of our lives. I said I'd keep quiet, but he had to work to stop his evil desires. He said that he would.

"Once again, a few years passed, and I sensed he'd gotten a hold of himself, but I come down to his basement area to find a girl tied to a cot. He uses the same line on me, so I shut up. This pattern, it goes on for years."

"How many were there?" asked Dakota.

"From what I saw in his little photo collection over there and from what I witnessed, I counted thirteen including Rebecca and Maddy."

"So when does Maddy come in?" asked Dakota.

"Right," said Lillian, gathering her thoughts. "You see, in the typical Freddy fashion, he misunderstands something I told him and goes too far. I was a member of Pastor Shaw's congregation. Freddy hadn't attended church in years, even though he was the one who needed it the most. One day, as we were running errands, I asked Freddy to stop by the church for a moment. I wanted to drop off some items for the church yard sale they were having the following day. Anyway, Madeline was outside the church with her grandfather and Freddy saw her. I got back in the car and said that she was the type of girl I wished he would have been interested in back in high school: a nice Christian virgin, instead of his own sister or any of those other blond sluts he drags home. I told him it would have been nice to see him fall in love with a sweet, smart girl like Madeline, get married and have babies. Then, I told him how disappointed I was that his behavior meant I could never attend my own children's weddings and I'd never have any grandchildren.

"He took this to heart. About three weeks later, he tells me that he has Madeline in the basement. I yell at him and beg him not to kill the pastor's granddaughter. But he says that Madeline is going to be his wife, just like I said. I don't want to go along with it, but I listen to his plan.

"He was going to keep her here, treat her real nice and then they'd get married and have tons of grandchildren for me to help raise. I don't like what he did but at this rate, we couldn't let her go. She would tell and that'd be the end of us. This way she'd get to live. I planned to put the house up for sale, after the wedding. I found a minister from a church in the desert to do the ceremony and then we'd move to this compound I found out about up in rural Oregon. We'd live off the land and be happy there. Maddy had not been any trouble while she was here. Freddy and I treated her really nice. Only punishing her when she needed it. She was always helpful around the house. But one night, she must have overheard us talking about moving and how she would stay with us for a long time. She panicked and ran out the backdoor. Freddy chased after her. I couldn't see much from the window, but there was a struggle and Freddy said he had no choice but to kill her."

"Is she buried out there with the others?" asked Sean.

Lillian nodded. "Yes, she's on the left side of the greenhouse. It's a shallower grave. Freddy would dig her up from time to time to visit her."

Sean bolted past the old woman and out of the house. Dakota and Capri ran after him. He knelt to the ground by the greenhouse and began dragging handfuls of dirt out of the earth. Dakota opened the door to the greenhouse and retrieved a shovel.

Sean took it from her and dug and dug and dug until the bones of his daughter were fully revealed. He fell to his knees and cried. He crawled down the two-foot drop and climbed over her bones. He held her rib cage to his chest and whispered "I'm so sorry" to her remains.

Dakota and Capri were too focused on the sad sight before them to notice that Freddy wasn't dead. He was awake, walking behind them with the tire iron in his white-knuckled fists.

He struck it along the side of Capri's head, causing her to fall into the grave with Sean. Dakota turned and saw Freddy's murder-hungry face coming closer. She jumped back across the grave and picked up the shovel from where Sean had left it. She swung it at Freddy, but he ducked. He tried to grab her wrist, but she wrangled free from his grasp.

She swung the shovel again, and this time it hit him. He fell to the ground. She hit him again and again. Blood and mud flung up from the ground and covered Dakota's skin and clothes.

She hit him once more. This time, she angled the shovel so the sharp side hit his throat. She hammered it down on him until the sharp metal severed the flesh on his neck down to the bone.

She didn't stop until Sean and Capri held her back.

"Look," said Capri. The night sky around them was suddenly illuminated with flashing red and blue lights. Sirens rang out and the sounds of boots thudded against the pavement outside.

Lillian came rushing out of the house and into the backyard. She looked down and saw the dead and bloodied body of her son and she screamed. She screamed the scream she had swallowed inside her the day Freddy killed Rebecca — and every other day he brought home another woman to rape and murder.

Two police officers pushed through the backyard's gate, demanding everyone put their hands in the air. Dakota dropped the shovel and stepped away from Freddy's dead body. One officer went over to Lillian, who had fallen to her knees. Two other officers escorted Dakota, Sean, and Capri out of the property and into a cop car that was waiting on the street.

Inside an ambulance, Cassidy sat with a blanket wrapped around her. She asked the officers to see her sisters and they let her walk to the car.

"Thank God you're all right," said Cassidy.

"No, thank God *you're* all right," said Dakota, feeling a pang of guilt for not worrying about her sister's whereabouts until now. "What happened? Where did you go?"

"We ran up the stairs and we were walking towards the front door when his mother woke up and started yelling at us. Capri pushed me forward and told me to go get help while she bore the abusive screams of the old hag. I ran out of the house. I went to the next-door neighbor, but they weren't home. I went one house down and told them everything, but they didn't believe me. Finally, the third neighbor who had heard me screaming and begging outside, let me in to call the police."

"I'm so glad you're okay," Dakota said, hugging her.

Capri got out of the back of the cop car she had been placed in and joined her sisters in the hug.

"I'm so sorry I got you all tangled up in this. I would have never started the investigation if I knew it was going to put you in danger," said Dakota.

"It was awful," began Capri. "But you got him. He can't hurt anyone ever again."

Two emergency responders wheel a metal stretcher out of the backyard. On top of it, lay Frederick King, Maddy's killer, covered in a black body bag.

Chapter 17

Dakota was nervous. She didn't like public speaking and preferred the black and white text of a newspaper to serve as a buffer between herself and her audience. But there was no avoiding her audience now.

Santa Monica's mayor was going to give her a key to the city for her bravery and investigative reporting. She was expected to give a speech about her accomplishments. Not only that, but she agreed to have the episode recorded and posted live as the finale to *ShadowCast*, giving her audience some much-needed closure.

Debi was in the bathroom with her daughter. She held Dakota's face in her hand while she patted champagne-colored eyeshadow on her eyelids. Dakota sat still at her mother's vanity, wearing a black and violet business-style dress Cassidy loaned her for the occasion.

Debi pulled out a soft pink lipstick and applied it to her daughter's lips in quick even strokes.

"There," she said. "You look gorgeous."

"Thanks, mom," said Dakota, looking at herself in the mirror.

Even though Debi's makeup brightened Dakota's naturally pretty face, her anxiety over the speaking engagement left her complexion looking pale and ashen.

"I can tell you're nervous. Stop it. You'll be fine. We're all so proud of you and we'll be right up front, cheering you on," Debi said, as she kissed the top of Dakota's head. Dakota smiled and the two women walked downstairs.

Ken was waiting with the car out front. He had the backdoor open and was standing at attention like an old-fashioned footman.

"M'Lady," he faked a bow as Dakota came near. "Your chariot awaits."

"Oh Dad, knock it off," laughed Dakota.

"Come on, you're the guest of honor today and you should be treated like a princess," he said, as he held open the door for Dakota to enter.

The Kilroys arrived at the ceremony. Several rows of chairs were set up to face the stage with a podium.

When it was time to start, the Mayor grabbed her hand and the two of them walked out on stage. Dakota took a seat behind the Mayor, alongside other town officials, as he got up to the podium.

"Good morning, friends, family, and neighbors," he began. "Today, we are gathered to honor a Santa Monica native who has risked her life to uncover the dark truth that had been lurking in our backyard. For twelve long years, the disappearance of Maddy Montgomery had plagued the minds of many in this community. There were very few leads that could point to where Maddy could have gone. No one knew what had become of her. If she had met foul play or died as a result of an accident. Now, both the Montgomery family and the Santa Monica Community have answers, thanks to the investigative talent and tenacity of one young woman, Ms. Dakota Kilroy." The Mayor clapped his hands causing the rest of the audience to applaud.

The Mayor ushered Dakota to the podium. Dakota rose to her feet feeling a sickness in her stomach. She wanted to throw up, she wanted to turn and run off stage. *Suck it up and do it for Maddy*, she told herself as she approached the microphone.

"Good afternoon everyone," she started. Nervousness quaked in her voice, but she forced herself to steady it. "When I moved back here to my hometown of Santa Monica just two months ago, I wasn't in the best of moods. I thought I was a failure. My career as an investigative journalist in New York was at a standstill. I was unemployed and after not finding work for three months, I had no choice but to move back home. I was devastated, angry, and ashamed. But now, I'm thankful for all the bad luck I recently endured because if fate or the universe — or even just dumb luck, hadn't led me back here, I wouldn't have been able to look into Maddy's case. As many of you know, Maddy was my best friend in high school and was one of the most special and unique persons I've ever met, even to this day. She was kind, loyal, talented, beautiful, and smart, but most of all she was herself, unabashedly Maddy, all the time. Even in high school, when everyone is trying to look cool and grown up, Maddy stayed true to herself."

Dakota took a breath and collected herself. Her nerves were quieting down but still not enough for her to feel comfortable.

"For years," she continued, "the pain of not knowing what happened to my best friend burned a hole inside my heart. It was too painful for me to even read a newspaper article about her case or even look at an old photograph of the two of us. But coming back home, I had no choice. My house was full of memories of her, driving by the places we'd hang out: the park, at school, at the library, it all forced me to think of her. And after investigating corruption and crime on the streets of New York, I was finally ready, both intellectually and emotionally, to find her.

"I won't go into the details of case but we all learned that it was the serial killer, Frederick King, who took Maddy. In an effort to tamper with my investigation, he planted evidence on Maddy's loving stepfather and grandfather. Now, with Mrs. King's confession and the evidence left at the King residence, we can confirm this man is not only responsible for the disappearance and death of Maddy Montgomery, but twelve other young women and girls. I'd like to read the names of the thirteen women who lost their lives to this horrible man over the last four decades. After I've finished, I kindly ask you to take a moment of silence to honor their passing and their surviving family members.

"Rebecca King, 1969
Marie Kennedy, 1974
Patty Flores, 1977
Hedda Mårtensson, 1979
Linda Baker, 1984
Rhiannon Cooper, 1988
Sophie Ross, 1990
Amber Kincaid, 1995
Natalie Silverman, 1998
Brittany McKenna, 1999
Maddy Montgomery, 2001
Cheyenne Jones, 2012"

When Dakota finished the list of names. The audience bowed their heads.

After a moment of silence, Dakota started again. "When we continue to discuss his crimes or his psychology, let us not forget the real lives that were taken, the pain and torment he caused, and the family members and friends of his victims who have lived for so many years uncertain of what fate their loved ones met and the emptiness their deaths will always leave in their hearts. I want to end today's speech on a positive note. I want all of you out there who have been affected by a missing person's case or by unsolved murder to know that even if the odds are stacked against you, there is still hope that the case may be solved. If you can find the strength in your soul, don't stop questioning what happened, don't stop looking for answers — because you just might find them. Thank you to everyone who listened to *ShadowCast* and to those who allowed me to interview and record you for my investigation. Thank you, the Montgomery family for letting me dig up these painful memories once more so we could finally put our questions to rest. And thank you, Detective Muldowney, Detective Carter, and the countless other law enforcement and legal professionals that have helped with this case. Thank you everyone for being here today and caring about finding justice for Maddy."

As Dakota ended her speech, the Mayor came up next to her with a large golden key attached to a large wooden plaque. He handed the key over to her as several newspaper reporters snapped photos.

•   •   •

After the event, the Kilroy family with Sean returned to Ken and Debi's house. The air was mixed with both joy and grief. Cassidy and Capri would have to come to terms with the terror they had been subjected to at the hands of Freddy King. But they all were relieved to know such a horrendous man was buried six feet under in a government-owned cemetery.

Dakota's phone rang.

"Hello?" she answered.

"Hi, is this Dakota Kilroy, the host of *ShadowCast*?" a man's voice asked.

"Yes, it is. May I ask who's calling?" she replied, for fear it was some crazy fan.

"I'm Mike Perkins, head of talent acquisition for PRA," the man said.

"PRA?" she asked.

"Public Radio of America."

"Oh my God, I love you guys!"

"That's good to hear," Mike laughed. "I'm reaching out to you today to discuss the possibility of us syndicating your show as part of our larger family of talk shows."

"That sounds like an amazing opportunity," said Dakota.

"We have several ideas for you. We loved what you did with your first season. We were thinking every season could last about eight or so episodes, you investigate a cold case and try to get answers. You could travel to do interviews or have experts come on as guests, whatever makes sense for you. Anyway, we'd love to have a meeting with you at our offices in New York," Mike explained.

"If I were to take this, would I have to move back to the city?" she asked.

"Yes, we would highly prefer you to come into the studio on a regular basis. It's a lot to consider, so why don't we schedule a meeting with the two of us and see if it's a possibility?"

"Sure, I'd love to," said Dakota, trying to hide her excitement.

"Great, I'll have my assistant call you back in about an hour to schedule something. Lovely talking with you and hope to see you soon," said Mike, as he hung up.

Sean came over to Dakota. "Who was that?"

"That was PRA. They want to pick up my show and distribute it to a national audience." A huge smile was stretched across her face.

"That's amazing!" he hugged her.

"And I'd have to move back to the city if I want to take the job," she said.

"Really?" he asked, his face lit up.

"Yes, I can't wait," she smiled. "Oh crap. I forgot. I don't have an apartment; I'd have to go through the hell that is apartment-hunting again."

"You don't have to do that," he said.

"I'm pretty sure I do if I want to live there," she said.

"No, you could live with me. My place is big enough for the two of us," he said sheepishly.

"You want me to live with you?" she asked.

"Yes," he said.

Dakota was taken aback. "So soon?"

"Listen, Dakota. I'm crazy about you and at this rate, I'm 44 years old. I don't have the luxury of being a commitment-phobe like I did when I was a 20-something party boy. I want a future with you, and I want it to start as soon as possible," he said.

She stared at him.

"I know it's weird that I'm the biological father of your friend but..." he began.

"You don't need to explain yourself, Sean. I want a future with you too. Our relationship and how we met may be a bit unconventional, but I don't want to give up on us," she said. "So yes. I'll move in with you."

•   •   •

A month later, Dakota came home to her new apartment on the 35th floor of a sleek high rise in Midtown West. She had just finished her first recording at PRA. She was assigned a case about a dirty cop and the death of a young man that he may or may not have caused. The case excited her. She knew she would be able to work as an investigative journalist again and this time for the long haul. She couldn't wait to get her hands on all the evidence and crack the case.

She put her key in the stainless-steel lock outside her apartment door and opened it up. The place was a palace compared to what she had been living in before. It was spacious enough for a full-sized living room with a fireplace, a dining room, kitchen, and an outdoor garden. The master bedroom included a pillowy king-sized bed that looked out over a wall of glass where the city lights twinkled below.

Inside, the sunset was filling the room with a warm light. On the fireplace, there was picture framed in gold and silver of her and Maddy in their school uniforms.

With Sean still at work, the place was quiet. But Dakota didn't feel alone in the apartment. She wasn't much of a believer in the supernatural, but she could feel Maddy's soul

with her in the room.

ShadowCast

She was there, in every fleck of orange-gold sunlight casting in from the window, streaming rays of light over their picture. Maddy was proud of her friend and she was now resting in peace.

The End

About the Author

V.P. Morris is an award-winning thriller and horror writer and podcast host. Her interest in true crime and criminal psychology inspired her debut novel, *ShadowCast*. When she isn't writing, she is enjoying her time with her husband, son, and their rescue dog, Oscar.

Note from the Author

Word-of-mouth is crucial for any author to succeed. If you enjoyed *ShadowCast*, please leave a review online—anywhere you are able. Even if it's just a sentence or two. It would make all the difference and would be very much appreciated.

Thanks!
V.P. Morris

Thank you so much for reading one of our **Psychological Thrillers**.

If you enjoyed our book, please check out our recommendation for your next great read!

The Tracker by John Hunt

"A dark thriller that draws the reader in."

–Morning Bulletin

"I never want to hear mention of bolt-cutters, a live rat and a bucket in the same sentence again. EVER."

–Ginger Nuts Of Horror

View other Black Rose Writing titles at www.blackrosewriting.com/books and use promo code **PRINT** to receive a **20% discount** when purchasing.